Betsy

AND

Catherine

AN UNCOMMON FRIENDSHIP

HELEN GAILEY

ISBN: 979-8-89031-564-9 (sc)
ISBN: 979-8-89031-565-6 (hc)
ISBN: 979-8-89031-566-3 (e)

Library of Congress Control Number: 2019907590

Because of the dynamic nature of the Internet, any web addresses or links contained in this book may have changed since publication and may no longer be valid. The views expressed in this work are solely those of the author and do not necessarily reflect the views of the publisher, and the publisher hereby disclaims any responsibility for them.

THE EWINGS PUBLISHING

One Galleria Blvd., Suite 1900, Metairie, LA 70001
(504) 702-6708
1-888-421-2397

Contents

CHAPTER

1

A Joyful Childhood

It felt somewhat grand to be the lady of the house even if it was only for a short time. Blakewood House had known my service for many years. The ordeals that Lady Catherine and I endured over the past year have bonded a friendship that began in our childhood.

When we were children Catherine told me the baron had spoken firmly to her, "You must stay away from the servant's children. They are not of our class. You don't see your mother befriending Mrs. Bramley, the cook, or me befriending Woods, the butler. You have got to know your place, Catherine."

We were six years old when Catherine told me we were not to play together anymore, we were only to smile at each other in passing. Nothing else.

I passed on this information to Aggie and Tom. We were all disappointed, but there was little we could do. I told my Muma and she confirmed the baron's word. "Servant's children should not mix with those they serve. It's not our place, Betsy. We are under their employ. But don't mind, dear one, you have your brother and sister. And you can always come into the kitchen and I can be giving you things to do if you get bored. When you see Catherine, just smile as you pass each other."

Several days later, when I passed Catherine on the stairs, I did as Muma asked. But, when she passed me, she whispered to me, "Meet me outside after breakfast."

I was overjoyed, but also a little anxious. Both of our parents had told us we weren't to play together.

I always knew Catherine was willful because she always wanted to play tiggy and didn't really care what I wanted to do. That didn't bother me much. We just liked to be together.

Tom and Aggie often followed me around. Tom was tall for his five years and Aggie was but four. So, when I went out the back door they did also.

There she was, sitting on a garden seat next to the lily pond. Catherine was short for her age and had lovely honey colored long hair. In comparison, I was ever so tall. The baroness always ensured Catherine wore the finest of clothes. Different to us, we wore hand me downs.

As I sat down next to her, she said, "I don't care for what Father says. We can still be friends. We can play in the yard. He won't know. If he or Mother come out, we will just have to run away from each other."

I responded, "I am not too sure, Muma said we were just to smile at each other in passing."

"Oh, don't be a stick in the mud, Betsy. No one will need to know. Let's play hidey. I shall play 'he'. I'll count to ten while you hide. You better hide good cos I'll find you."

And so the year rolled over. Sometimes my da would see us as he was busy keeping the grounds looking presentable.

He'd say, "You know you little-uns shouldn't be playing together."

But his words were of little use. We would all run away and laugh about it. I don't think he ever told Muma, as nothing was ever said to me.

Several times Catherine's father, the baron, reprimanded her. She would be kept inside for the day for disobeying him. But Catherine took very little notice of his words. I think he really didn't have much conviction behind his words as he didn't enforce them. I recognize now how fortunate we were to live in such a goodly household. Throughout my childhood and adolescent years, Catherine never spoke down to me.

Indeed, the grounds were large and there was plenty of room for childlike fun.

Games of hide and seek, ball games and other simple kinds of fun were all joys that we shared as we were young, Catherine, Aggie, Tom and me.

When she was a child, Catherine would say, "Father's talk about class is silly. We are friends. What more needs to be said?"

By the time we had reached adolescence, her tone was more guarded. "I suppose we shouldn't talk so freely when other people are around, but I mean no slight by saying that. We are tried and true friends, there is to be no distinction about class. I will stay true to you from now and forever. Will you do the same?"

My childlike loyalty rang true as I replied, "Most definitely! We are one."

Blakewood House was a large estate. It had been built to house several families, not just my fellow servants, but a family of high prestige. This house had seen a baron, his lady and their dear daughter grow to adulthood. Prior to that the baron's uncle, Sir Henry Kensington and his lady had the manor house built for themselves and their four young daughters. When Sir Henry died, his wife soon followed. All his daughters had married into nobility and all had homes of their own.

As custom would have it, Blakewood House was left to the oldest male relation, our baron, Baron Kensington. The baron and his family were living in Sheffield at the time as he owned lands there. He and the baroness decided they would like a change, so the baron appointed a foreman to keep his lands in Sheffield in order and to collect the tenant's rents. This allowed him the freedom to move into Blakewood House in London. His estates in Sheffield were larger, but the benefits of living in London, with its political and social opportunities, made the sacrifice worthwhile. Yet, from time to time, the baron and baroness would travel up to Sheffield to see that everything was in order and to collect the monies owed by the tenants. I knew that the baroness also took time to be with her family on the outings.

As chance would have it, our dear baron's title might have been a title only. His father had spurned him for secretly conveying food stuffs from their Manor to give to the more unfortunate in the nearby village and for the unforgivable fault of falling in love with her Ladyship who was a mere peasant girl at the time. Baron Kensington Senior was somewhat of a tyrant. He was a cruel and oppressive ruler over those who worked for him. To the great good fortune of our Baron Kensington, his father took ill and died within the space of three months. Although he had publicly declared he would leave our baron penniless, he left no will and by law and custom our Baron Kensington inherited great fortune.

Although she was a commoner by birth, Lady Kensington had all the social graces of a lady. It was rumored amongst the servants that Baron Kensington's sister took her under her wing and taught her the manners and etiquette of society so she could appear socially with Baron Kensington. It was a scandal at the time but, as many who came to know Baroness Victoria Kensington became truly aware, she was a caring, loving righteous soul.

Blakewood House was the largest in a complex of buildings that covered ten acres of land. Such a big area kept my da busy tending the grounds. The main house was two stories and built of stone with many rooms. The baron's family lived in the upper area and the ground floor consisted of servant's rooms, the kitchen, and the servant's eating hall, and the front entry area. There was a small seating area in the front entry and then a flight of stairs. To the right was a hall leading to the living and entertainment area of the house and to the left the families' sleeping quarters and several spare bedrooms There was another wing of the house, but I never had need to see it until Catherine was married. We servants never knew how much the house was worth, but it was rumored the entire estate was worth many thousands of pounds.

My parents had served the Kensington household as servants since I was four. Their previous employer had passed away and his widow no longer wanted to maintain the house. She moved on to live with one of her children. My parent's services were no longer needed. The late master's widow was concerned that all the servants would no longer have employment and let it be known that my Ma was an exceptional cook, Sarah a good kitchen maid, and my da, an excellent groundskeeper. The Kensington's had heard, and Muma, Da, and Sarah, the kitchen maid, were invited to meet with the baron and the baroness. They were employed on a trial basis for a brief time and impressed the baron and baroness enough that they had remained on their staff since that time.

At breakfast, after grace was said, Woods said he needed to pass on a compliment. As he rarely shared anything with us, our chattering immediately stopped.

He said. "Mrs. Bramley is to be complimented."

We all sat still and waited for him to continue.

As he added sugar and milk to his porridge, he continued, "While I was serving the evening meal last night, I overheard the following remark when the baron and baroness were entertaining Lord Morticut and his good lady. While their words were only spoken in jest, Lord Morticut asked the baroness if she might swap cooks with them. They thought the food was delicious."

Both my muma and my da looked pleased.

Woods continued, "I haven't always passed on compliments, Mrs. Bramley, but I must tell you, you are very well respected for your culinary talents by many of the baron's guests."

It has been sixteen years since my dear Muma's death, I do miss her so.

All who knew my dear muma and da respected and loved them. That was indeed true of the baron and his lady, which was extremely rare. Not so many families in London had much time for their servants. I don't believe I fully realized this until I had reached adolescence and came to know how other homes were run.

Admittedly my parents were from poor stock and had no social standing, but I took comfort in the knowledge they were honest, hardworking souls who had loved me dearly. Having such wonderful parents opened many opportunities in our lives, some which they never foresaw. Such opportunities were a rarity amongst other servant's children. I know of no others who had the good fortune to experience schooling and live in a fine household, even if it was just the servant's quarters.

This was most contrary to custom. Servants' children were often looked upon as a nuisance, more mouths to feed, more beds to find. As I came to know personally, the baron and baroness had better Christian values, indeed they had love in their hearts for my entire family.

Just before she turned seven Catherine came up to me looking very sad. "Mother and Father are hiring a governess for me, so I suppose I won't see you as much as I'll be learning sums and stuff."

I replied, "Oh rats! I'll miss you Catherine. We will just have to make time. You won't be with her all day, will you?"

She responded, "I am not really sure."

I spoke with childish hope. "Well, when you find out more you can tell me."

"Mother and Father said she's coming next Monday." I asked, "Have you seen her?"

"No, but Mother and Father have. They say she is young, friendly, and seems very knowledgeable."

"You'll have to see for yourself then!" I replied.

That Monday afternoon Catherine came running to me.

"She seems friendly, but she gives me hard sums and expects me to write my name. I would much rather be with my playtime friends."

I was somewhat exasperated as I considered that Catherine was telling the truth. It was common knowledge that those of noble birth were taught to read and write.

I said, "I don't think we can be the same playtime friends that we have been. But still, there will be time on the weekends. You must tell her she's got to show you what to do. You need to learn how to read and write."

Catherine responded, "Oh I have, Betsy, but she expects too much of me."

I assured her, "Give her a week or so and tell your mother and father, but for goodness sake don't tell them I told you that. I will be in deep trouble from your parents and mine if they know I said anything about it."

We were very young then, but I remember Catherine's worrisome attitude.

"You are right of course. Yes, I must see how things go. If need be, I will tell Mother and Father that Miss Alexandra is too demanding. You mustn't worry. Why would I mention your name?"

When the baron came down to address us one morning as we were eating breakfast, we all looked at each other and wondered what we had done wrong.

"From now on the baroness and I have agreed that Betsy, Aggie, and Tom are to join Catherine when she takes lessons from Miss Alexandra. Normally a child such as Catherine should be educated with children of the same class, but despite our instructions, we can see that she longs to be with her play friends. We are hoping that Catherine will take more interest in her work if she is with you children. Catherine will tell you where you need to be and at what time. Betsy, do you understand what I'm saying?"

I stood there in shock for several moments. I could not even process the thought. This was not possible! I was sure my face was flushed, and I stammered to find words to reply.

"Sir? Do you mean we are to have lessons?"

"Yes, for Catherine's benefit."

I expect the baron understood my confusion completely. He waited while I stumbled for words to answer. Finally, I gathered enough presence of mind to stutter out, "Yes, sir, if that is your wish. We will do whatever your Lordship requires."

I elbowed Aggie who stood silent at my side.

"Yes. Sir! It will be grand," she finally said.

Then, as I glared at Tom, he also repeated the words, "Yes, Sir."

Inwardly we were all very pleased, and I expected our parents would be also. But I was wrong. My parents were not pleased at all.

My muma was more vocal than anyone. "It's a pity, such a pity. People of our class will mistrust you. You will stand out in the community. People will tell you, you are 'putting on airs.' This sort of education will set you apart from your peers. You will be different to other servant's children."

Then Woods, the butler, had his say, "I think you are wrong, Mrs. Bramley. I learnt to read and write and here I am a young butler at thirty in a notable household. My lessons have bought me a good wage and a position of responsibility."

Then my da, "I don't be knowing that it's fitting to be educated when your parents are in service. The way you talk will be different and, truth be known, people will either disown knowing ya or they could be taking advantage of ya."

Then my muma, "We can't do much about it or can we?"

Woods the butler again, "I expect you could. You could share your concerns with the master, but I think you are silly to deny your young'uns such a wonderful opportunity."

Then my muma again, "What are you thinking Betsy?"

"I want to be with Catherine. I want to learn how to read and write."

Then Tom backed me up, "I want to learn too."

Muma stated, "You are but children. You don't understand how this reading and writing will affect your lives."

Then Da, "If they use their brains it might work out alright. I say Woods is right."

Then ma said with resolution in her voice, "Alright then, but you three kiddies are not to hold anything against me if you be having trouble when ya get older!"

The next day as we were climbing the stairs to the room which had been set up for classes I saw Catherine. How we hugged each other and felt so pleased we could be together!

The room had a number of tables and chairs in it and we couldn't look out the window as it was nearly to the ceiling, but it let rays of sunlight into the room.

Miss Alexandra came into the room. She had a nice smile and her blondish hair was tied back. She wore a brown skirt and a beige blouse. She carried a brown cardigan.

"Welcome to Betsy and Tom."

And then she looked at my sister and said, "You must be Aggie then?"

"Yes, Missus that's me." Aggie was only five, but she was an adorable little girl.

There were good times and bad with Miss Alexandra but eventually, we all learned to read and write.

Apart from the time when Catherine went away traveling with her cousin, we virtually grew up together. It seemed Catherine's parents slowly approved of our friendship. I expect they must have. Otherwise, I can't see why they allowed us to take classes with her. Apart from lessons and helping in the kitchen, Catherine and I always seemed to find each other. I expect the baroness finally became resigned to the idea and judging from the baroness's past it was understandable.

On days when I was free from kitchen duties and schooling, Catherine and I could be found up in the attic telling tales and giggling and laughing over silly things. As time progressed so did our stories.

We talked and laughed about the imaginary men whom we would marry and perhaps attend court with. Other times we would imagine that we were traveling abroad together and numerous men of high standing would be seeking our acquaintance. We would sleigh on the slopes of Switzerland. We would bathe in the seas of Italy. In our romantic imaginations, we would dance amongst the tulips in Holland. We might even find a home in America and settle down with a rich landowner. Our imaginings took us all over the world. I knew it would never be true for me, but…Catherine, she could and maybe would travel. Little did I know back then how the next decade would unfold.

CHAPTER

2

Memories

Though years have passed, the memories are still fresh in my mind. I paused for a moment and could feel the tears welling in my eyes. So long ago, yet the hurt is always deep. While taking a few days off for a one time visit to France both of my parents died when the ship they were on capsized in a sudden squall while returning to England.

The baroness and the baron had my siblings and I come up to the parlor.

Her Ladyship had tears in her eyes,

The baron addressed us, "Children…we have very sad news to tell you, your dear mother and father were killed in a squall as they were returning home from France on a ship."

I found myself saying, "No it can't be true…they said they would be home in time for my birthday tomorrow."

The baron responded sadly. "Unfortunately, it is true. We have had word from the transportation company they traveled with."

Tears were running down my cheeks and I could hear Aggie crying as she tugged on my dress.

Tom was fighting tears but soon his grief could be heard.

The baroness put her arms around us.

The baron raised his voice, so he could be heard above our weeping.

"You will not be treated as orphans, you will remain in the household and take on duties if and as you wish."

How keenly I felt the loss of my dear parents. I think I sobbed silently to myself for many weeks. Aggie seemed to take it much harder than I. There were times, many months later, when her sobs could be heard at night as we lay in our little beds in the tiny room we shared. I would try to comfort her, but doing so would make my heart ache even more. She was so young to be without parents. I hoped her future would be sure.

I felt confident in the knowledge that the baron would keep to his word. The thought of being an orphan terrified me. I know, now that I am much older, we could have been cast off into the workhouse and shown very little love and care. I'm not so sure Aggie knew what an orphan was, but Tom most certainly did. Tom seemed distant for a while and I could not really tell what he was feeling concerning his future.

But he repeated my very same thoughts, "At least we have each other and work here. But I'm not so sure about working in service. We will just have to see how the future unfolds. I am to start working with Woods in a weeks' time. He's hoping I might become a footman. He asked me a few weeks ago before this bad news."

I said, "I've been working with Muma in the kitchen. I wonder when the baron will take on replacements."

Tom seemed more grown up for his age when he said, "I heard that Woods is taking care of it. It's going to take a bit of getting used to. Don't be fretting Betsy. Muma and Da wouldna' want us to fret. They would be wantin' us to be happy."

As I looked at Tom, he still had a twinkle in his eye. I felt sure he would make a good life whatever the circumstances. Tom was a people person, but I can't say the same for Aggie. I supposed, as she was the youngest, she would feel the hurt a little more, if that was possible.

When I met Catherine outside, her parents must have told her the bad news because she put her arm around me. "Betsy I am so sorry for your loss, but you must be strong. Don't let the sorrow and pain rule your life."

"Oh, I know you are right," I replied, "I know I must be strong and be a good example for Aggie's sake. It's true what Tom said. Muma and Da wouldn't want us to be unhappy."

As we sat on the garden seat in silence it felt comforting to be with someone who had complete empathy. The silence between us at that time spoke volumes.

I thought of Catherine and the differences between us. I was much taller and ungracefully thin. Catherine was much shorter, but she always looked elegant. The baroness made sure she wore the finest of clothes. Catherine and her mother would often spend the day shopping, or they would seek out a dressmaker and there would be fittings and then certain materials of different colors were chosen.

Such things were foreign for me. Lord Kensington gave Woods a monthly stipend and my muma would take me where you could buy cheap second-hand clothing. Sometimes we found a bargain, but generally not so much. With my muma's death I wondered who would take me shopping now.

Listening to Catherine that day made me see that there were other differences as well. Catherine spoke with a cultured voice and I spoke as the other household servants did. I took Muma's words to heart and tried to speak like others in the kitchen. I tried to be common although I imagine taking classes with Catherine took some of the edges off servant talk.

Catherine's whole countenance was cultured. As she comforted me, I felt inadequate and realized I had much to learn. And so, on that day, sitting on that garden seat, I vowed to myself to become more learned. I hoped I would make my parents feel proud even though they were gone.

As Tom had said, Woods found a selection of people to fill the two vacancies, Cook and Groundskeeper. I believe the baron and baroness interviewed those who Woods had recommended and within a week the positions were filled.

I was fourteen then and was already accustomed to helping in the kitchen with my muma.

I found it somewhat more challenging to get used to the new cook, Mrs. Mclintoch.

She told me her parents had moved to England from Scotland to be near relatives when she was fifteen. Nevertheless, even though a good number of years had passed, she still had a strong Scottish brogue.

As I don't know who the other applicants were, I don't know if she was the best choice, but I knew time would tell.

She was a motherly soul aged about fifty, with red hair, and was perhaps a little overweight. It didn't take long for her to fit into the Kensington household.

She wasn't backward in sharing her opinion and had strong principles, but she was nice, just not my dear mother who I adored. Of course, I thought at the time that she didn't have the skills my mother had. Her cooking was good, but not as exceptional as my mother's had been. But she was easy to talk to and caring of us as we grew. She always referred to Aggie and me as dear girlies and Tom, a dear boy. She was highly organized, just like my muma, but stricter; every food item had its place and pity anyone who put things away where they didn't belong.

Aggie had little to do apart from attending to her schooling. However, she soon started to wander amongst some of the other homes which were nearby and began to meet other servant's children. While she continued to take the hurt of the death of our parents deeply, the new cook, Mrs. Mclintoch, became a mother figure for Aggie and me so the pain of our parent's deaths eased a little for both of us. As time progressed, I was pleased to see Aggie making friends easily. She often told me stories that the other children in the neighborhood would tell her and we would laugh together.

Mrs. Mclintoch told her, "Make sure you take care lassie and don't be wandering off too far. You had better be telling me when you are about to go and where you are going, we need to be knowing where you are."

Aggie was obedient. Often, when I was working in the kitchen she would come in and tell Mrs. Mclintoch where she was going. Over time we noticed a pattern to her wandering. She often wandered to the second Manor on the right. Mrs. Mclintoch and I would share a knowing glance with one another.

One day as I was walking in the garden with Catherine, Aggie bought one or two friends to play in the grounds.

Even I knew that it would be looked upon severely if the baron knew.

I had to take Aggie aside and whisper, "We'll be in trouble if the baron finds out you bought other servant's children here, especially while Catherine is here. You had better go to their grounds."

I felt badly about it, but we couldn't anger the baron who had treated us so kindly. Aggie nodded, but she seemed a bit puzzled. Nonetheless, she did as I asked and whispered something to her friends. Within a few moments, they were gone. On some levels, I wasn't sure why, but I knew that the baron didn't want it known that his daughter was playing with servant's children.

One night as we were getting ready for bed Aggie told me she had found a true friend. A young man by the name of Eric.

She looked at me doubtfully and said, "I want to marry him."

I responded quickly, "You are far too young to be marrying anyone."

To which Aggie replied forcefully, "Other folks do. Why not me?"

I asked. "How do you know this Eric is a responsible person. How old is he?"

Aggie was sitting on her bed as she looked up at me pleadingly and said, "He is eighteen. He has a good job. He works as a footman for the household two buildings to the right of here."

"You know, Aggie, marriage is for the whole of your life!"

She responded eagerly, "Yes, I know. It will be so wonderful to have him to care for me and I for him. He takes time to listen to me. I think he understands me. He is very genuine. We have kissed several times. I do love him."

I said, "If you are serious about it, you will need to speak to the baron then."

I was pleased with her response. "Yes, I shall do so. I think I better ask Woods to arrange it for me."

Two days later she reported, "Oh Betsy, he asked me lots of questions, but he did say yes."

He said, "I see no harm in it if you feel sure it's the right thing for you. You know marriage is a lifetime event and it shouldn't be looked upon lightly. I shall speak to Eric's employer and get his opinion."

Aggie was ecstatic. "Can you believe it? Eric will be so pleased."

She told Eric that he too should do the very same thing as she had done. He should seek out his Lordship where he lived and ask his permission.

The baron sent for Aggie a week later. "I have spoken to Eric's employer. He goes to the same club as I. He speaks highly of Eric. So as far as we are concerned you can arrange a wedding date. You will take a position as a kitchen maid in Eric's household. We will miss you Aggie, but we are happy for you."

When I told Catherine she commented, "How wonderful that she has found someone who will love and care for her. She is younger than either of us. I hope there will come a time soon when you or I might find a good man to marry. Remember when we used to pretend all sorts of fantasies that would lead to the loves of our lives?"

I replied, "Yes, and I expect such fantasies could very well come true for you, Catherine."

Her answer, "We can dream dear Betsie, we can dream!"

It all came together; Aggie and Eric were married. Although her husband was young, he was decidedly good looking, sensitive and very caring of Aggie. I was so pleased for my sister.

His parents were also in service. I met them when Aggie and Eric were married. I found them to be friendly, loving and caring just like my dear Muma and Da. The actual ceremony took place in an Anglican church in the nearby village. All the servants in Eric's household and ours were invited to a fine feast at Blakewood House.

Many a household would shun the idea. Indeed, they would think it scandalous for servants to have a wedding feast. The whole idea was totally absurd and unheard of.

The baron and his dear wife defied custom and several weeks prior to the wedding, the baroness made arrangements for Aggie's marriage to be followed by a wedding feast.

Mrs. Mclintoch had all of us helping in the kitchen in preparation for the fine feast: cold cuts, vegetables, pies and sweetbreads of varying shapes and sizes. His Lordship sent out for several cases of cider for the feast. How thankful we all were.

Yes, Aggie was indeed privileged to have been treated so, being the daughter of a former servant. While the area was a tad too small, we all squeezed in and had a lovely time celebrating in the servants' hall where two long tables were set up with linen table clothes and some fine china and silverware which was normally reserved for the baron and his wife's use.

Along with those in service where Eric lived, we were a merry group, as we ate, drank and celebrated. Everybody was pleased for the wedding couple's joy in each other. I was content that Aggie had got over the loss of our dear Muma and Da, and she had a certain future with Eric.

Aggie moved over to Eric's household, but it was not for long. On one of Aggies visits to Blakewood House, she looked rather sheepish when she confided to me, "Eric is not interested in continuing his life in service anymore. He has decided we should move up to Cheltenham. He has a brother there named James who is involved in some type of carriage business and they want to join forces and work together. And with my reading and writing skills, I will be a great asset to them."

I had to reluctantly agree. "If that is what you both want then that is what you should do. Cheltenham is a fair journey from here, I hope I will get to see you."

Aggie replied positively, "Of course. James, Eric's brother, comes up here often to see his ma and da. He was Eric's best man at our wedding. Don't you remember? We will visit often."

That night, as I lay in bed, I thought to myself. Yes, Aggie was fortunate to have someone to share her life with. I was confident that she could make a good life with Eric wherever they were.

I knew I would miss Aggie, but I was happy for her. Nevertheless, I shed several tears that night in the knowledge that dear muma and da were gone and now Aggie. Of course, I hoped that we would see her often. I hoped she would be true to her word.

In the years following our parent's death, Tom took to going down to some of the riverside taverns when he wasn't needed at Blakewood. He told me he heard many a sailor's yarn about their voyages to different lands in the world. Even as a child Tom had always said, "When I grow up, I am going to be a sailor."

As he came of age, Tom determined that he would make his yearnings to be a sailor come true. In due course, he took his leave also. The baron gave him two pounds to see him safely on his way. I haven't seen Tom for ever so long. I wonder if he ever thinks of Aggie or me.

When I reached the age of sixteen, a few years prior to Aggie's wedding, the baron and the baroness sent word via Woods, that they wanted to see me. As Catherine and I were meeting in the garden that morning I told Catherine that I was to meet with her parents after lunch.

The baron addressed me: "Catherine is of the age now where she should have a lady's maid. We wondered if you would accept that responsibility? Unless, of course, you have other plans."

Obviously, I responded, "Yes, I would love to."

The baroness said, "We hoped you would say that. Thank you, Betsy."

Then the baroness added. "Sometimes Catherine can act too...", she strung out the word as though struggling to find the exact thing she needed to say, finally settling on "'spontaneous' for her own good.

Keep your eye on her Betsy. Being the only child, I think we may have spoilt her somewhat."

Then the baron had his own thoughts, "We will want you to be in uniform, so I will tell Woods to arrange that. You will be paid thirty pounds a year and will also be privy to household news. If we have dinner guests, you might be needed to help serve."

His words were music to my ears. Now Catherine and I had license to be together more often.

When I was dismissed by the baron and baroness, Catherine was waiting for me in the hall. She came up and hugged me and said, "I knew what it was all about, but I thought if I told you this morning you wouldn't have acted surprised."

I responded positively, "Yes, I am very excited."

Catherine was always more vocal when she was with me, "I think it is wonderful. Now we don't need to meet only in the garden, we can be together as we please."

I hastened to say, "Not strictly as we please but more often that's for sure."

My uniform arrived. I was to wear a white bonnet and a blue dress with a white collar and a starched white apron. Woods gave me two changes of clothing and said, "If you need something more you are to tell me." He asked, "How do you feel about your new position?"

I answered with a smile, "I am thrilled and looking forward to helping Catherine."

As we had grown up together, I cannot remember a moment when I didn't put Catherine first in all that we did. I enjoyed dressing and caring for her and giving her advice when she asked. My goodness, she was my good friend back then, not just someone whom I served.

One day Catherine said, "Betsy let's pretend. Let's pretend we are mannequins."

"What's a mannequin then?" I asked.

She folded her hands and did her best impression of Miss Alexandra, our governess. "It is a kind of doll that is used to display clothing for people who might be shopping. And, more exciting, people put new clothes on them and show them to people who might buy. They dress them up and show off their clothes to everybody, I heard Mother talking about them the other day."

She continued "There is a box of old clothes up in the attic. We could invite Mother and Father to our showing and even some of the servants."

I replied, "You are just bored Catherine. It would be most inappropriate for your mother to see you doing silly things with me. Do you want to make trouble for me? Your mother would send me out to the street shoeless if you even suggested such a thing! She would not believe that it was your idea! You have got to get used to this silly class distinction. As I remember your father told you many years ago."

"Oh, Betsy you are always too practical. If we want some adventure in our lives we have got to go after it."

I replied with a smile, "I hardly think that prancing around in some old clothes is adventurous."

After laying out her night clothing, I told Catherine. "I will return in the morning with your breakfast."

Catherine had copied her parents' breakfast habits. They too always had their breakfast bought to them while in bed.

It was Catherine's parents who bought us back to reality. I found it a little strange when I was summoned to the family parlor along with Catherine. As well as the baron and his wife there was another guest in the room. I wondered who she was. She looked very stylish. Such a fine stylish woman as I had never seen before. Guessing her age, I thought she might perhaps be in her early forties.

She carried herself with a calm, cool and collected demeanor. Her skirt was fashioned stylishly, black cotton with a white ribbon and a tiny rose pattern. Her blouse had buttons that led their way up to her stand-up collar with wide cuffs. The yoke and shoulders were gently gathered to create an expression of elegance itself. She wore a delightful black hat with a feather. Although the weather was warm, she wore black laced ankle boots.

Catherine told me later that she was a cousin of the baron. She had lost her husband in the Revolutionary Wars in 1792.

Catherine's father looked at her saying, "Catherine, your mother and I have decided that you should spend some time with your second cousin traveling abroad. She will teach you the social graces and upper-class-cultural rites in preparation for entry into society."

The baron spoke directly to me when he said, "We can't help but notice Betsy that you and Catherine have formed a friendship over several years. We have asked for you to be here to save Catherine from telling you and feeling sad because of it."

I was immediately concerned that he was going to send me elsewhere, or perhaps dismiss me altogether.

He continued, "My cousin has a large group of servants traveling with her, so your services won't be needed."

He must have understood my alarm as he hastened to put me at ease. "My wife's personal maid is unwell and will not be able to continue in her duties. We are hopeful that you will stay on at Blakewood to attend to the baroness. When Catherine returns, we hope you will return to your proper place with her."

While Catherine's eyes gleamed at the thought of traveling with her second cousin, I hoped she shared a little of my sadness that we would be parted. As I was dismissed, I could feel silent tears building inside me. I tried to cheer myself up. Blakewood was my home and I was thankful to both the baron and her ladyship for the care which had been shown to me and my family.

As I went to put some of her clean clothes away Catherine was sitting at her desk in her bedroom.

She remarked, "Dear Betsy, I will miss you so much."

I whispered, as I knew full well I would sound tearful, "And I you."

In fact, for the seven days which followed before she was to depart, we would look at each other and then, tears would trickle down our cheeks.

Upon the day of her departure, as I laid out one of her prettiest gowns, Catherine and I said very little as I helped her attend to her toiletries. I was thankful for her promise.

"We will rekindle our friendship, dear Betsy. Please always be in my life. Promise me!"

I replied, "Of course." Nonetheless, I wondered if her traveling would take her away altogether. No one mentioned how long she would be gone. Perhaps the baron had given his cousin directions. Catherine seemed to think it would be just a month or so but as it turned out, six months passed by before Catherine graced the walls of Blakewood House again.

During that time, I assisted the baroness. I came to know that she was friendly and caring of all those around her. Apart from the time she comforted us when my parents died, I had perceived that she was stand-offish and aloof. As I got to know her better, I concluded to myself we sometimes make judgments which are totally incorrect.

While Catherine was absent, I spent more time in the kitchen and I also came to know Mrs. Mclintoch better.

She asked. "Do you have a special someone then?"

I responded, "It's highly unlikely! Where would I meet a special someone?"

Her reply, "There's a lot of servants here about. Surely you should be meeting up with someone."

I answered, "I'd have to be going to the local pub to be meeting someone. I would rather read than do that."

As Mrs. Mclintoch was beating eggs, she told me, "You know, lassie, when I was young, just like Aggie, I met the love of me life. We didn't have the wedding that she had, but we were both able to take a week off from our work. We went down to South Hampton and had a grand time. His name was Thomas. Oh, how I loved me Thomas. We both worked in the same household so there was no conflict with time. For a good twenty years, we worked together. He, being a butler, and me a cook, we saved enough to buy a little place of our own."

I wanted to know more about Mrs. Mclintoch, so I asked, "What about children? Did you have any children?"

She looked sad. "I wish that be true lassie. One or the other of us couldn't have children. We tried for several years and then he gave up trying. He started drinking too much and eventually he was let go from the household where we worked. I don't know where he is now. I thought he really loved me. Anyways, I started out as a cook and be it sure, cook I shall be until I've got the grass above me."

So, my days were filled with assisting the baroness and reading. I had much more time to myself. I wondered when Catherine would return.

CHAPTER

3

Changes

After six months I was able to see the face I loved. She seemed changed. To my eyes, she had acquired a new grace and elegance. She was so beautiful that I felt pangs of envy. I was quick to notice she carried herself with the fineness that becomes a lady. I was surprised that she continued to treat me as I did her. After she had been home for just an hour or so, she confided in me that she had met a special someone. I remember her words. They left me feeling at a loss, it was like my world was crumbling before me.

"Dear Betsy, guess what has happened to me? I've fallen in love with the dearest man on earth."

The look on my face must have conveyed to Catherine that I was deaf and dumb. I could barely find words to answer.

I asked, "What? What do you mean? You met someone? Do you mean a man?"

She smiled joyously, "Yes, of course! What else could I mean?"

I finally grasped that she was sharing the romantic moment we had talked about as children.

I asked, "Where did you meet him?"

Excitedly she said, "On the ship coming home. He is Lord Edward Bannister. He is a Lieutenant-Governor over the North-Western Provinces in India. He spends some of his time in London but often travels abroad because of his duties for England."

I questioned, "What would he be doing abroad then?"

Catherine was hesitant. "To tell you the truth dear Betsy I am not sure. He told me he had contacts with the British judiciary system in India. I'll have to ask him more about it as I'm sure Father will want to know. Anyway, he's going to be courting me. He is a few years older than me. I don't know if Father will be pleased about that."

For a moment I was transfixed with fear. I thought selfishly that I was going to lose the dearest friend I would ever have. It hurt so fiercely that I could hardly breathe. She would marry this nobleman and I would suddenly lose my place and my purpose in life. I thought to myself that Catherine might really forget me altogether and put our friendship aside. But she looked somewhat pensive when she took my hand.

"You won't be put out by me seeing Edward, will you? I have told Edward that you will always be my dearest friend."

I could see Catherine meant what she said as we hugged each other tightly. The fear left me, and I quickly reassured her. "I will be at your side as long as you wish. How can I ever repay the love and kindness your family has shown to mine? Besides we are forever friends."

I smiled when I said, "Remember our childhood oath? We swore to love and care for each other always?"

"Oh yes, I do remember! I am so happy knowing that you hadn't forgotten. I was so disappointed when you didn't meet me at the ship. I wondered if you no longer cared."

I wanted to laugh. "There were obvious reasons, Catherine. I doubt very much if it would be appropriate for a common servant to be there.

If that had not been the case I would have been there with bells on. So, tell me what he is like."

"When he smiles, he is indeed charming. So handsome and sensitive to my needs and feelings. He is well groomed and immaculate in his dress. He shared much of his personal information with me. Although he said he spends much of his time away traveling to India I was immediately drawn to him when I met him."

When Edward courted Catherine, he often spent time with the family. I remember the first time I met him I felt drawn to him. It was an unusual thing for guests to talk to servants, so of course Catherine had been truthful when she told me she had told Edward that she and I were sworn friends.

"You must meet him, Betsy." She declared. "We will be in the drawing-room after lunch."

"I wonder if it is appropriate for me to just come. Perhaps you should send for me?" I replied.

"Oh, very well, this class thing is so annoying. I have very little time for it."

After lunch, I stayed near the kitchen and as expected a bell rang from the drawing room. Woods was immediately on his feet and when he returned, he said, "Miss Catherine has sent for you Betsy. She is in the drawing room. I don't know what it is all about. She also has a gentleman friend with her."

I felt nervous as I knocked timidly on the door. I had imagined him to be tall and dark and just a few years older than Catherine. When he stood as I entered the room, I was surprised to find that he wasn't particularly tall. He had tidy blonde hair and a well-manicured mustache and there was a twinkle in his eye as he spoke. He was incredibly handsome, with a thoughtful face that had little wrinkles of laughter near the corners of his mouth and eyes. He was somewhat older than I had expected.

As Catherine introduced us, he stood and remained standing and didn't sit down until I was seated. After the initial introduction, he said, "I am delighted to meet you, Betsy. Catherine has sounded your praises often. I almost have a feeling like I know you well."

I was thinking madly to myself, it's no wonder Catherine fell for him. He was so good-looking and seemed very personable. Normally I don't feel shy when I meet new people but, this time, I felt both shy and awkward. Nevertheless, I forced myself to respond.

"Yes, My Lord, Catherine speaks highly of you also."

I wanted to tell him that Catherine had fallen in love with him but certainly, it wasn't my place to do so. He asked, "You are living here at Blakewood House then? Do you help Catherine? How long have you been living here?"

"Nearly all of my life sir. It has been a happy time. I didn't become a lady's maid to Catherine until I was sixteen, two years before my sister Aggie was married."

"You have a sister then. Does she live here?" he asked.

"No, she has moved on with her life," I replied.

As he walked to the fireplace to put another log on the fire he asked, "And should Catherine leave Blakewood, do you think you might move with her?"

In reply, I said "Indeed, my Lord, many years ago Catherine and I swore to be friends forever. Nothing has changed."

Later that night when I was helping Catherine change into her nightie she asked, "Don't you think he is wonderful?"

"Yes, he certainly is a gentleman. Do you know anything about his background?"

"Yes, he was born in Yorkshire, but he has spent several years abroad with his uncle who is quite elderly. They spend most of their time in India as Edward is taking over his Uncle's position as a Lieutenant-Governor over the North-Western Provinces in India. Also, Lord Edward has distant cousins. They are Scandinavian. He told me he sometimes visits them."

"He is very good looking. Do you know anything about his mother?"

"Yes, Betsy, his mother died in childbirth. His close family consists of a much older sister and a younger brother, Henry. His father died a few years ago. His father was a noble, so, as he is the eldest surviving legitimate male, he inherited his title and that included the right to a seat in the House of Lords."

I replied, "My, that's something to be proud of."

"Edward told me he inherited a great deal of wealth when his father contracted pneumonia and eventually died."

I pondered, "That must have been a sad time for his family."

Over the winter of that year, Catherine's mother, the baroness, started to become sickly with influenza. The doctor was called several times but the only thing that seemed to help her was Mrs. Mclintock's fine broth along with one or two hours of sun each day. Often the baron would carry her outside to sit in the sun. Her health improved a little, so I was surprised when Catherine came down to my little room one night to inform me of big changes that were being planned.

"Oh Betsy, Mother and Father have decided to move back to their country estate near Sheffield. They think the country air might help Mother's health improve."

I said, "Yes, I know she has been poorly."

Catherine continued, "Father didn't say I had to go with them, but he might. As you know I am seeing Edward almost every day now and can't bear the thought of parting from him."

If she wasn't with him, she was talking to me about him. I could have become quite jealous. I imagined having a gentleman adore me so much would have felt like heaven. But no, I loved Catherine and wanted to see her happiness. I think Catherine must have spoken to Lord Edward about it.

Just a few days later, when I took Catherine's breakfast to her room, as soon as she saw me she excitedly said, "I wanted to come down last night and tell you, but I knew I would have to wake you if I did.

Good news, good news, dear Betsy, Edward has asked me to marry him and he has spoken to Father. It's going to work out splendidly. We will marry before Mother and Father leave for the country and then we will live here at Blakewood House."

How my heart felt comforted! I could see a fine outcome. I responded eagerly, "Oh, that will be grand!"

"Edward is going to purchase Blakewood House from Father. Just think, I will soon be called Lady Catherine Bannister. I love Mother and Father dearly, but will be so pleased to carry Edward's name."

I was relieved to know that Blakewood House would continue to be my home. My familiarity with Blakewood gave me a sense of belonging as I remembered nothing else.

There was much talk amongst the servants about the forthcoming wedding, but it took a few weeks before things seemed to be organized.

Mrs. Mclintoch told us at tea one evening, "If we are to make this a grand day for Lady Catherine, we all need to work together to follow the instructions her ladyship has given me. We will need to open the west wing to prepare for the guests staying over. Her Ladyship has authorized Mr. Woods and me to take on more kitchen maids and housemaids as we see fit. There will be a pre-wedding evening meal and then a late morning wedding followed by an afternoon of entertainment and good food.

She questioned Woods asking, "There'll be sixty for the dinner and a hundred and forty for the wedding day, how many additional servants can you see we might be needing?"

Woods replied, "Surely a woman of your ability should know such things, perhaps you should ask Betsy here. Her mother was a real wiz at organizing."

"That's silly," she replied. "I hardly think Betsy would know. She's a lady's maid."

Woods spoke candidly, "Well then I suggest it's up to you to determine."

As they were speaking, I felt a little tension in the air.

Mrs. Mclintoch replied tersely, "Very well I will. Mr. Woods, you take note now. Look for four temporary kitchen maids and six temporary housemaids."

Woods reply was rather matter-of-fact. "How soon do you think we'll need them?"

As Mrs. Mclintoch stood and removed her apron she said, "It's best to be safe. two weeks before."

Woods responded, "Very well then, I will need to hire several to help serve also, but I won't need them until the actual days of the festivities.

"There will be lots of baking and cleaning going on at Blakewood. We have eight weeks to be doing everything. The evening meal will be in the house, but they are going to hold the wedding feast outdoors."

I wondered what they were going to do if it rained and expressed this very thought to Mrs. Mclintoch.

She smiled wryly. "Then lassie, we will have it inside and we will need to alter our plans. I've noticed that you and the Lady Catherine have formed quite a friendship. You will have to keep a bit more distance from Catherine when she is married. That's something you will have to get used to lassie."

I responded, "Catherine and I have a good understanding. We have been friends for many years. She has already introduced me to Lord Edward. He is aware of our friendship."

"Be that as it may, you need to remember, Catherine will be a married woman and she must give her husband priority. Plus, whoever heard of a noble taking notice of the likes of us? It's a wonder the baron didn't squash the idea a long time ago."

"Anyway, I won't need to start ordering food yet. But there will be plenty of work for us all."

Throughout the coming days, everyone in the household seemed to be excited and full of anticipation. I knew it was true that I would have to be a little more distant from Catherine. I tried to put that thought out of my mind. In the following weeks, apart from my duties as a lady's maid I was involved with cleaning and assisting Mrs. Mclintoch to be sure she didn't forget something. I don't know why she had faith in me, but she frequently looked to me for advice.

Fortunately, Blakewood House was large and there was sufficient room to seat sixty people. I helped with preparations for the tables with fine china and silverware, some of which had to be purchased new. The glassware was mostly crystal and was custom finished with the baron's family crest on it.

Earlier on the wedding eve, the house was opened so that florists could see to their wonderful floral arrangements. A mountain of food and wine was purchased. A day or two before the dinner, those of us in the kitchen worked rolling pastry, preparing delicacies and peeling fruit and vegetables. We didn't have the facilities to cook several roast dishes at the same time, so another large oven was purchased. Money didn't seem to be an object.

The night before the Wedding Eve, Mrs. Mclintoch spoke to us all as we were eating our meal.

"I believe everything is coming together as the baron has asked. Don't you agree, Mr. Woods?"

Woods looked up from his meal and said, "Yes, I agree with you. But be encouraged. Everyone, we must follow the master's orders. We must make it a wonderful occasion that no one will forget."

A seamstress was bought in to make Catherine's dress. She was prim and proper and took to her work as soon as she arrived. She bought several rolls of dress materials, allowing Catherine to choose which she liked best. As the dress was coming together Catherine often asked my opinion.

When I brought in her breakfast she asked, "Miss Pinkerton is coming this morning. Would you come and have a look at my dress when she comes? She comes to my room at ten."

"I'll be here," I said. "I'll get Lizzy to come and make your bed up before she comes. Mrs. Mclintoch wants me to help cleaning the silver today so can you dress yourself?"

"Of course. I know how everybody is so busy in preparation for my big day. I do appreciate it. You are all so very kind."

When I returned to Catherine's room she was standing in front of a mirror. She had chosen a thin muslin.

She asked, "Do you like my dress, Betsy?"

I was truthful, "Yes, I like the muslin. It's light and will be ideal for this warm weather."

"Do you like the sleeves?" she asked. And then continued on without waiting for my answer, "I am going to have a long train."

I replied. "Yes, I like the puffed sleeves, but I wonder do you need such a long train?"

"Oh, Betsy I have dreamed of having a long wedding train all of my life. Besides, Mother agrees, and Miss Pinkerton does also."

I don't know why Catherine asked me. I think she wanted validation that she had made the right choice.

Catherine said she would ask her mother and the baron if I might be a guest at the wedding and later at the wedding festivities. There was never any chance this would be allowed. I knew what the answer would be. Anyway, I was asked to help serve with Woods and those he had hired to assist. I was content. I knew that by serving alongside Woods I could share in Catherine's joy, watching her and seeing the guests.

Many hours went into preparing fine food for the dinner.

The guests took up most of the large drawing room where an aperitif and drinks were offered. A variety of seafood had been bought up from the docks. Mrs. Mclintoch had us prepare tasty morsels on squares of pastry and other delightful treats. When dinner was served, the guests moved into the dining room to enjoy duck, pheasant, chicken, beef, lamb and a grand array of vegetable dishes. Sweet pies and small bread puddings were offered for dessert. All the desserts were made from fresh fruit that had been bought in from the countryside. There was fresh whipped cream in abundance. Mrs. Mclintoch had done an outstanding job, almost as good as my own dear Mother might have done.

The following day, when I helped Catherine dress for the wedding, she looked a little flushed.

"Dear Betsie, these past weeks have just flown by. We haven't talked a lot. I am so thankful that Mother and Father have accepted Edward as they have, and I have seen the way he brings a smile from you. You do think my marriage to Edward is the right thing, don't you?"

"Are you having those pre-wedding jitters?" I asked. "You asked me that very same question yesterday. Of course, your Edward is a very fine person. No one could want for a better man."

"I hope you might find such a man Betsy. You deserve to. Someone of fine character just like Edward."

"We will have to wait and see. To be truthful, I don't have much desire to marry, but who knows what the future may hold?"

The following day, when Edward and Catherine took their vows, my thoughts began to change. Yes, I would like someone to care about me. Someone who would share my thoughts and put my feelings ahead of their own. Eventually I resolved that thinking in such a manner was foolish. I was happy in my situation and it was unlikely that I would ever meet a man like Catherine's Edward.

All the servants who were permanent in the household attended the marriage ceremony and what a joy it was. Everyone loved Catherine.

The wedding was beautiful. The sun was shining and there was a soft breeze which made the train of Catherine's wedding gown rustle as two of her young cousins followed holding it. Catherine was radiant. How happy she looked! When it came time for their wedding kiss, Edward took her in his arms so gently. I thought they made a wonderful couple as they walked down the aisle together.

All the guests slowly ambled to the area which had been set up for the festivities. A dance floor had been set up on the lawn.

I asked Woods about it. "When was that bought in? I was looking over the area last night with Mrs. Mclintoch and I didn't see a dance floor."

"It was made in pieces that could be assembled in blocks. A few of the villagers put it together early this morning. They have been working on it for several weeks." He replied.

The wedding tables looked grand. The long wedding table was at the center and four very long guest tables were on each side of the wedding table. They were covered with flowers, fine china and silverware of varying types. As the guests were seated, I was overjoyed to be able to serve the wedding table. Often, Catherine and I exchanged looks. There was delight in her eyes, the same delight which I felt for her.

While the guests were eating, there was a pianist and a fiddler playing festive music.

After the guests had eaten, Lady Catherine and Lord Edward took to the dance floor and danced a waltz while all looked on. I thought to myself again that the bride and groom were well suited. Many of the guests joined them in dance and I believed they all had an enjoyable time.

Clearing the tables of dirty dishes was just the beginning of the cleanup. The newly hired kitchen maids had a mighty job. They had remained, cleaning dishes, from the previous night to ensure there would be enough silverware and fine china for the wedding day. Clearing the garden area was also quite a job. Eating utensils of all sorts had to be taken in; rubbish done away with; many white soiled tablecloths and servants attire meant the days ahead would be full of laundering and starching. Tables and seats had to be removed and so on. It was a huge undertaking, but no one complained. We were all so pleased the wedding and festivities went off so smoothly. During our evening meal that night the baron came down into our eating area and thanked us all personally.

I felt a little disappointed after it was all over, and I did miss Catherine, but just two weeks later we were called to assist the baron and her Ladyship as they made preparations to travel to their country home. They took some of their finer furniture as well as their bone china, glassware and some linen and cutlery. There seemed to be endless bags of clothing. As there was so much of everything, another larger coach was hired just to carry much of their baggage.

As they were about to leave, we gathered around their coach. Her ladyship had tears in her eyes when the baron said, "You all have been good and faithful friends and servants. My wife and I shall miss you all dearly. May God bless you all. We will be back for a visit when Edward and Catherine return."

Coughing softly, her Ladyship hugged each one of us. When it was my turn, she spoke tearfully to me.

"Dear Betsy. What a joy you have been! I will miss you so. You have always been so kind, so willing to please. Please promise me that you will continue to care for Catherine, especially when Edward is away."

"Of course, your ladyship, I love Catherine ever so much."

"Thank you, my dear, make sure you look after yourself also."

I nodded my agreement. I thought if I even just said the word, 'yes' I would break out in tears. I had grown very fond of her Ladyship.

We all stood watching as their coach made its way toward the large gateway of Blakewood House.

Mr. Woods helped us all return to the moment, "You are all to stop your sniffling. Ya heard the baron then. He said they would return for a visit when Lady Catherine comes home."

While waiting for Catherine and Lord Edward to return, I had little to do. Sometimes I would go to the local pub where I would play darts and have a shandy with other servants. I gained a good deal of knowledge about many of the Lords and Ladies living in the district. I got a proper view of life and the way people lived it. There was one young man who often sought me out for a chat. I somehow think he fancied me, but he struck me as being full of himself. I just humored him and took our friendship lightly. Much of the time I preferred to read.

Time edged its way along slowly, but the day finally came when we welcomed both the Lady Catherine and our new Master home. They had many bags. Catherine had purchased many new clothes and it took some time before I finished helping her put them all away. There was one parcel which Catherine wouldn't let me touch. As she caught my eye, I could see she was filled with glee.

"Dear Betsy, for you I purchased a fine dress. As she handed the parcel to me, she said, "It's mauve. I thought the color would go well with your dark hair."

I opened it quickly and as I put it up to my body, I could see it would fit well. "Catherine, how kind of you! Thank you so much."

"Oh, Betsy its nothing of any consequence. If I had my way you would have ever so much more."

Catherine was quite excited as she told me of their time in Europe and the many different cultures she had experienced. I envied her a little and secretly hoped that someday I might get the opportunity of at least crossing the channel to spend some time in France or Spain.

Catherine and Lord Edward settled into a lifestyle appropriate for people of their station in life. Most days Lord Edward would disappear to his office in the heart of London. He'd be gone for most of the day. On some such times, Catherine would decide to plan a charity dinner, which really meant she would spend time with Mrs. Mclintoch and me. Often peals of laughter could be heard coming from the kitchen.

Catherine really had no idea how to plan a charity dinner, but both Mrs. Mclintoch and I would merrily guide her and, eventually, a fine dinner would be the outcome. Catherine saw to it that the money raised was given to the poor. Looking back now, I really don't think we had any idea how the poor lived. Nevertheless, planning those dinners was a real joy. Indeed, those were grand times.

CHAPTER

4

Three years later

And now, how I berate myself! I should have been able to save Catherine and myself. What must the baron and his dear wife think of me? I promised her Ladyship I would care for Catherine and I failed in my duty. I am greatly disappointed in myself.

As I was musing, I heard a tapping on the door. I hurried to answer it, hoping it would be company. Whoever it was, I hoped they would take my mind away from the ordeal that Catherine and I had been through.

As I opened the door, a familiar face greeted me. The kind face of Edward's elderly sister made my heart warm. Miss Bannister had never married and had been a mother figure to Edward when their mother had died in childbirth. Catherine and I always admired her for her stylish manner of dress and her kind manner of speech. Today she wore a tailored blue dress with a bonnet to match. She carried a small bag which also matched both her shoes and bonnet.

I said smiling warmly. "Why Miss Banister how good it is to see you!"

Her reply, "It's wonderful to see you Betsy, after all this time."

I asked, "Would you like to come through to the parlor? There's a fire in there."

"Yes," she replied. "It is very cold outside. Thank you."

We both took a seat near the fire.

As Miss Banister sat down she said, "You poor dear! What a wicked ordeal you've been through! And oh, the poor dear, Lady Catherine.

She continued, "I've just come from the manor. Edward stopped by this morning. He said you both had been treated very badly and Catherine has lost her memory. I wanted to ask questions, but it seemed he had no time to answer. He told me you are to be treated like family because you stood by Catherine's side endlessly. He told me you were no longer to be a servant and said he is going to purchase a home nearby for you. He mentioned that you were both servants in Australia and when he arrived to rescue you the Governor there was already expecting him. Beyond that, I couldn't fully make head or tail of what he was saying, only that it had all been such a terrible mistake."

I responded, "Yes, as I think on it, it was a wicked mistake."

Miss Bannister continued, "Edward said he was in a rush as he wanted to see Henry, our brother, and then he needed to be at Catherine's side as they were traveling up to Sheffield to see her parents. I presume he and Catherine have left already. I was disappointed not to be able to see Catherine but pleased to know you were both safe. Edward told me to come and see you. He said you would be the Mistress of Blakewood until they returned. He said you would tell me all about it."

"Yes, it's true." I replied. "Edward is determined I should be treated with respect and was no longer to be a servant. Over the past year, in circumstances beyond our control, Catherine and I wound up on the other side of the world. He may have told you that we were sentenced as convicts and sent to Australia on trumped-up charges."

Miss Bannister replied, "Yes, he told me before he went to get you. He said you and Catherine were sent to Australia on a convict ship. How horrid that must have been!"

Betsy shuddered, "It was not a joyful journey. Indeed, quite the opposite. Catherine and I and many other innocents were treated harshly, and we nearly lost our lives in the crossing."

Miss Bannister said earnestly, "We were so worried! When you and Catherine had been gone for two days, your Butler, Woods, came over to ask if I knew where you were. I had no idea, so we checked with Catherine's parents and friends. And early on we contacted the Police Commissioner and reported that you both were missing. We also sent word to Edward, but there was some delay. It took nearly fifteen weeks for the pouch to reach him."

"Catherine's parents were greatly distressed. Her father came down to London. He worked with the constables questioning everyone. The news was everywhere. It caused quite a disturbance throughout London. There was news of it in the Times. In the end, the authorities had just about given up by the time Edward returned to London.

"You might not believe it, but Edward turned London upside down looking for you. He went through the interviews the constables had conducted and followed up on them to be more thorough. The constables questioned many more people and Edward put up a reward of a thousand pounds for anyone knowing of your whereabouts. When the interrogations didn't provide much, Edward hired a team of private investigators to sift the information he collected and to develop new leads.

"Eventually it paid off. Edward took a hand in the interrogations himself and developed a lead that took him down to the docks. There were rumors about a pair of unusual prisoners that were condemned and sent to Australia. There was a convict who the authorities claimed was insane. It was rumored she pretended to be a 'lady' and that she had a woman who claimed to be her maid with her. The dock hands who reported this were apologetic, but thought it was good for a laugh at the time. Edward wanted to know names, but nobody could help him there."

Betsy responded thoughtfully, "While we were traveling home on the ship Edward told me how he discovered our whereabouts, but I would like to hear what you have to say about it. Can you tell me more?"

"Yes, of course dear, I hope I can remember it all. My memory is not what it used to be. It's a somewhat involved tale. Edward went through the records of prisoners who had been sent to the Colonies in Australia. There was a judge named Wilkens who sentenced many of the convicts. Edward had past dealings with the man and wondered if you had somehow run afoul of him. He put two and two together when he saw your bogus names on the court records. Thank goodness you had used your real Christian names!

Evidently, this judge Wilkens was a corrupt man who obtained his position by extortion and bribery. I guess this is not all that uncommon. I have heard there are some among the law profession who profess to be honorable and righteous, yet have had no real formal training and corrupt the legal profession.

In their earlier encounter, Edward and some others of his peerage had collaborated to bring charges against Wilkens. Edward personally confronted that Wilkens man. I believe there was quite a scene. Edward made him look bad because he was a scoundrel. Wilkens had brought charges against many innocent people for crimes they didn't commit. They were given the choice of facing the hangman's noose or paying a large fine. The fines were outrageously high, and many were hanged for little or no reason. Some were able to raise the money and that

Wilkens fellow pocketed much of it himself. Edward publicly exposed him as an extortioner and a liar. A constable was dispatched to arrest him, but found the man gone, and no one able to find him.

Apparently, everyone thought Wilkens was gone, but, somehow, he worked his way back into the legal profession again. He evidently had information about a scandal involving Lord Dunston and was blackmailing him. He used what he knew to get Lord Dunston to secretly arrange a quiet posting that allowed him to become a magistrate again.

His authority was more limited than it had been. He couldn't condemn people to the hangman's noose. But it seems to me he determined the future of many a poor soul."

Edward was furious when he realized that Wilkens had not only escaped justice the first time but had corrupted the legal system by acquiring authority again. When your names came up in the court register from Judge Wilkens, Edward thought it was an impossible coincidence. Your name shows up in his court register at exactly the same time you went missing.

Edward took precautions when he made this discovery. He arranged for a watch to be set at all the places Wilkens was known to frequent. When his whereabouts was known Edward brought the Chief Commissioner with him to collect the man. Edward then questioned him fully. In the face of Edward's fury, and realizing Edward had the power to destroy him, Wilkens admitted that he had tried a woman who pretended to be something she was not. He pretended to have the best interests of England in mind and claimed he was only executing the mandate given to him to get the riff-raff off the streets. He also admitted that it was about the time of Catherine's disappearance.

The Chief Commissioner also took a turn at questioning Wilkens. As devious as that wicked man was, the Commissioner kept at him until it finally came out. In a moment of anger Wilkens admitted Catherine had told him who she was, and when he realized she was the wife of his longtime adversary, he took the opportunity to exact retribution for the trouble Edward had caused him in the past. After this admission, the Commissioner immediately arrested Wilkens and he was jailed and put in irons, with his fate to be determined when Edward returned from Australia.

Edward let it be known that the disappearance of his wife was the fault of a dishonorable Judge. He was so angry! He went to his contacts at the Times and had them devote a complete edition to exposing the vile practices of Wilkens. He shared some of the harsh realities of Catherine's ordeal. Not that he knew how Catherine was really treated then. The Times declared Wilkens to be satanically evil.

Upon learning of your whereabouts, Edward immediately arranged to board a ship bound for Australia. He had no notion of what had happened to you once the convict ship had left England, and he refused to delay his search in order to hold those responsible to account. His only thought was to find you as quickly as possible. He took ship with the HMS Florencia and arrived in Sydney to find that the governor already had word of you."

Miss Bannister continued, "Edward told me this morning that a man by the name of Lord Mars sent a note to the Governor in Sydney town telling him that an English noblewoman who had been wrongfully sent as a convict to Australia was, in fact, staying on his estate. Her husband, an English noble by the name of Lord Edward Bannister, might send an inquiry. If this happened, Lord Mars asked the Governor to inform Edward that Catherine and her ladies' maid were both in his household. Mars wrote that he didn't think Catherine was well enough to make the journey back to London because she was only then recovering from a nasty lung infection. Lord Mars had separately sent correspondence to Edward, but Edward said it was waiting for him at his return and must have reached London sometime after Edward left for Australia. I really don't know.

Edward was so pleased! He knew exactly where to find you both. Of course, he is truly distraught by the way you have been treated. He told me that Catherine has lost her memory. Although nothing was said, I can see that Edward blames himself. And, I must admit, I think he was wrong leaving Catherine. It's not as if he needed the money. I suppose we all make mistakes. I hope for Edward's sake he will have the right priorities in the future. I also hope that dear Catherine's memory will return, and she might be the happy soul she once was."

"It has been very traumatic for Edward," I responded.

Miss Banister spoke candidly. "Yes, my dear, it has, but far more traumatic for you and Catherine."

"Yes, you are certainly right, Miss Kensington. On the ship, as we returned home, Lord Edward was at Catherine's side most of the time. And, when he wasn't with her, he was very somber. He always appeared more cheerful when he was in her company. Nevertheless, I agree with you, I think he feels he is to blame."

I continued. "Edward told me how he was able to find us, and he assured me that I would never need to be in service again. He told me he would find a small house for me nearby. But, apart from that, he spent his time with Catherine. They had a standing invitation to eat at the Captain's table with the officers of the ship, but Edward declined because at times Catherine needed encouragement to eat. And, truth be told, she would often say silly things. He felt it would not be appropriate to expose Lady Catherine to their judgments.

Lord Edward came up on deck most days for a short time, and occasionally Catherine would accompany him. The Captain and his officers would try to draw him out in conversation but to little avail. He always inspected the food which was taken to the cabin he shared with Catherine and they dined together."

"Normally I would join them during the evening meal. Catherine continued to eat very little but gradually she has regained her appetite. Thank Goodness."

Betsy continued. "There is an obvious change in Lord Edward. He is certainly not the man I once knew when he is apart from Catherine. But when he is with her the Edward who I was introduced to returns. He seems very disillusioned in his own countrymen. I am sure he didn't know how badly convicts are treated and how his wife was treated. I suspect he is deeply upset that his beloved England has dealt him such a cruel blow. He brightens up when in Catherine's presence. I am pleased they are able to visit Catherine's parents together."

Miss. Bannister responded. "Yes, I noticed he was somber and somewhat troubled. I asked him how it had all happened. He said it all had been a terrible mistake and I should see you, Betsy. He said you would tell me about it. I am hopeful he will stay by Catherine's side as often as possible. He adores Catherine. He was very unhappy during the time you were missing and would often spend time with me. Not that I, a little old lady, could help him much."

I considered this before answering. "He seems far better now that he has come home and Catherine is with him again."

Miss Bannister responded, "He told me Catherine was very insistent and determined to see her parents. I would have thought she would have wanted to spend more time at Blakewood to recuperate after your voyage from Australia."

"There was more to the situation than you might think," I replied. Yes, we tried to coax her to stay. But she had forgotten that her parents lived in Sheffield. When we first returned, she believed her parents would be here, at Blakewood. That was a mistake we should have rectified before it happened.

When we arrived, Catherine ran up the stairs and rang the bell. Woods answered the door. I think he was mystified when Catherine didn't recognize him."

Miss Banister frowned as she said, "I am cross with Edward. I hope he will use his brains and stay close to Catherine."

This reminded me that Edward had already made that decision. I remarked, "Before all this trouble, Edward said that this trip he was making would be his last trip to India."

Miss Bannister scowled judgmentally as she said, "I would hope so. Look how scandalous it has been. It's a wicked state of affairs.

She continued, "Tell me Betsy, where were you in Australia? Please tell me what happened?"

"I have gone over everything with the master numerous times. Even though the ordeal seems to haunt me, I am sure Catherine would want you to know. I owe it to her, to share her tale with family who will listen. I am sure Edward will see to it that Judge Wilkens hangs."

I smiled sadly at Miss. Banister when I said, "In response to your question, It's a long story. I don't know where to begin. Perhaps I could read Lady Catherine's journal to you. It's upstairs.

Lord Edward wants it to stay at Blakewood and has set conditions for how it is to be handled. He has given me permission to refer to it as often as I wish, but no one is permitted to take it out of Blakewood. And, when not reading it, it must be returned to its appointed place in his bedroom. I think he is going to use it as a reference when he confronts his peers about the matters it reveals. But then again, he may think it too personal to do even that. I'll run and get it. Make yourself comfortable, I won't be but a minute."

Coming back, I noticed that Miss Kensington had moved to a seat nearer to the fire. I sat down opposite her.

She said, "I do appreciate this Betsy."

I said, "It doesn't much look like a journal. It's really just a collection of papers. Lord Marsden, the master whom we worked for, wasn't much into writing, so it's the best I could find for Catherine."

"Even when she was very sick, Catherine wanted to write her story down for Edward to read. Every time I look at her writings, I remember Catherine's face during those last few weeks just before Edward came. She looked so pale and fragile as if just a slight breeze would take her away. She was delirious for a time and even I couldn't understand her words. It brings tears to my eyes."

"If it makes you upset Betsy perhaps you shouldn't."

"No there is no need for tears now. Fortunately, Catherine's health started to improve momentarily when the master told her that Edward was on his way."

"Catherine would want me to tell you. I am sorry you couldn't see her when we came back. Although she still looks frail and weak, she was most insistent that she wanted to see her parents. Lord Edward agreed because he thought the country air would help her. I think he is hoping Catherine might regain her memory if she sees her mother and father. I expect he and Catherine will be a third of the way there by now. Lord Edward said they would stop in at an inn overnight as he didn't want the journey to be too taxing on Catherine's health. I am sure that Catherine's parents will welcome them both with open arms."

Miss Bannister replied, "Yes, her father was very upset about it. He stayed here, at Blakewood House, when he was in London searching for you. He told me Catherine's mother had not accompanied him because she was in poor health. Let's hope she and Catherine are a good tonic for each other."

Catherine's Journal

As I turned to face Miss Bannister I said, "As you listen, you will understand why Lord Edward is so horrified by poor Catherine's ordeal. He had no idea that ordinary people were being condemned as convicts and then treated so cruelly. He was horrified to discover how badly Catherine had been treated."

I began to read:

"It seems like an eternity since I have enjoyed the calm peace and heartfelt joy I felt while enjoying a drink and a cozy chat with Edward, my dear beloved. I so look forward to the day when I might see his face again; when I might enter the doors of Blakewood House again. Our home is a fine and stately place where there is much warmth, especially when Edward is home.

Edward's presence seems to overshadow everyone who enters those fine doors. For me, home has always generated deep feelings of geniality and comfort. Edwards's gentle and peaceful manner is surely a sign of a man of a good and fine character. After only a few months of marriage, my dear Edward was asked to become a Lieutenant-Governor over the North -Western Provinces in India. Previously he had served as an aid to the Lieutenant- Governor, Edward's uncle. As a result, we only see each other for six months of the year. In the two years we have been married we have not had a lot of time together. Nevertheless, such times are wonderful and joyous as we spent them together.

Sometimes Edward would ask me to sing while he played the piano. We would visit with friends in London to play cards, attend parties, attend concerts and whenever the opportunity of a ball arose, I would purchase a new gown and we would always be among the first on the dance floor. Edward and I often held charity dinners for the poor. Nothing fancy, of course, just a gathering of friends and associates to enjoy a meal together where donations were made to some of the poor houses. Back then I really had no idea how much in need those poor people were. How my view of life has changed!

When Edward told me of his overseas travels, I could hardly imagine the life he led. He asked me if I would go with him to India, even though we both knew it could prove to be a nightmare. My health had been fragile as I had just suffered my second miscarriage. In the end, we decided it would be unwise.

How he has adored me! Our times of lovemaking were so dear! He was so gentle, so kind. When it came time for him to leave, we both tried to hold back tears. I can remember him saying, "My dearest Catherine this will be my last trip. I cannot bear these separations any longer. I have given the Home Office notice that I will not be able to continue in this position after the year's end."

Considering all that has happened, I feel I am such a stranger to the life I once lived. So many times I ask myself where am I? Who am I? How life has dealt me a wicked turn in fate! I have wandered from paths of frivolity, comfort and security to endless days of depravity and intolerable grief. Oh! What a twist in fate these last months have been! Those other convicts and guards on the ship used to say I was a mad woman. Perhaps I am. These past ten months have been a total nightmare. It is I! I must take the blame for the hellish predicament which befell poor Betsy and me. Will I ever forget that fateful day when this terrible ordeal began?

After breakfast one morning Betsy asked: "Do you have any plans for the day Lady Bannister?"

So formal! It has stuck with me. She called me "Lady Bannister" like I was some elderly dowager. Betsy was not generally so formal. Her sudden formality struck me at the time.

I replied, "Oh, Betsy don't forget we are friends. There is no need to address me in such a manner; it is alright when we are in company, but not when we are alone."

My goodness, we were good friends then. And now how these past months have bound that friendship. I do love her and have relied on her so much. Nonetheless, in answer to her question, I said, "Remember a few days ago when we chatted in jest, that we might go over to the East End to have a look around and look at their shops?"

Betsy replied, "I don't think we should be seen in such a place, Catherine. You never know what trouble we might get into."

I replied, "Oh fiddle stix! You are such a pessimist! I think we should disguise ourselves, so no one will know who we are."

I think I called it 'pretending to be streetwalkers.'

Betsy rejected this as nonsense, "No, it's not a good place to be. I doubt very much if Lord Edward would approve."

I disagreed with Betsy and responded, "We don't want anybody to know who we are in that area. We will need to use made up names. Anyway, who will ask? This will truly be an adventure. I doubt if we will like anything they have, but maybe I might get a look at the way the other half lives and truth be known, I am sick of always having my clothes tailored for me."

Betsy argued with me, "Catherine you know we shouldn't go there. The place is full of thieves and vagabonds."

My peevish reply was, "Well I will go alone then."

Betsy said crossly, "Oh my goodness, you are so determined. I promised Lord Edward I would care for you. How can I keep you safe when you have these silly ideas?"

I replied cheerfully, "You will have to come with me then because I am going no matter what you say."

I know Betsy was truly concerned, but she said, "Well perhaps we should go when it is not raining, but I do not condone the idea."

I know Betsy only said that so I would forget the idea, but I was determined and said, "Betsy, you are such a 'stick in the mud'. If it's a sunny day then we will go tomorrow."

The following day the sky was blue, and the sun was shining.

We left Blakewood House early in the morning hoping that no one we knew would see us. We had rehearsed what we would say if we saw anyone we knew.

We discovered it was a fair walk.

We thought it unwise to go by coach to the poorer area. From a practical standpoint, we knew that if we did, Tod, the coachman might reveal our indiscretion to you, Edward upon your return from India. And now, Edward as you have found us and have read my writings, you will know how shamefully I acted.

If only I had listened to Betsy! All the trouble which followed would never have happened!

Before we went, I made Betsy swear that she wouldn't tell anyone. Betsy told me it was a long walk, so we decided to walk there and get a cab back. Indeed, it was a very long walk. Much longer than I had anticipated.

Please, dear Edward, don't think too ill of me! I thought it was going to be just a bit of fun. Betsy and I dressed in some old clothes. We put extra rips in our dresses to make them look older and worn. I even practiced speaking like a commoner with Betsy. Betsy told me to drop some of my consonants when talking and make my words sound different. What was it she said?

"Ya 'otter be "ore carin' if ya be 'inking it be 'rite."

We had a good laugh over it.

Although the sun was shining, it was cold. Betsy suggested we should wear cloaks to keep us warm. We searched until we found some amongst the old clothing in the attic.

Dressed as we were, we avoided the servants and left by a side door in the drawing room.

Lady Ashcore, who lived on our street was just about to leave her house as her driver pulled up with her carriage.

She greeted us and said, "My goodness Catherine, where are you going dressed like that?"

I was quick to respond, "Some friends are hosting a play, "Relief for the Poor". We are going to a rehearsal."

Lady Ashcore responded, "It's early to be doing such things."

Catherine spoke, "Oh, not so much. It's a good thirty minutes' walk. I like morning walks."

Lady Ashcore said, "Yes, I do too, it clears the mind."

Lady Ashcore smiled at Betsy who had the good sense not to speak. If she had done so, Lady Ashcore would have indeed wondered why I was keeping company with a servant.

When we started our walk, we passed many elegant houses in squares and there were broad straight streets built north of St. James Palace.

Betsy asked, "Have you ever been in there, Catherine?"

"Hardly," I replied. "You need to be Royalty if you are to go in there."

"I wonder how old it is!"

"I know all about it. Father told me when we used to take walks together when I was young.

"The palace was ordered by Henry the 8th, on the site of a former leper hospital dedicated to Saint James the Less. The palace was built between 1531 and 1536 as a smaller residence to escape formal court life. St James is arranged around a number of courtyards, including the Color Court, the Ambassador's Court, and the Friary Court. So there, Betsy," Catherine said smiling, "I bet you didn't think I knew all that."

We walked down through the more prestigious part of London. Then the houses and shops started to look shabby and there were grassy slopes where we picked up clumps of grass to throw at each other.

Catherine declared, "I don't think I have been this far from home walking. This is an adventure, Betsy. Do these houses have water connected to their homes as we do?"

Betsy smiled amiably and said, "This is something I know. In the 17th century, wealthy people got piped water. It came by canal from the countryside. Then it came by hollow tree trunks under the streets. You had to pay to have your house connected... so if you are poor, no water."

"So, Father has to pay for us to have water?"

"Yes, I think so."

As we were walking quite a few Hackney carriages passed us.

"Maybe we should have got a carriage, Betsy. This walk seems way too far. My feet are not used to walking so far."

Smiling, Betsy said, "So, we should give up and return home?"

I replied stubbornly, "Not so, we have not started our adventure yet. We have got money, why don't we wave down a carriage"

"I don't think so," she replied. "Then the driver would know that we came here and would think it strange and possibly tell others. Even though I find this adventure totally ridiculous, we need to be careful. We don't want to embarrass Edward or bring disrepute to your family."

I had no intention of giving up and said, "You worry too much. It will be fine."

As we walked near the dock area, there was a strong smell of fish in the air. People were huddled around fires, wearing layers of thin rag clothes, I can't see how they kept warm. It was bitterly cold with a cruel wind blowing from the north; I felt so sad for them! Their faces were dark and miserable and there was a distinct smell of raw sewage.

I asked Betsy, "Don't they have some provision for getting rid of the waste?"

She replied, "There has been talk amongst the servants of having it flow into the Thames. But I am not really sure."

I said, "It's terrible how these poor people live. Something should be done. I will most certainly tell Edward about it."

We went into one shop where lady's hats were displayed.

Betsy whispered to me, "Better not try any on."

I asked innocently, "Why not?"

Betsy said, "I've heard consumption is rife in these parts.".

More reason why we should have left. Why we didn't leave right then, I just don't know.

As we made our way through the cobbled dirty streets of Whitechapel, it disgusted me to think that poor folk lived like this. The streets were alleyways, the shops were dingy and chaotic; men and women were yelling trying to sell their wares. I saw two women vomiting in the street. Little ones were running about in bare feet with no one to care for them. There were feces just lying on the cobblestones. It was a filthy dreadful muddle, a horrid sight. Betsy and I promised each other we would visit one more shop and then leave. From what we had seen most of the clothing was raggedy and not very clean. I thought to myself, "Who would want to buy such rubbish?"

There was an objectionable odor to most of the clothing. But then in that last store. I spotted a bolt of cloth. I told Betsy, "It doesn't smell, and it is just the color I have been looking for."

I was not expecting to have such a find. My seamstress should be able to make a fine dress from this."

"Betsy whispered to me, "Just buy it, don't make any fuss."

I had Betsy speak to the shopkeeper, "If ya don't mind mister could me friend buy that there bolt of cloth?"

He smiled at me and responded, "Ya that cloth 'as come all the way from India."

Betsy whispered to me, "As if it would have come from India, in a place like this."

I wanted to be sure that it was the right color because the shop was dark and dingy, so I took it out to the street to see it in daylight.

Betsy glared at me as if to say no.

Then it happened. The shopkeeper's words, "Excuse me Mrs. Where do you think ya be goin' with that there bolt of cloth?"

Forgetting how Betsy told me to speak, I replied "I am trying to see the color in the light of day."

The storekeeper responded, "A likely story that be, who in the 'ell do ya think ya be, talking like that. Do ya think by pretending to be a toff ya gunna make me be thinking, I'm go-in above me station and I'm gunna let ya off? Ya must think I'm a right nit."

"I think no such thing, I am not pretending anything, indeed, what a ludicrous idea to think that I should steal." No matter what I said he didn't believe me.

Betsy said, "She really is a Lady. It is silly accusing her of stealing."

But he wouldn't listen. Betsy, the shopkeeper and I were out in the street. The shopkeeper was carrying on. He grabbed hold of Betsy and called to two young louts who were passing by.

I tried to get Betsy free of him, but he held her tightly.

We tried to explain. I told the shopkeeper, "I will give you twice what the bolt of cloth is worth. Give up on this silly idea. Stealing is certainly not my forte."

I reached for my purse in my pocket, but it was gone.

I looked at Betsy exclaiming, "Betsy my purse is not in my pocket!"

I thought for a moment, it must have been when we went through Whitechapel. There must have been a pick-pocket.

I told the shopkeeper, "Someone must have stolen my purse. I will bring you the money tomorrow, but I will not take the bolt of cloth."

But he just wouldn't take note of anything that I said. Upon further reflection, I feel that it was his way of lashing out at the upper class. I had heard these poorer folks viewed nobles as selfish and hardhearted. I couldn't be sure of where I'd heard this. At the moment I thought it must be something Betsy had told me.

I really don't remember clearly what happened next. I think the shopkeeper, who was holding each of us, called to two louts passing by and told them, "Give them a going over. They're pretending to be toffs so they can get free fabric."

One grabbed Betsy and the other grabbed me. They pushed us into a deserted alleyway. The taller of the two said, "This'll be right fun."

He told his friend, "You deal with that-un (meaning Betsy) and I will be doing the same to this un, but be sure you slap em', no punches."

They pushed us to a more secluded spot along the alleyway.

When he pushed me down, I heard myself shrieking as I fell to the ground. As I lay there, he leaned in threateningly and grabbed the front of my dress and pulled me up and struck me in my stomach. I gasped for air and almost collapsed from the pain. I could hardly breathe. He came at me again, slapping me about my face and arms. I backed away as quickly as I could, putting my hands up to try and ward off his slaps.

Little good that did me. He seemed to enjoy treating me in this manner.

"Why are you doing this?" I sobbed in disbelief.

He smiled an ugly, gap-toothed smile, dragged me several feet along the cobblestones, and threw me to the ground again. When I tried to crawl away, he pulled me up menacingly. I realized that he was holding back, if he wanted, he could have hurt me much more seriously. He slapped me again, splitting my lip and making my ears ring.

All the while I could hear that Betsy was also being mistreated. I heard the painful blows as they struck, followed by her whimpers.

I wanted to help. I couldn't believe that these ruffians could treat us like this. I was both helpless and indignant. How dare they!

Even in those moments of horror, several things rushed through my mind. What would Edward say? What would Mother and Father say? What would my friends say? Why did I put Betsy in this situation?

Forgetting my own danger, I tried to protect Betsy. I pulled hard against the young man's grasp, but I couldn't escape. My hands and arms were badly scraped from the cobblestones. He slapped me on my face several times until I could tell that one eye was swelling.

After another slap to my face, and more blood running from my lip, he pushed me down on the cobblestones again.

"Well now, yer' ladyship'," he drawled. "We had better not kill ya, but you will be remembering not to go around pretending you ain't just common folks."

He laughed and said something to the other ruffian, and they were gone.

I looked over to Betsy. She looked as if she had experienced a similar battering as I. After a while we were both able to stand up. We looked for a constable but couldn't see one. Walking along in pain we finally found one and I called out and beckoned to him. He came up and said, "It looks like you's have been in trouble."

I then commenced to tell him what had happened to us.

His response was not very helpful. I wanted him to go after the ruffians. Instead, he asked, "What shop were you getting the fabric from then?"

I pointed in the direction of the shop, and while we were both hurt, and despite our protests, he pushed us along towards the shop. As we stood in front of the shop he said, "Now we shall see what the shopkeeper says."

He pushed us into the shop and asked the shopkeeper, "Have these two women tried to purchase something from 'ere?"

The shopkeeper replied, "Ya. You can be sure, constable."

As he pointed at me, he said, "That one there pretended to be some toff and when it come time to pay for it, she ain't got the money. I reckon she was tryin' to get me to be givin' it to 'er cos she says she's some toff."

The constable asked, "Why are they in such a sad state?"

The shopkeeper said with conviction, "There's no doubt, they were tryin' to steal a bolt of cloth from me and some young lads passing said they'd be fixing them for me. I dunno know what they'd be do-in. I 'ad to be with me shop."

The constable's response was most unjust. "Mmm, we shall see they get dealt with properly."

He quickly herded us through the narrow alley ways to a building which looked grim, dark and foreboding.

Whispering to Betsy, I asked, "What can we do?"

Betsy said reassuringly, "Don't worry. When they come to judge us, we can tell them the truth."

As we were pushed into a dark and disgusting smelling room, I protested strongly, "You have no right to do this! My husband is the Lieutenant-Governor over the North-Western Provinces in India. He will see you pay for this injustice."

The cynical retort from the jailer was to be expected I suppose, "Yes, Lady what's your face, I'm sure he rules the world!"

Just before he slammed the door, he told us, "Ya will be stay-in 'ere tonight. Ya's will be sentenced tommorry."

Then the door was slammed behind us.

The first thing that hit us was the foul smell of dirty bodies and feces. As our eyes were able to focus in the dimness, we found we were amongst many women and children. The little ones ranged in age from babies to about twelve years. There were some who seemed younger than us, others seemed to be about our age and others were obviously older. Though we were dressed like them, we certainly didn't smell like them, nor did we speak their coarse dialect.

The room that we had been pushed into bore little resemblance to any other I had seen before. The floorboards were bare, the walls were badly stained and there was just one long wooden bench, upon which about half of the women in the room sat. Others sat huddled on the floor, some holding their babes. There were several buckets in the room. I looked enquiringly at Betsy who looked back at me in dread.

This was the beginning of the endless depravities that would come our way in the months ahead.

Over the next few hours, Betsy and I looked at each other often. She whispered to me, "Don't talk. If there's any talking, I'll do it. These women have no love for nobles. I worry things will go badly for us if they find out who you are!"

Though I held my tongue, I doubted her. The women seemed friendly enough. One of the older women asked, "What they be holdin' ya for then?"

Betsy began to tell them our tale but as she conversed with them, I felt so angry that I didn't heed her advice. I spoke out "We shouldn't be here, it's a complete injustice."

They heard me speak and, as I told them what had really happened, they scoffed and scorned. We were quickly shunned. Betsy hushed me.

"You should speak quietly to me, but to no one else."

Betsy and I tried to keep to ourselves in what little room was ours, but it was a fruitless task. Some blankets and pillows were stacked up against one wall and I noticed most of the women had taken some.

I looked pleadingly at Betsy and whispered, "Whatever are we going to do? My body aches all over."

Betsy whispered back, "I'm hurting too. When we were crossing the office, I took a piece of paper, ink and a quill and put them under my cloak. We might be able to get a note out to someone we know to help us."

In the faint light, I was able to scribble a note to Edwards's brother, Henry. I folded it and put Henry's address on it and gave it to Betsy.

"We'll have to wait for an opportunity to get someone to take it to him. Have you still got that sovereign in your shoe?" Betsy asked.

Ever since I was small, even before I knew Betsy, I had always kept a sovereign in my shoe thinking it to hold some magical power. The old grounds man we had at the time told me he found it when he went to fairy town. I suspect he found it amusing. I was so gullible I believed him and asked him if he would take me to fairy town. His reply, "One day little one, one day."

I took the sovereign from my shoe and handed it to Betsy. Some lucky sovereign that turned out to be!

Aside from being Edwards's younger brother, Henry was also a lawyer. Even though he was young, he was very capable and much sought after. I was certain he could help us.

Some of the young prisoners and young women with babies were released the following day before breakfast. Betsy made a beeline for one of the older girls. She looked to be about twelve.

Betsy, trying not to be too forward, asked the girl, "Can ya read then?"

The girl replied, "Ya, some."

Then Betsy spoke to her in a whisper, "If ya got any goodness in ya, an ya know God is wat-chen' ya, then please be tak-en' this 'ere note to this address and 'ere's a sovereign to be thankin' ya. Will ya be doing it then?"

I heard the girl's response, "Where did ya get that then?"

That wasn't where Betsy wanted the conversation to go. "Never you mind. It's gotta be taken to that there address. Will ya do it then?"

"Surely will, miss, for that there sovereign."

Betsy handed her the note and the sovereign.

The girl smirked, "Ya can be sure, Miss; I'll be doing as ya say. I be know-in' this address. Ta then."

She rushed off with the others who were set free.

There was a lot of crying. Some of the young-uns were separated from their mothers. It was painful to watch. I had heard some of the women talking the night before. Some were being punished for minor crimes. Stealing food for their little ones. How wicked it all was.

After the children were taken from their mothers, there were many that didn't eat. The jailors bought in large pots of oatmeal. It didn't have the sweet smell of the porridge Mrs. Mclintoch made, but Betsy urged me to eat. As we hadn't been given any food the previous night, I was hungry and took a scoop from one of the bowls. It was food, but little else could be said about it. I wondered what I looked like. There was no mirror to see. My face hurt. My lip was split and had bled a little during the night and it still felt badly swollen.

In a moment of vanity, I worried what I looked like. What would Edward think?

I asked Betsy, "Tell me how I look."

I think she spoke truthfully, "You have a large bruise on the right side of your face and your lip and eye are swollen."

Betsy asked, "And what of me? Tell me what I look like."

"Not so good. You have bruising on your face and your left eye is swollen," I said.

I continued, "I hope that girl will get our note to Henry."

Many months later, as I reflect, I expect the girl took the sovereign for herself and Henry never received the note. Those first days we waited with great anticipation. Nothing! … I rarely ever wished evil on anyone, but as I began to lose hope, my thoughts were not so pure. Apart from the depravity, I can't be sure which thought made me more indignant: that no one would believe us or that the girl would simply pocket the money without even trying to help.

Throughout these past many months there have been numerous occasions when I have been the victim of evil, some of which seems pointless to relate. Nonetheless, I shall endeavor to put some of my tale on paper. When I first acquired this nasty cough, I thought I would recover quickly. But my cough has been accompanied by a lingering tiredness that has gotten worse over time.

I am determined to put my tale in writing. I doubt if I can remember everything and, as I have often said to myself, "What point is there?" No one will fully understand the evil things we went through. Nonetheless, I shall return to the corruption of our legal system and how this nightmare continued.

After the morning meal, we were herded into another building, just a few yards from the wretched building where we had spent the past night.

There was quite a group of us sitting on chairs waiting for the judge to come. I noticed that the constable who had grabbed us was also sitting in court. We waited a good twenty minutes and then a young bailiff announced, "All rise, the right honorable Judge Wilkens."

A stout man wearing a wig walked to a desk in front of us. He had beady eyes and a pointed nose and walked with a slight limp.

The bailiff then declared, "All be seated." He gave further instructions. "When your name is called out you must stand."

The judge called out a name and referred to his notes, "Mary Bliham."

An older woman stood. She was a ragged little gap-toothed figure barely tall enough to see above the railing as she stood before the judge.

"It says here that you were caught stealing from a baker. What have you got to say for yourself?"

She replied, "I just wanted some bread for me grandkids. Their mother, my daughter, was taken by smallpox and I have no work. I had nothin' to feed em."

"There's no excuse for stealing no matter what we deal with. What then of the poorhouse? Do you think you are too good to ask for help?"

She seemed very genuine when she replied, "I can-na not work ya lordship. Me hands be pains all the time."

She held up her hands and they were very misshapen, red and swollen at the joints.

The judge showed little compassion when he said, "Mmm. You should have had your friends help you."

She answered, "I ain't got no friends who can be sparing a crumb."

The judge replied coldly, "It's off to Newgate with you, and then to Botany Bay."

I whispered to Betsy, "What a sentence! Sent to the other side of the world for stealing a loaf of bread."

Betsy whispered quietly, "I have heard they are trying to colonize Australia."

I replied, "Yes, I know, but what a wicked way to do it."

One by one, several women were called and told similar tales.

Finally, Betsy and I were called.

The judge asked, "Which one of you is Catherine?"

I spoke out, "I am."

As he addressed me, he referred to his notes, "You are charged with stealing and bearing false witness. It says here that you and your accomplice were caught stealing and you have been pretending to be another woman."

"Please listen to what I say," I responded. "My name is Catherine Bannister. My father is a baron, Robert Kensington. He owns land in Sheffield. My husband is Lord Edward Bannister. He is Lieutenant-Governor over the North-Western Provinces in India."

That judge started briefly when I mentioned my name, as though it had some special meaning for him. His demeanor changed, darkening by the moment as he listened to me. He pursed his lips and stared hard at me for a few moments.

"Yes," he said. "I have heard our great country has dealings with India, but you are making ridiculous and absurd claims. What noblewoman would be found in that part of town? Be done with this foolishness." As the judge growled out these words, his features seemed bestial.

The troopers and court clerks looked sharply at the judge. This was clearly out of character for him.

I begged. "If only you would check? PLEASE, good sir?"

I continued. "It has all been a terrible mistake. I would never commit such an unforgivable act. I gave a false name because I didn't want it to be known I was in that part of town. Please check with your superiors."

The judge snarled. "You are nothing but a trollop; I don't need to ask my superiors for such a case as this. I would be laughed at and scorned."

Looking at his notes, he seethed, "You treated the constable who charged you contemptibly. He had to get help to apprehend you. You kicked and scratched. You tried to run away. Look at your face woman. It is the face of one wanting to flee."

"Yes, it is true we did try to leave. But the shopkeeper had two loutish ruffians beat us. That is the reason why our faces are puffed up and bruised. You see my face? The shopkeeper had two ruffians beat us. That's how Betsy and I came to look like this. My goodness, you have no understanding of what really happened."

The judge asked the constable who had arrested us to stand. His eyes flashed as he asked, "Did you write this report of the incident?"

"Yes, sir, I did. And all that has been discussed is true."

I spoke again, "You must know Henry Bannister. He is Edward's brother and a prominent lawyer. Assuredly you must know of him."

The judge shook his head slowly, dismissing my words without seeming to consider them. His frown deepened and he laughed snidely. "Not likely. What a tale you are trying to spin. I have not heard of such a person."

I continued, "You could have a messenger sent to Blakewood House to seek out the butler, Woods, or any of the servants. They can identify us and verify that we are who we claim to be. They will surely establish our innocence."

He responded sarcastically. "So now you have put your friends up to telling lies for you."

Betsy, who had remained silent while we were being accused, suddenly found her voice, "She looked straight at his beady eyes and said, "She tells the truth, your honor. I have been a lady's maid to Lady Catherine Bannister for a number of years."

Her affirmation hung in the air, the judge looking sharply at her, weighing and dismissing her with a sweep of his eyes.

In the end it made no difference. The judge didn't so much as raise his chin. In a voice oozing with contempt, he said, "I want to speak privately with the constable who charged you."

The constable who had bought us in approached the Judge.

The judge whispered to the constable, but Betsy could hear what was said and she repeated his words to me.

"These two women are to be put away on one of the hulks, but they are to go to Newgate prison first just like the rest of them. You are to ensure it is done in strict secrecy. There are NO excuses. They are not to speak to anyone. Her husband is the one who ruined us several years ago. Do you understand? If you need money to secure this quietly, see me. No one is to know they even exist. If you need to spread lies about them, then do so."

The constable nodded. "I'll see to it," he said.

The judge turned back to face us. "You have presented a ridiculous tale. I don't know how you thought you could get away with it."

With unexpected passion, he passed down his ruling, "This court is not lenient with criminals and thieves. You are found guilty as charged."

He continued, "In another time you would both be sentenced to hang. You may be grateful that I am in a merciful mood. You are bound for Botany Bay and be grateful of that!" And then he banged his mallet on his desk.

How it sent a shiver right through me when he said, "Guilty as charged!"

He motioned impatiently to the bailiff. "What are you waiting for? Get them out of here."

Betsy told me later that the bailiff scowled and looked at his feet, knowing that something was off about these matters. I felt sure the bailiff knew who Henry was. Henry was a notable figure and the judge would be aware of him even if Henry had never spoken to him.

I whispered to Betsy, "It was a judgment that allowed no disagreement. What a bitter and evil man!"

This horrid man, this wretched excuse for a magistrate, accused us of lies, stealing and of using a false identity.

I cried out as we were dragged out of the courtroom, "My husband will find out about this and you will be held to account!"

As we were being shoved into a small cell by ourselves, I cried out again. "You are mistaken. My husband will see that you are punished for this injustice."

As the guard was about to lock the gate, he added his own snarky comment, "And so will the king of England."

I asked, "Well what of it, Betsy? What can we do?"

I could feel the despair in Betsy's voice as she said, "I don't know. Perhaps there will be an opportunity later to get word to Mr. Bannister."

We were put in a cell, away from any other prisoners. We just sat there, holding our arms around each other.

My mind was everywhere. I am haunted by the memory of that judge! The cruelty and anger I saw in him have left dreadful memories in my mind. Quite apart from the rage I felt at the appalling conditions of the jail, I raged at Judge Wilkens till I had no more tears to cry or breath to speak. I swore endlessly that he would have to pay for our contemptible treatment.

Later that evening, they bought us soup and two slices of bread. The soup was tasteless, but we dipped our bread into it and ate it anyway for we hadn't eaten all day.

Not really speaking to Betsy or anyone else I said, "It can't be true! He can't send us to Australia! How will Edward find us? I hope someone will rescue us soon, I am totally fed up with this stupidity."

The following day, a guard gave us each a bowl of porridge and told us to be ready to leave for Newgate.

As they were taking Betsy and I and several other women to Newgate jail in a closed wagon, we had a few moments when we could speak to the others going with us. Betsy asked one of the younger women, "What do you know of Newgate prison then?"

She spoke quietly, "I 'ave 'eard talk of it. Its laid out in two sections: a 'common area' for poor prisoners and a "state area" for those able to pay for better living."

Betsy commented, "That's daft. Why would someone be paying to be in jail?"

I thought the very same thing.

The frail woman replied, "Some prisoners are in irons all the time and some be paying for their irons to be taken off."

I whispered to Betsy, "Surely that won't happen to us."

Betsy replied, "I hope not, Catherine. I hope not."

When we climbed out of the wagon at Newgate prison, the guards ordered us to stand in line and one of them spoke to a jailer. I don't know if he was in charge or not. It was just the impression I had. They ordered us into the jail, and we were put into a large cell with a group of other women.

Many of the guards spoke roughly. They were unkempt and we couldn't help but notice some gave off an offensive odor.

When it came dinner time, it was soup and bread again. This time the soup had a bit more flavor.

They had all the women come out of the cell and form a line to get their food. There was some banter between the guards and some of the prisoners. Indeed, I was shocked to hear some of the women offer themselves to the guards.

Their response would often be "Wait ya time lovey, we'll be takin our pickens when the time is right."

Obviously, the time was right just before candles were extinguished.

Several of them unlocked the holding cell and a few women whistled at them. My goodness, I thought, how degrading!

One of them a short fat little guard looked in my direction.

"Betsy! Help!" I whispered.

Betsy called out, "I wouldna' be lookin' in 'er direction, she's got the crabs."

The guard replied, "Well, I don't fancy you. You're way too tall for the likes of me."

I remarked, "Thank you, Betsy. How did you know what to say?"

She whispered, "You hear all sorts of talk in the servant's hall."

The following day the guards were tight-lipped and no reference was made to the night before.

One such guard, who was ladling out our porridge, wore a black eye patch over his left eye.

Speaking to me, he said, "So my lovely, you'll be waitin' for me tonight?"

Betsy responded quickly. "She's been poorly. Leave her be."

The guard responded indignantly. "And what right have you to be speaking for her?"

Betsy's response wasn't quite blunt enough to curb his sense of entitlement. "Tis not likely she would be speaking to you."

Though I was seething by this time, I held my tongue. It was clear that this particular guard would not be easily dissuaded.

"Let her speak for herself. What ya be saying, lovey?" he said.

Despite Betsy's advice. I said, "Yes, I will speak. You are despicable and loathsome. How people like you can take advantage of women prisoners, I know not. I want nothing to do with you or your type."

I expected him to take offense at my language. It didn't happen. He didn't seem bothered at all. I think I was more affected than he was.

"I heard there was a mad woman amongst ya," he said with a self-satisfied smirk. "I'll be takin' me pick tonight then. Look forward to it."

The guards were not the only ones listening to our conversation. Before I finished there was a hushed silence around us.

Another prisoner came up to me. "Don't ya be thinking that you are better than us. Keep your opinions to yourself and begone with your airs and graces."

Betsy and I ate our porridge in silence. Then Betsy stared at me as she said, "How can I help you if you continue to speak?"

I knew Betsy was right, but I wasn't used to being openly disrespected. I said, "It makes me sick to see so much bad treatment. Not only from the guards but from other prisoners."

Betsy looked straight at me and said, "I know what you say is true, but we need to be focused so that we don't draw unwanted attention to ourselves."

Betsy and I were singled out a little later. We were put in a cell by ourselves. That seemed odd at the time. There was no explanation for it. We were just ordered to come to the door of the cell and then taken away to the other cell.

The guard who collected us from the original holding cell was also a different cut than most of the other jailers. He seemed respectful and well groomed, with a well-trimmed mustache and beard. His clothing was neat and seemed clean and freshly pressed.

As he locked our new cell, he told us, "You will be transferred to one of the hulks on the Thames in a day or two."

Betsy was quick to ask, "Please good sir, what are hulks?"

"Hulks are prison ships on the Thames where prisoners who are sentenced to Australia are held until the next available ship is ready to make the voyage. I expect you'll be there a month or so, but I can't be sure. Then it will be three or four months on the ship before you get to Botany Bay."

While I knew we were sentenced to the colonies, the reality of it struck me more deeply when the guard said it in such a matter of fact way.

I felt dazed. How would Edward ever find me? I felt desperate and suspect Betsy felt equally so.

I had never realized that the journey would take several months. I guess I should have known. It just didn't occur to me until the jailer said it that way. I doubted I could survive so long. I felt sure my death was imminent.

The next few days at Newgate are lost to me. I just can't remember. Perhaps that's a good thing.

Nevertheless, I do remember that over the next few days the pain inflicted on us by the ruffians at that shop seemed to slowly subside and the bruising on our faces also faded.

When the time came for us to be taken to one of the Hulks, we were escorted from our cell to a large wagon with metal bars. I watched the other prisoners closely as we were forced into the wagon. I saw pain and discouragement settle on each of them as they were herded roughly along and prodded to take their place inside what amounted to a rolling cage.

For myself, I dreaded everything about this. It felt very demeaning to be in a prison wagon where everyone we passed could see us. I wanted to hide, yet I wanted to see someone I knew. Unfortunately, as we looked through the bars of the wagon, we didn't see anyone, only children making faces at us and jeering as if we were evil heretics.

As the wagon made its way through the streets from Newgate prison to our destination on the Thames, I went over and over the trial in my mind. The judge's name kept re-occurring in my thoughts. "Wilkens."

I shared my thoughts with Betsy. "I keep going over that judge's name in my mind. I feel sure I have heard that name before. Have you?"

She replied. "No. I can't say that I have. Perhaps Lord Edward mentioned it to you?"

I kept pondering it and then concluded Betsy was right. Edward must have mentioned it sometime."

Lifting her eyes from Catherine's notes, Betsy stopped reading and addressed Miss Banister.

"And so, that is how it all began Miss Bannister. I feel sure it will take several more hours to read Catherine's journal fully. I can't really offer to let you take it home to read. Lord Edward told me it mustn't go out of Blakewood. I rather expect Lord Edward is going to share it with his colleagues in government so they will see how badly convicts are treated."

Miss. Bannister smiled at Betsy, "My eyes are not much good for reading anymore. Why don't I drop by another morning, and then you could continue to read and tell me about your ordeal? Perhaps I could join you for lunch? I know Edward wouldn't mind. That's, of course, if you have free time?"

"Yes," I replied. "I have nothing very much to do these days. I will welcome your visits. Lord Edward was insistent; I am no longer in service. He believes my service to Catherine must have been very comforting to her. I told him it was only out of my love for her that I tried to be strong for us both.

I asked. "When would you like to come again?"

"Shall we make it every second or third day then?" Miss Bannister asked.

"Yes, of course," I replied

As she started to stand, I asked, "Today... Can you stay for lunch today?"

"That would be lovely," Miss Bannister said. "But I have an appointment to see a physician. Perhaps I could come the day after tomorrow; Wednesday. I'll come by at ten in the morning if that suits."

"I shall look forward to it," I replied.

I thought to myself that it would be nice to have a new friend, even if there was a big difference in age and class. It was also true I didn't have much to do. It seemed I was neither one thing nor the other. Being a servant, one was on call for much of the time. But now the servants obeyed me. Not that I had much to ask of them.

I decided I would spend time with them and help when I saw the need. I had the strong impression they wanted me to share some of my past experiences with them. While I didn't always read from Catherine's journal, I almost knew every word that Catherine had written and would describe some of our experiences when I shared a meal with them.

I was sorry that Mrs. Mclintoch was no longer employed at Blakewood. Sarah, one of the pantry maids, told me she had taken ill and had moved to be with her sister who had a cottage in the country. Woods, the butler, hired a new cook before we returned to England. Mrs. Featherstone seemed a little officious but handled her new position with vigor.

Right at ten on Wednesday morning, Miss Bannister rapped on the front door. Woods showed her to the parlor where Betsy was waiting.

"Miss Bannister, how nice to see you again," I said.

"Dear Betsy, I am delighted to see you. You'll have to start calling me Elizabeth. You said yourself that you are no longer in service. It matters not that there are a few decades between us in age. I hope you might think of me as a friend. Catherine will be pleased, I'm sure."

"Thank you, Miss Bannister." I said. "I agree. Catherine would be ever so pleased." Then, belatedly realizing I should have done as she asked, I said, "Oh, I should have said Elizabeth, I think it might take some time for me to get used to the idea. I have always admired your grace and presence. I feel awkward addressing you by your Christian name, but I expect I'll come to love the idea. Please take a seat and make yourself comfortable."

I picked up Emma's journal.

"Now where were we up to? Oh yes, here we are. I marked the place where we had left off. Just to refresh your memory Elizabeth, Catherine has written these things for Edward to read."

6

The Hulks

"Dear Edward, as I write the following, please know that the order of the events written here may not be reliable. I have written them as I remember them. They are all horrid memories

There had been talk among the other prisoners on our way. A hulk was a ship that was no longer seaworthy. They were temporary jails holding prisoners as part of the process of transportation to the colonies. Thinking back now, I remember one of the jailors had told us that.

When I saw where they were taking us, the 'hulk', where we were to be imprisoned, looked like it had seen its day in traveling. One of the masts was missing and the paint was peeling. The smell of rotting timbers and a dank and musty odor wafted across the docks in front of the wreck.

Though I have sailed some, I am only vaguely familiar with what is required to sail a ship. Even so, I could tell that this prison ship would never make a voyage again. And while it was clear that the ship would never make it out of port, there were many times when I thought I would never survive to make the voyage either. As I look back now, I am surprised the horrors we faced on the Hulk didn't bring me to my death.

How we hoped that we might find an opportunity to get a message out for help again. We didn't have any writing materials and all the guards were rough and brutal men. There was little distinction between them. Certainly, there was no compassion or thoughtfulness from any of them.

When so much time passed, we realized Henry had never received our message. Yet we still hoped. After we had been on the hulk for a week, Betsy spoke to one of the guards as he was taking our fetters off one morning.

"Would you be kind enough to get me some writing materials so I can write to my family and tell them where I am."

The guard responded, "Where do you think I am to be getting such things for the likes of ya? I canna not read and write me'self. I s'pect you can do no more. Let me see. I'll be seeing ya tonight and should ya take to being with me I might see what can be done."

After he had removed more fetters from fellow convicts, he left. I looked at Betsy, amazed. "You know what he wants Betsy?"

Betsy spoke quietly and surely, "Yes, but we have no choice. And besides I have been with a man before. What else can we do?"

I knew she spoke the truth. There we were on the brink of disaster. In my mind, I could only see a wretched future. Betsy and I approached the evening with dread.

As that very same guard was putting on our fetters that night, he told Betsy he would come and get her a bit later.

Betsy made it clear to the jailer, "I want the writing materials first."

His response was only vaguely reassuring, "I can't get them for you tonight, but I will in a day or two."

Betsy was determined. "When you've got them, I will be with you. Otherwise, I will scream my lungs out if you try anything."

As he walked away, he said, "I can have anyone I please."

So that attempt to get writing materials was fruitless. But, in a way, I was pleased. I was astonished at the lengths that Betsy would go to.

One of the more outspoken women called out, "None of us be liken' these 'ere arrangements so we'll have to be sticken' together."

Most of the other woman agreed, and we joined in the clapping and murmurs of agreement. After her remarks, there seemed to be some sense of congeniality from the group. By listening closely to the chatter, I found out the hulk we were assigned to would hold about one hundred convicts in wicked conditions.

The hulk was a dreadful place. Shortly after boarding we were ordered down into the quarterdeck. Descending into the dank space, the smell of unwashed bodies and feces hung thickly in the air.

Betsy whispered to me, "I heard one of the guards say some women have been on board for sixteen days. Some are in cells on the lower deck because it's said they are very evil in character."

The quarterdeck was divided into uneven areas by bars of iron. Convicts were herded into the larger area behind the bars and there we learned that the smaller area in front of our cage was the guard's station. In our prison, there were a few benches and some straw on the wooden floor. This became our wretched home for several weeks.

I noticed what appeared to be a pile of tattered rags. "Look, Betsy, what are those things stacked up against the bars?"

"I have no idea she said. "Looks like they could be blankets."

I thought that if that was all the blankets available it was far too few for our numbers. A pained look passed between Betsy and me as the guards went around and put us all in shackles. Those horrid things pressed upon my ankles so dreadfully. We could walk, but each step we took would send slivers of pain up to our thighs and hips and then back down to our ankles.

It was at this moment we were introduced to one of the most wicked of our jailers. Grotesque in appearance, a short, cross-eyed, plump little trooper addressed us from the guard's area.

"My name is Tottenham. I am assigned to accompany you to the colonies, so be sure you follow the rules on the hulk and then on the ship we will be assigned to. You'll be fed three times a day and you'll be set to work daily starting from tomorrow. You will wash before breakfast and after the evening meal. Guards will bring your meal tonight, but tomorrow you'll be responsible to prepare the food.

When not in irons, you will be under strict guard. If you obey and do as you are told, you will be treated respectably. Mind you, anybody who disobeys will be severely punished. We will put you in the coal hole with half rations. Some wrongdoings may not be treated quite as harshly, but lesser violations will result in having your heads shaved."

I looked at Betsy. She whispered, "I would hate to have my head shaved."

Women sat together in groups on benches and on the floor. When someone moved, you could hear the horrid rattle of chains. The was a constant murmur of voices, a babble of evil swearing and blasphemies.

I could stand fully, but Betsy couldn't. She was five or six inches taller than me. There was only about five and a half feet between the floor of the quarterdeck and the upper deck.

Some hours later they bought food. Indeed, it was a miserable excuse for food.

We were told to take a tin cup and hold it out for one of the guards to ladle soup into. We were also told to take a single slice of coarse dry bread. I looked pleadingly to Betsy, though I hardly know what I thought she could do. As much as I felt repelled by such food, in my thoughts, I could still hear Betsy's urgings.

She said, "You must eat. We'll never get through this if you don't."

When I heard Betsy say that, I realized that she thought we wouldn't be rescued.

The soup wasn't as bad as it looked. A short young guard who ladled the soup told us, "You better eat up, you've got lots of work to do on the morrow."

A little later it was wash time. Some fiasco that turned out to be. Over a period of several days on the hulk, we settled into a routine.

A few of our number were ordered to bring several small tubs of water each morning and evening. Indeed, it was very little water for two hundred women to wash in. I decided I would prefer not to wash unless I was the first or second to a tub. That was a very rare occasion. After several days of not washing, I didn't much like myself physically, let alone emotionally. One of the women guards noticed that I held back when it came to wash. She was tall with long brown hair tied back. Her facial features were plain but somewhat foreboding. She was dressed in black and was someone I wanted to stay away from.

She spoke sternly, "You'll be on half rations if you continue to disobey orders missy."

I was angry and had forgotten Betsy's council. "I can't be washing in foul water that's been used by other people."

"You must be that mad one I have 'eard talk about. You won't be pretending ya be some toff with me. I won't stand for it."

The tone of her voice became louder and more shrill as she spoke to all of us in the area. "There's to be no pretending here. Ya may be thinking you is better than anyone else, but here ya is just another convict. So ya all will be doing as ya should or it will be a whipping with the lash. The head guard here is stern; mark my words."

As candles were extinguished that first night there were whisperings amongst the convicts, but I didn't hear them. I had become preoccupied with my own sorrow.

Apart from the adverse sleeping conditions, feelings of panic and terror overcame me, and I spent most of the night sobbing. I felt so hollow, fearful and totally ashamed of my actions. Betsy tried to comfort me, but to little avail. Why, why didn't I listen to Betsy? I condemned myself over and over!

I was in anguish in both my body and mind. I kept asking myself why? Why didn't I listen to Betsy? How can I describe such feelings? I know not!

"Oh shame, shame on me!" I exclaimed mentally. Sometimes disaster strikes, a person's life is changed through some accident of fate. The person might be an innocent victim, brought to harm by circumstances beyond their control. I had no such excuse. Our situation was entirely a consequence of my own arrogance and stupidity. I couldn't find words to express my regret and deep disillusionment in myself.

Those feelings remained with me for many months. Poor Betsy! She must have wanted to scream at me. Look what my foolishness put upon her. She could very well have spurned me. A more faithful friend I could never find.

After some time, I had no more tears left. As my sobbing quieted, I realized I wasn't the only one. I heard others weeping. I imagined they had left loved ones behind.

My impression of their crimes was shaped by listening to them plead for themselves as Betsy and I had done. I knew for a fact that many of them were being sent to Botany Bay because they had stolen food or clothing when they were cold and hungry. In some cases, they only wanted to feed and clothe their little ones. I concluded that we have a wicked and evil judiciary system in England! I wondered if Edward had any knowledge of it.

Over the nights that followed, we were expected to wash each evening. The guard who had spoken to me a day before and a shorter woman with a mole on her cheek ordered some of our number to bring in the small tubs of water. The second guard was also dressed in black. I concluded it must be a uniform but was not sure. I hurried to be one of the first to a tub. I felt it was rather demeaning undressing in front of everyone. Betsy pushed her way in behind me and tried to make herself a shield from those who were behind us.

Our daily routine soon became monotonous. At Blakewood House, Betsy and I had been accustomed to doing as we wished. We would read the same book and then exchange thoughts about it as we took walks about the grounds. Other times, I spent time with friends and then we would shop. Of course, we never shopped in the east end. At times Betsy would shop with me and that was perfectly acceptable. But now, in these regimented circumstances, we could only do as we were told.

Meal preparation was also monotonous. About ten women would be chosen to go to the ship's galley to prepare our breakfast, a thin gluey mix which was supposedly porridge. It was most distasteful. It consisted of a few crushed oat grains in a gluey mass of grey liquid. Betsy made sure I always ate the oatmeal and the coarse lump of cheese they sometimes gave us.

I found myself whispering to Betsy, "Remember the oatmeal Mrs. Mclintoch served with sugar or honey? I wish we could have that now instead of this."

To which she responded, "I wouldn't be thinking of the past Catherine. It will only eat at your heart. We must find a way to get word out for someone to help us. I have been trying to think of a way. Who knows when they'll be taking us to Australia? We might die before we ever leave England, judging by the rumors about this place."

We were almost worn out just from having to move around in shackles to stand in line to get breakfast. But some of our number started to make a line when a large copper pot was bought onto the prison deck.

"Tea, Catherine. You like tea," Betsy said.

Yes, it was true. I always liked a cup of tea. But this tea? My goodness, I can't fully describe the taste. It was very weak and salty and there was no sugar or milk to be had. I heard another prisoner say they had mixed some of the river water with fresh to make it. It smelled like rancid river water and I was unable to bring myself to drink it. Obviously, Betsy shared my judgment and neither of us partook of tea again while we were on the hulk.

Despite this, Betsy still encouraged me to eat. "Catherine the tea is putrid, but you must try to eat."

As we bit into our biscuits, I exclaimed, "They are very bland!" Bland. How strange that sounds now as I remember it. Tasteless, hard, almost inedible. Those are other words I could have used to describe our meals.

Betsy put her finger to her mouth and hushed me.

I was unfamiliar with how biscuits are made but listened to Betsy's explanation when I asked. She whispered, "They are a mix of flour and water with a dash of salt and a small amount of lard.".

They were tasteless. Nevertheless, as Betsy said, we needed to eat them. I took just enough tea to soften the biscuit, but my stomach reeled. I just couldn't eat mine and offered it to Betsy. She frowned and urged me to reconsider. "We need every bit of energy we can get. Who knows what is ahead of us?"

I hoped that they would feed us better for the mid-day meal.

After we had eaten, several convicts were chosen to take the used mugs and bowls back to the galley to wash and dry them. We guessed that the ship's galley must be at the far end of the quarterdeck because those whose duty it was to prepare our meal and wash our utensils reported that they were not required to go up or down any stairs.

After the copper pot had been taken away, and those on galley duty had returned, a guard I hadn't seen before came down to our deck accompanied by four others. He was stern and spoke with a faint tremor in his voice as he told us. "When your shackles are removed, you must go up on deck one by one. Once there, you are to line up. The ship's crew will instruct you. When your shackles are removed you will be under strict guard. The crew has orders to shoot anyone attempting to escape. And, as you see, we all carry a musket or a pistol. We will shoot and have no hesitation about it."

As the guards loosened our shackles, I sensed a great feeling of relief amongst our number.

We followed each other gingerly as we climbed up the wooden stairs. No one knew what to expect. What a sight we must have been, with tattered hair and wearing the ugly misshapen smocks that were given to us at Newgate.

The same guard who addressed us earlier told us, "As you get off the ship, make a line of two across and the troopers will march you across to the workhouse over yonder street there."

As we were getting into line, I heard complaints, "Now what in the 'ell will they be 'avin us do? … It ain't right, all this is to be the end of us.… You'd think they 'ave better stuff to do, than to be watchin' o'er us."

Watch over us, indeed they did. As we walked down the gangplank another trooper called out, "Ya women need to hurry along and march across the road to that there big brown building, Ya all's to be 'picking oakum.'"

Fortunately, Betsy was by my side. "What is oakum?" I asked.

She replied, "I am sure I don't know, I have never heard of it."

We were marched to an older building across from the docks. As we were led into the building, I noticed the area was uniform in that chairs were set up in rows and there was a definite walking space between each line of chairs. Piles of old rope were bunched together and pushed up against a wall.

Troubled and not knowing what this was about, I asked Betsy, "What do you think they want us to do?"

She replied, "It looks like we will see soon enough."

I said, "Make sure you stay by my side, Betsy? I'm feeling very nervous about this."

I thought the guard who spoke to us earlier had remained back at the hulk, but no, there he was standing pompously in front of us, his mustache twitching as he spoke.

"You see there are many stacks of old and tarry lengths of ropes in front of you. There're six lengths to each bundle. Each one of you is to come up and take a bundle of rope then return to your seat where you'll pick it apart and un-spin it back to loose fibers with your hands. That's what we call 'picking oakum'.

I suspect many of you have done this before. You will come, row by row, to take your bundle and return to your seats to commence. Make sure you gather a full bundle. The guards will check what you take and then they'll be watching to see if you do it right and fulfill your quota of work. You'll have to do your quota, or they'll be no lunch for any of ya. You will put your bundles of fiber in the large bins you see on my right."

The process seemed silly and disorganized to me. They asked for us to go up front and take a bundle from the pile, yet we had just passed the pile on our way in as we were directed to claim a seat.

Row by row we went to gather up the old ropes and then return to our seats. As the trooper had said, a bundle consisted of six or seven ropes that had been cut into a yard's length. Some women took to the task easily, even though I could hear swearing and cursing around me.

I tried to unravel the coarse rope, but I made little headway. It was totally unfamiliar work and I didn't do well with it. My hands were soon rough and sore.

I whispered, "Betsy you seem to be doing far better than me."

She replied cheerfully, "Oh don't worry, I am used to this sort of work. Just untwist the fibers as much as you can. As soon as I am done, I'll help you."

Despite Betsy's offer, I knew there was a time limit. I had to try! Some women were taking their piles of fiber up to the large bins that stood to the side in the building. Ignoring the pain in my hands, I was able to untwist four lengths of rope. One of the guards said to me, "Ya better be doing that a bit faster missy, or else you'll be having this herd of females after ya."

Fortunately, Betty finished hers and quickly worked to help me finish mine. Even so, we were among the last to finish. As I carried the fibers to the large bin another guard said, "You'll have to be a bit faster next time."

The guards had set up a few tables upon which our lunch was laid out, such as it was.

Some people might find ox-cheek soup appealing. That's if it had a mix of healthy vegetables and barley in it, not just a scant pea or two. Nevertheless, seeing Betsy's glare as I started to walk away from the table, I turned about and took a mug from among many on the table. The soup looked dark and grey as a fellow prisoner ladled it into my mug. The biscuits on the table were just like those we had been given earlier in the morning. I took one but felt I would be sick to my stomach if I ate it.

Day after day while we were 'picking oakum' our midday meal consisted of that soup and a course slice of dry bread or a biscuit to go with it.

Often the biscuits were moldy and green on both sides. Sometimes I could not control my response. My stomach would heave involuntarily. Some prisoners would try and scrape the green off, but truthfully, it was hardly food that one would give a pig.

After lunch, a few male convicts bought in more stacks of ropes.

Some of the women wolf-whistled as the men came in. But their stay was short. After they had bought in their bundles, they were ordered outside and then they were gone.

The head guard was tall and wore a full uniform, gray trousers, a red jacket with a white sash around his waist. He also wore a black hat most of the time. And, of course, he and all the other troopers carried muskets.

'Picking oakum' occupied most days. As the days stretched into weeks, the monotony almost became unbearable. Many of the women would utter foul and dirty words, such as I had never heard before. When they marched us back to the hulk, the bitter wind struck us and often the women would run. Even Betsy and I ran. The smocks we wore were thin and we had no cloaks.

Our evening meals weren't much either. Some convicts were ordered to the galley to prepare them. A thick slice of ox-cheek, another biscuit or a slice of mealy bread and a mug of weak, salty-tasting, tea. Occasionally our evening meal was made up of rice and peas and, on such times, we were given cheese.

Disease was rampant and spread quickly in the wretched confines of our prison. We lived in constant fear, watching those around us fall ill and die within days. I attribute our survival in those horrid conditions to luck and perhaps the good fortune of having been healthy at the time of our arrest. Most of those around us were fragile to begin with, thin to the point of starvation before they ever arrived at the hulks. They fell like wheat to the scythe and within a few weeks, our number was halved. Our numbers fluctuated, with new arrivals taking the place of those who fell to disease and malnutrition.

On several occasions when we were 'picking oakum,' someone would keel over. They were taken back to the hulk but that did little good to revive them. I had bitter feelings towards those responsible for our conditions. No matter that many of those souls were rough and ill-bred. They were God's children.

There was a short stump of a doctor who would offer a shot of brandy to those who were ill, but this had no obvious effect for good. Bodies of different shapes and sizes were carried away by their fellow prisoners. There was no burial ceremony, just another body tossed onto a cart. After they were carted away, I don't know what became of their bodies.

How cold and callous our jailers seemed! I counted it a blessing that, aside from hunger, Betsy and I continued to have good health.

As the weeks passed, Betsy and I also began to lose weight. Betsy became more and more alarmed. She would often say, "We need more food, we will die from starvation."

Along with the awareness of death, our bodies ached from the shackles and lying on the floor. The guards established a regimen that divided us into two groups. The first group was responsible for preparing the food and the second for serving the food and cleaning up. Several times I was chosen. It was an easy chore, but it irked me to see food in such a large quantity that was obviously so displeasing to all those who ate it. Despite Betsy's glares I rarely ate after I had been told to serve.

The pain of those shackles made movement excruciating as we went back and forth to get our breakfast. I hated the pain and torture they caused. Fortunately, it became a part of our daily routine to have the troopers remove those horrid things. As we climbed the stairs to fulfill our duties, it was refreshing to feel the fresh air on my skin and to be free of those ghastly shackles for the day. At times I would look upon a bird and envy it for its freedom. I had little hope that I might ever feel joy again. I often wandered mindlessly through the day thinking "If only I could get a message to Edward."

Our next opportunity came several days later while we were on our way to picking oakum. Unbeknownst to me Betsy had scrounged paper, pen and ink and created a note to Henry. It had Henry's name and address and she had written where to find us. While we were making the trip between the hulk and the poorhouse it was often common for scruffy children to laugh and make fun of us, poking their tongues out and yelling out stupid things. This time, taking a chance, Betty grabbed one of them and said, "If you be wantin' to make some money you'll take this to this lawyer and be sure he'll be given ya a penny or two for doing as I bid."

Who knows what that ruffian did? Obviously, as I look back now, the note never reached Henry.

I asked Betsy in amazement, "Where did you get the writing materials?"

"The gate was opened a few minutes early yesterday morning. I took advantage of a brief distraction that took the guards away and I snuck into the guard's office. I suspected that guard who I asked to get the writing materials had no understanding or compassion. He could have done as I had asked. All the guards here are the same. They only think of themselves. By the way, I told you a lie. I have never been with a man. I was dead scared but didn't want you to know."

Betsy made connections with a few of the other prisoners. She said, "You know, Catherine, it wouldn't do us any harm having a few friends around us. Most of these women are much like the servants at Blakewood House. Given the opportunity, we might talk to a few of them."

I wondered what I would have in common with them. And then, of course, I realized. I doubted that any of these women wanted to be on the hulk and bound for Australia any more than we did. It was on this premise that I tried to befriend one or two.

How dreadful that turned out to be!

One asked, "Who ya pretending to be, talkin' like that?"

I wasn't about to make up a story, so I started to relate what had happened to me. Several of the women took notice and a few of them gathered round. Because I didn't speak the way they did, they thought I was putting on airs. None of them believed me. They soon laughed me to scorn, deciding I was crazy.

Oh, how they ridiculed and taunted me; one or two of them tried to mimic my speech. They agreed amongst themselves that no judge in his right mind would sentence a "lady" to such a bad end, so I must be a mad woman. The judge should have sent me to the lunatic asylum. Betsy told them my story was true and she met with a negative response also. I remember how they cackled like hens, "Right luv, you humor her, she'll be leaving you a fortune when she goes. Ha!" Poor Betsy.

What a misery it was to return to the lower deck each day; a dark, drab and contemptible place. A gradual numbness crept into this depressing existence, for as I was accredited with being "mad" I determined I would no longer seek contact with any of the other women. In my isolation, I somehow felt safe.

Very few words were spoken by anyone below deck. Betsy and I would exchange whispers and others did also. Nevertheless, it was a place of isolation. I concluded that God required all of this as a penance for getting Betsy into so much trouble and for being so stupid. To this day I am amazed that my health remained good throughout this period.

During that time on the hulk, Betsy and I waited in great anticipation and hope that Henry would free us. But as the days and weeks passed and there was no word, a feeling of deep despair grew in me.

Dear Betsy was always hopeful and she was forever ready with an encouraging word. If ever there was anything pleasant in that foul hole of human horror, Betsy would find it.

After several weeks of coping with such horrid living, the head guard addressed us, "You will be transferred to the HMS Barringer leaving England on the 4th September 1832. Not all of you will go as there will be a limit on numbers."

I took this news badly, knowing full well we couldn't get any further word to Henry in the time.

Giving voice to my fears I told Betsy, "If we are separated, I shall surely die."

I noted a quiver in Betsy's voice when she said, "We will keep together."

I prayed so fervently to be saved! Although I went to church weekly while I was growing up, I hadn't come to know Deity in any way. Over these past months as a convict, I always had a prayer in my heart. I implored our Maker; "Please, please may we be saved! Keep us from this horrible plight."

In my continued isolation, looking at the women around me, I realized we were all much alike. I expected there were many on the hulk who dreaded having to leave England. What of the mothers who had been torn away from their children? What justice was there in our dear country? I know not.

In my fitful sleep that night I saw Edward's face. However, when I woke, the familiar stench made me cover my nose as I realized, with horror, where I was. From that time to this, sleep has been my only respite.

We desperately hoped for some way to escape and looked in vain for some sign that Henry had got word from us. Betsy told me she was going to make one last attempt. She showed me the note she had written as we had one more day of pickin' oakum. As before, she grabbed one of the young boys who was making faces at us as we walked to the storehouse.

"Do you know what is like to do a good service for somebody?" She said.

"Sure do Ma'am, we is Christian,"

"If you be takin' this note to this address, then God will be lovin' ya and you'll get a penny."

He answered, "Sure will. I want a penny."

Betsy and I hoped, surely this time Henry will come.

That night on the hulk was to be our last. I had mixed feelings. I was glad the hulk was no longer to be our home but found no comfort in the thought. I found only fear in thinking what the future might hold.

Before the guards came to put our shackles on, both Betsy and I were ordered to see the head guard. We looked at each other in fright. What had we done that we shouldn't have? Questions racked our minds.

As we stood before him on the upper deck, he looked annoyed and spoke with disdain. "We have been watching you both closely while you have been on this Hulk. Twice you have tried to notify a lawyer of your whereabouts and twice we have intercepted your notes. As if any lawyer would want to know the likes of you."

He looked at me contemptuously. "You truly are a mad-un. Whatever control you have over Betsy Longwood is surely evil. Should either of you endeavor to cause trouble while on the Barringer you will no doubt lose your lives. Be warned and go now."

When we were back on the prison deck, I spoke to Betsy with tears in my eyes, "To think, all this time we have been hoping Henry would help us. Why have they been watching us?"

Betsy replied "Maybe he was just saying that to frighten us. Remember what I overheard the judge say to the constable. Maybe they are watching us more than we think. Don't think about it, Catherine. What good will it do? But know that I share your grief."

When we were ordered to go aboard the HMS Barringer, the ship that was to take us to Australia, we knew it was pointless to look for Henry. As I reflect on that time now, the hope that Henry would find us had given me a reason to live.

Betsy never gave up hope. Even when they shackled us below decks, she tried to reassure me. "We will get by, Catherine. As long as we are together, as long as we have each other."

I wondered if Betsy really believed what she said. I wondered if she felt any resentment against me for needing her so.

Breakfast the following morning was the same. Nonetheless, I sensed many of our number were pleased to leave the hulk. I was certain they also wondered what the future would bring.

7

The Voyage

Fortunately for me, Betsy and I were allowed to remain together. We were part of a large group of about one hundred women making our way to the gangplank in single file. There were two large tubs of water on deck with a type of sheeting around them. I was appalled when one of the new troopers said, "You are to strip completely and wash your hair and body in the large tubs of water and make sure you dry with the cloths which are provided. You will be given new clothing afterwards. Put it on and follow the orders you are given. Move, all of you, now. There is to be no dilly-dallying. We have no time for slackers on this ship. You will have female guards to watch over you while you wash."

I didn't fancy being naked, even if it was only in front of women, but Betsy started undressing and glared strongly at me.

The clothes which had been given to us at Newgate were tossed aside. As I recall, I wished I had never seen those clothes. They were a part of the beginning of this whole ordeal. I felt humiliated standing there naked. The morning air was very cool, making this ordeal even more horrid. I shivered and trembled. I don't know if it was from the cold or the situation we were in. Both, I think. It was so demoralizing.

The ship's crew cackled, even though they couldn't really see us. I have never perceived nakedness as being attractive or appealing, and now our nakedness revealed that we were an emaciated and unsightly lot. We were given course hemp smocks to replace the smocks provided us at Newgate. We were told by the senior female guard to take another set of clothing for the journey ahead. I bathed as quickly as I could. I hated everything about it.

I hadn't considered that we might have female guards. To my surprise, if it can be called that, two women watched over us as we washed in the icy water. The more senior woman was stout, with black hair. She was tall and could have passed for a man in the right light. Her facial features were coarse and looking at her dressed in black didn't present a pretty picture. Indeed, when I realized I was staring, I turned away and focused on my place in line.

The younger guard was a lot more pleasant. She had blond hair, tied in the back. She stood about five feet four. She was far better looking than her senior counterpart. As she handed out the cloths for us to dry ourselves, she smiled when many of us thanked her. Both female guards carried a short flail. I expect they knew that, if there was trouble, they only needed to call out and male troopers would come. As we dried ourselves and were dressing in our rough clothing, the more senior woman told us.

"Don't forget to gather up a spare set of clothing."

A few minutes passed and then she spoke out again, the tone of her voice sending a chill amongst us, "The captain and the Head Trooper will address you tomorrow when you are at sea, but it is right for me to say now. You all are to watch out. We won't be troubled if we need to discipline ya. If hell's to be your fate, then we shall see it happen."

I whispered to Betsy, "She must be one of Satan's creatures."

In reply, Betsy said, "Yes, woe be to us, Catherine. Woe be to us."

The younger guard motioned for the troopers to come.

A few of the troopers came from behind the sheets and ordered us to go to the prison deck. It was a slow process, yet Betsy and I were among the first to see our home for the next several months.

The prison deck was like a real prison with bars between us and the guards. It bore some similarity to the prison on the hulk. There were many rectangular benches made of wood. I looked at Betsy, the question in my thoughts unspoken.

She said, "I think they are to be our beds. I wonder will there be enough."

I complained, "I would rather have hay and sleep on the floor."

Betsy responded, "We will have to make the best of it. There is at least some provision for our sleeping, though I doubt if there will be enough room for all of us. At a guess, it looks to me like some of us will be sleeping on the floor. We don't have much choice, Catherine. We'll have to see what they tell us to do."

Before they closed the gate to seal our place behind the bars, the guards put shackles around our ankles. A shiver of fear passed over me.

It was the first time I had seen Betsy angry. She said, "I can't believe they mean to keep us shackled. We should be free of such things. I hope they are not going to keep us in shackles for the entire voyage."

Betsy closed her eyes, maybe to regain her composure.

My own thoughts were more pitiable. "These shackles are so heavy, much heavier than we had before."

Something in me broke. I ignored Betsy's scowl when I spoke to one of the male guards who was standing watch.

"I need to speak to the captain."

"Oh, do you now? I be thinking he'll not be wantin' to see one such as you. You, a criminal? How silly can ya be? Ya don't seem to be knowin' ye'r place. Ya don't seem like ya know much at all."

The guard leaned menacingly towards me putting the butt of his musket on my neck. "Besides who do you think you be? A convict speaking like she's a queen or some such thing. A convict speaking to the captain? I've never 'eard of such a thing."

I was oblivious to the threat and, ignoring Betsy's efforts to quiet me, I plunged forward. "You don't understand. There has been a horrid mistake! I am a lady of nobility. I have been misused, mistreated and belong at Blakewood House. My husband is Lieutenant- Governor over the North-Western Provinces of India and my father is a well-known baron and he resides in Sheffield. Something must be done."

The guard shook his head disbelievingly, clearly surprised that his threat had left no impression on me.

"It will go better fer ya if ya keep ya silliness to yourself. I 'eard there was a mad-un amongst ya. Surely it be you! I'll be telling the Head Trooper. He'll be 'avin words with ya."

He asked, "And what be your name then?"

I spoke boldly, "Catherine Bannister but you have my alias name of Catherine Lancaster."

As the guard walked away, Betsy was at my side. "Oh, Catherine! I warned you to keep silent. This will mean trouble for us. Why can't you trust me?"

Though I had some doubts, I tried to stay resolute, "I have tried ever so much, but here we are convicts, being sent away as criminals to some foreign strange land where we don't want to be. How will Edward ever find us? And that's if we are still alive at the end of this, something which I very much doubt. I am totally exasperated."

Betsy responded, "I know how hard this is. Your despair is mine also, but we need to be cautious. I doubt if anything good will come of this."

When the 6th bell rang, the guards bought down several large containers of soup, meat, bread, and tea. The prison door was left open as each convict went up to get their food.

As Betsy returned from getting hers, she commented, "I think our meals might be a bit improved. This soup looks like it has got more than a single pea in it. And the meat looks more inviting, not as dry or as wizened as much as it was on the hulk."

I answered, "I surely hope so. Time will tell."

After our evening meal, our fictitious names were called out by one of the new guards whom I had never seen before. He was a big man, taller than most, and wore a uniform that looked like it hadn't been cleaned in a month. He waited impatiently near the door to our prison.

"Catherine Lancaster and Betsy Longwood, you are to come forward."

He spoke louder than he needed to, "Follow me yer' hear!"

I exchanged looks with Betsy. I could tell she was forcing a smile, but I could also see she was worried. Maybe we were going to get some justice finally. Both of us walked forward and followed the guard. Our movements were slow because of the shackles, but my determination was strong. I think Betsy was more worried than I.

Climbing those rungs of the ladder to the top deck was painful and difficult. but this time I felt I had a purpose, so I moved as swiftly as those dreadful shackles would allow. When I reached the top deck, the guard grabbed our smocks and pushed both of us to a cabin on the upper deck. Despite the guard's rough treatment, I hoped Betsy and I might be saved, and I would be returned to my proper place.

There was a desk and behind it sat the squinty little cross-eyed man who spoke to us when we were on the hulk. He wore the uniform of a trooper.

"You may not remember me," he began. "I spoke to your lot on the hulk. I oversee all discipline on this ship. My name is Tottenham, you shall call me Head Trooper Tottenham."

He spoke sternly and I felt the contempt he had for us.

He asked, "Which one of you is Catherine Lancaster?"

I raised my chin and said, "I am, sir."

"It has come to my notice that you, Catherine, have already become a difficult convict with your pretense of being someone you are not. To assure that you learn your lesson, I have asked for your accomplice to be here to see what discipline brings.

Seeing his disposition, I was immediately alarmed. I realized I may have made another horrible mistake. I thought we might have the opportunity, at last, to speak to the captain, a man who might have noble connections. "You don't understand. There has been an evil mistake. I am Lady Catherine Bannister. I have been misused and mistreated for many weeks. My residence is in London. Blakewood House, you must have heard of it. My husband is Lord Edward Bannister, Lieutenant– Governor over the North -Western Provinces of India and my father is a well-known baron and our family name is Kensington. We must be released immediately. Betsy here will verify what I say is true."

He mocked me when he said, "Released immediately? Is that what you say, mmm? ... now what judge in his right mind would send you here if that be true? It says on your record you have been charged with stealing and false representation. I will not have this type of stupidity and foolishness amongst you convicts. You, Catherine Lancaster, must be taught to know your place. As for your 'ladies-maid', Betsy Longwood, she also will be disciplined. Should we permit the type of behavior you have displayed to go unpunished we would soon have chaos from your fellow convicts. Rather, it is important now, in the beginning, to set the right example. We won't allow criminals to lie and misbehave. We must deal with behavior like this now."

Turning to the guard who had escorted us he gave brief instructions. "Have their heads shaved." And then turning back to us, he briefly dismissed us with this warning. "There will be greater discipline if you continue with this twisted tale. Now get out of here."

"Please good sir, please!" I pleaded. "I just can't bear this! Won't you please just check. My home is here in London, Blakewood House. How will my family find me? Please check I implore you!"

"Guard! Get these two convicts out of here! I've no time for such nonsense."

We were dragged immediately from the room and left standing outside the door. The trooper who had accompanied us sent word for that older woman guard who had spoken to us earlier. She mustn't have been very far away as she appeared within moments. She seemed very matter-of-fact when she asked, "What are we to be doing trooper?"

He replied, "These convicts has been making trouble."

Her eyes lit up and she asked the trooper. "How am I to discipline them?"

Just the sight of her scared me. She seemed pleased that she could discipline us, evil woman that she was.

Speaking to the trooper, she said, "I hope it is harsh. We need to make an example of them."

As he held our shoulders in a tight grip, he said, "Head Trooper wants their heads shaved."

"Yes, I suspected something like that, so I have bought me razor with me," she said.

Turning to us she snarled, "Not even one night on the ship and ya need to be disciplined. You'll not be crossing us, do ya hear?"

Putting his hand on my head the trooper smiled as he said, "She's the mad-un who we 'ave heard about."

"And so we will teach you. I've heard about your airs and graces."

I responded, "I really thought someone in authority would believe me. I tell the truth."

The evil woman looked at me with that wicked scowl. "We'll make an example for the other prisoners. They will see what happens to those who don't obey the rules."

The two of them dragged us down the stairs to the prison. I lost my balance several times and scraped my knees and finally fell in a heap at the bottom of the stairs. From what I could see, Betsy received the same treatment.

That evil woman followed us with the burly guard beside her. She grabbed me by the hair and dragged me in front of the bars separating the prisoners from the guard station. She threw me down and quickly put a knee in my back to keep me there.

There was a hush among the convicts. They all watched from the other side of the bars and listened to what she said.

"Let this be a lesson to all of you. Watch and remember. Any prisoner who causes trouble will be punished. This here is one who thinks she is above us all. She is lucky. She should have been put in the coal room."

She held me, face down, on the floor with her knee in my back. She grabbed my hair and began making quick, careless, strokes across my head with her razor. Aside from the pain of her knee in my back, she took no care as she shaved my hair. Not only did I see my long honey brown hair fall to the ground, but I also felt blood on my face and winced with pain each time she managed to cut more than my hair.

All the while she was saying, "You are a criminal and a nobody. You should have got the lash instead. You'll keep your lies to yourself."

Speaking to all the convicts, she said, "You'll all damn well remember where your wickedness has bought you. We have no compassion for the likes of any of you."

With a final gesture of contempt, she rose from the floor. Then she grabbed Betsy from the vice-like grip of the guard and dragged her quickly to the floor next to me. Just as she had done with me, she put her knee in Betsy's back and held her by grabbing her hair. She roughly stroked the razor across her head numerous times. I heard Betsy gasp and saw blood oozing from the stubble where her hair used to be.

As all of Betsy's hair and mine lay on the floor, the evil woman growled, "You are to sweep this mess up and then go up and throw it into the sea. Your guards will then see that you return."

"I was so angry and tried to speak out, Your name? What is your name?" I demanded; my voice barely audible in the moment. The guard looked at me doubtfully, as though I was speaking a language she had never heard. My anger overrode my sense of self-preservation. "I will have your name!" I squeaked out, my voice failing me. "When I am found, there will be consequences for what you've done!" I stared at her defiantly for several seconds and watched her inner debate about how to respond.

A convict from inside the bars nearby suddenly whispered, "Her name is Brough. I heard someone say it was Brough."

The moment passed. The guard, Brough made the decision not to respond to my question. Instead, she spoke to the remaining guards. "See that they do it!" Without waiting to see that her instructions were followed, she left the prison deck and was gone.

For the first time in my life, I really hated someone. I can't find the words to describe my hate. In my eyes, guard Brough was the very personification of evil. The devil himself couldn't be more evil.

I looked around for a broom and the guard pointed to a broom. Betsy had already found a dustpan that was against the wall. She swept our hair into the dustpan and we looked at the stairs. How demeaning it felt as all the convicts watched.

One or two called out, "You can do it."

To which another added, "We'll get back at that witch somehow."

I felt a little heartened to know the other convicts empathized with us.

Climbing the stairs was very painful. Apart from the pain of the shackles, my whole body hurt because of her treatment. My face and hands were coated in blood, with more seeping from the injuries I'd taken. The same could be said of Betsy, who I could see was also in pain.

True to her character, she had no thought for herself, but she whispered to me, "I'll carry the dustpan."

Every step I took was accompanied by a burning pain starting from my ankles to my back and head. I struggled just to drag myself up the stairs. It must have been challenging to hold the dustpan straight as Betsy climbed.

As we reached the top of the stairs, I heard subdued murmurs from those who watched.

The bitter wind on our bare heads was so cold as we faced the night sky. Oh, how my head and back hurt! I really thought I would die.

We made our way to the side of the ship and Betsy tossed our locks into the dark blue sea. I felt like jumping over with them but thought better of it. All those who treated me so badly would someday have to pay for their cruelty. My Edward would see to it. Besides, I realized downheartedly, I couldn't even lift one leg to the height of the railing with those dreadful shackles.

When we finally returned to the prisoner's deck, I heard subdued voices from the prisoners. I felt humiliated. The guard opened the gate and pushed both of us into the prison.

Betsy held me by my elbow as I stumbled and made my way to our bench. I could see tears on her cheeks. I had caused this. It was all my fault.

As Betsy sat on her bench she motioned to me and whispered, "Here, sit here and rest your head on me. If anything, I think we have gained a little sympathy from the other convicts."

I whimpered and sobbed as silently as I could. Even the beating we had received at the hands of those two ruffians could not compare. I had never felt such pain. I don't know how Betsy coped. I knew she must have felt humiliated and full of pain also.

A little later several troopers appeared. They stacked a lot of tattered and torn blankets against the bars of the prison.

A guard spoke loudly over the many voices of the convicts. "We will unlock the gate so you lot can get your bedding here."

He pointed to some rags which were piled up against the outer wall on the trooper's side of the bars. I didn't have the energy to get mine, so Betsy hushed me saying she would get ours. We were allotted two tattered coarse blankets which were wrapped around a thin pillow."

The guard continued, "You will be responsible for keeping your bedding and clothing clean. Wash days will be assigned to you. I see many of you have chosen a bench. That will be your sleeping quarters throughout the voyage. Across from the convict deck, you can see the trooper's night station. Two troopers will be on duty so mind you be behaving yourselves. The troopers will be armed and have been given authority to shoot if necessary. There's to be no fighting or squabbling. Candles are to be extinguished by the eighth bell. As the bell is on the main deck we doubt if you might hear it. So, one of the troopers will also ring a bell on the quarterdeck as well. When you hear the morning bell ring you will receive instructions for the day."

He continued with his instructions. "Breakfast tomorrow will be made for you, but from then on you will be given meal duties. You will prepare food for the crew, the guards, the troopers, the free travelers and yourselves. When we have left the dock, you will have a bit more freedom. Some of you may have noticed we have lavatories on the deck. At night you will use the buckets, but during the day you are to notify a guard and he will see to it that you are accompanied to the lavatory. The guards will respect your privacy and will stand on deck and wait for you. Mind you, none of you are to take liberties."

Thank goodness they would stand on the deck until we finished. I doubted very much if that was always the case. Over time Betsy and I learned which troopers would respect our privacy. We would always seek them out when the need arose; While I hadn't shared my story with such men, I felt we had something in common with them. Betsy told me they were free men whose fare to the colony was paid if they fulfilled their duties on board watching over us. On arriving in Botany Bay, they would be allotted a plot of land to farm and take care of. Like us, their future was unknown, but at least they had their freedom.

There were murmurs amongst the convicts when candles were put out. There were ugly snorts of laughter and the smell of rum was strong as it wafted in the air from the trooper's area.

One or two of the women called out, "What will ya be getting' if you share some of that there rum?"

A rough voice responded, "We ain't out of port yet. You'll be havin' ya' turn."

Betsy was the only one to hear my whispers. "I don't know how they can bear it, groveling to those men like that."

Betsy replied thoughtfully, "Many of these women don't know any different. They have lived in the streets with nowhere to go. They take comfort in being with a man, any man."

I whispered, "I suppose they might get better privileges for acting so."

Betsy replied, "One good thing; we are sleeping near the back. Hopefully, none of those guards will come our way. Don't worry. Our hair will grow back. And, in a few days, the pain in our backs will subside. We'd better try to sleep now."

After a while, I could hear Betsy breathing heavily. I wished I could sleep, but desperation, hopelessness, and anguish tormented me. My body ached and my head felt very cold.

Apart from the snores and grunts on the first night, all was still. But many of the following nights we could hear shrieks of laughter and moans of delight coming from the guard's station. A guard would unlock the gate and call out, "Anybody wantin' any rum?"

Several women would reply, "I'll be wanting some," or something similar. They would make their way to the gate where several guards waited for them. I felt ashamed for them. I had no idea those of my own gender could act so low. But I remembered Betsy's words. Many of these women didn't know any better. Their lives had been hard, and they just lived on the street taking any opportunity they could that would make their circumstances better.

A lot of immorality took place on that ship. I shall not relate any of the details as they disgust me, but I was also grateful not to be chosen. For several weeks our hair was just stubble. We both had scars on our heads. I know we must have looked a sorry sight. Maybe that was a good thing.

I remember Betsy telling me, "I am not so sure all the women spending time with the troopers are volunteers. Make sure you at least appear to be sleeping if any of those guards come near."

I knew Betsy was looking out for me. Thank goodness we were never sought out.

Betsy asked. "Did you see where the lavatories are, Catherine?"
I replied, "No I did not."

Betsy told me, "I saw a little of them when they sent us to the prison deck before they put our shackles on. They are on the top deck. It looked like there are several of them. They are wooden seats over buckets. I hope it won't be our job to empty them. I don't think there will be much privacy as I saw four in a row."

I felt disgusted as I said, "Is there to be no modesty? They treat us like animals."

I didn't mind so much at night as we used several buckets along the back wall. In the dark, it felt more private. During the day we had to memorize the way to the buckets so that we would be able to make our way there in the dark.

Even though the odor from those dreadful buckets penetrated throughout the deck, the smell was not as vile as it had been on the hulk. Even now, while I am far away, writing these words, I can still smell the stench of that place.

Before the morning bell rang, Betsy shook me.

"Catherine, Catherine can you hear? They must have raised the ship's anchor. The ship is moving."

I know it seems a bit melodramatic as I say it now, but it was real to me and, at that moment, I felt tears begin to well up. How I longed to go up on deck to catch one last glimpse of my beloved England.

The morning bell didn't sound until an hour later. The same trooper who spoke to us the night before stood before us.

"You are to fold your bedding and leave it on your bench neatly. Before you go up on deck your shackles will be removed. There will come a time when they will be needed again. But, if you do as you are told, we won't have to bother with them until we are anchored near land."

I was pleased to have those awful things removed. As I looked around, I saw that I was not the only one who had suffered badly from wearing them. Many of the women had open sores where the metal had rubbed against their frail legs.

My ankles were badly chaffed, my head ached, and my aching back tormented me terribly. I looked at Betsy. Despite putting on a brave face, I saw that she experienced similar pains. I don't know how she could find a smile, but she did when she told me not to focus on my pain.

Crowded as we were on the main deck, I felt a sense of freedom. How bizarre, to think that not wearing shackles was freedom! Would I ever be free again? What lay ahead for Betsy? What was to become of her? She had a brother somewhere and a sister in Dover. If we ever escaped this horrid place, I would never outlive the shame I had brought on us.

The troopers held tight to their pistols and muskets as we made our way up on deck. I expect they were concerned that someone might break loose and cause trouble. But, I asked myself, what good would that do? As I looked out to sea, there was only a spot on the horizon where I imagined my beloved England was. The England I thought I knew before this ordeal. My dear mother and father, my friends, Oh Edward, I thought, where are you?

Perhaps I exaggerated the trooper's concerns, but I know there were some hardened women amongst us. I imagined they might resort to all manner of things if it took to their fancy.

While we were on the hulk, there was some type of fuss made over one woman getting more than her share of food. She was very friendly with one of the guards. Several of the women asked her to get extra food for them.

One of the troopers who oversaw the rations found out about it and the trooper who had been giving her extra food was disciplined and we never saw him again. There was a raucous argument among the women and the woman who started it all was tossed overboard by her fellow prisoners. As she was still shackled, she was gone in mere moments and, for all I know, her body made a good breakfast for some type of fish. I doubt very much if her death was reported to the authorities or anyone for that matter. Poor soul that she was.

When we climbed the ladder, I saw a few tables of food.

"Look Betsy," I said. "I thought we were to make the food."

She said, "After breakfast, don't you remember the trooper told us?"

"Oh yes, I wonder if the food will be any better than what we've had."

Betsy put her hands on my face and with deep concern said, "You must promise me. You need to eat a lot more than you have been. I don't want to get to that Australia on my own."

There was a pile of bowls, enough for all of us I would say, and several huge pots of porridge. We each took a bowl and then one of the women ladled porridge into it and then another would add a half teaspoon of sugar. After the short rations we endured on the hulk, the addition of a little sugar made the same thin porridge taste not nearly as bad as it had on the hulk.

Each convict on the ship was allotted a certain amount of food and, as the captain had directed, the food was combined.

I told Betsy, "I don't mind eating this. It seems quite edible. You know I think the women who served us must be free women. I have never seen them before."

Betsy agreed, "Yes, I think you are right. Their clothes look halfway decent, not like this course sackcloth we are wearing. Look, there are biscuits and tea also."

The tea was weak but still, it tasted as tea should. Most of the convicts seemed to be pleased and some thought we might be treated with a degree of humanity.

After the dishes were taken away a guard instructed us. "Ya' all are to form in four rows abreast and line up on the deck."

The guards showed us where to go, but it took some time to make an orderly group of us. We made a line from the front to the rear of the ship. That evil little cross-eyed man who had ordered my head shaved the night before stood above us on the forecastle.

"You will be silent as you are spoken to by the captain. Hush now. Hush." There was still murmuring but all was still when the captain appeared.

The captain was a tall, burly man, about six feet in height. His dark eyes were impenetrable, and his facial expression was hard. The way the crew reacted around him left little doubt that he expected complete and instant obedience to his commands. More, he seemed almost a cruel man, leaving the impression that he would not abide any leniency from his crew or the guards towards us convicts. He was wearing full navy uniform. I had seen men similarly dressed at social functions I had attended in London. He spoke as one who expected complete attention and it was clear that he was accustomed to power. His demeanor was haughty, self-important and prideful. These were conveyed to us as much by the tone of his voice as by the actual words he spoke. And, though I could dismiss his brusque aristocratic manner, I certainly did not understand his unmerciful tone.

He looked down from a higher level into our eyes and spoke. "While we have released you from your fetters, that by no means is a sign that we trust you. You are the lowest of the low, vagabonds, thieves, and murderers. Why they didn't hang the lot of you, I don't know. You are all in my custody until I hand you over formally to the Governor of New South Wales. While you are in my custody you will be submissive and obedient. We will not tolerate stupidity or foolishness."

As the captain spoke, I thought to myself, "It's true." I felt like the lowest of the low, though not for the reasons the captain had declared. It was my own stupidity and impulsiveness that led not only me but Betsy also, to this unspeakable existence.

My experience both on the hulk and this past night had taught me this: that any word from me would bring ridicule and worse, both to me and to Betsy. After what had happened, I pledged to keep silent as much as possible.

The captain continued. "Make no trouble among you. Be respectful and do what you are told. You are to be totally obedient to the troopers. They are onboard to guard you and make sure you follow the rules. If you make no trouble, you are likely to be alive when we see the shores of Australia."

There were murmurs from those of us standing there, but the captain ignored it and continued.

"Wrongdoings will be dealt with efficiently. Any wrongdoer will have her head shaved or will find herself thrown in the coal cabin to have one or two days to think on her wrongdoings. I daresay that most of you have heard of the cat o' nine tails. Any wrongdoings of a deeper nature…then it's five lashes you can expect to get."

He held that wicked thing up. It looked like a multi-tailed whip. I could just imagine the pain it could inflict. I was yet to see it in use. At the time I thought surely it wouldn't be used on women.

"Head Trooper Tottenham is the superintendent over all convicts. Make sure you heed his instructions and those who work with him."

He motioned for the head trooper to come forward.

That cross-eyed little man, Trooper Tottenham, spoke with a shrill voice. He stood about five feet six inches tall and puffed out his chest as he read from a parchment. As I had noted when I first encountered him, he gave the distinct impression he thought highly of himself.

"Hear ye, hear ye, all you convicts bound for Australia. The following are rules which you must obey.

All convicts must conduct themselves in a respectful manner towards all those in authority over them. You are strictly to obey such orders as the captain, the officers, myself and the troopers may issue."

As he pointed to them, he said, "You will see there is a large group of troopers, all of whom you must obey. They are at liberty to keep you confined if they see you acting badly. They all have guns of some description.

The prisoners must behave themselves always, but more especially when prayers are said at divine service on Sundays. Prayers will also be held up on deck each morning, weather permitting."

That meant we were able to go up on deck more often than I had imagined. That was a good thing.

Trooper Tottenham continued, "Cursing and all foul language, shouting, quarreling, fighting and stealing of any sort is strictly forbidden and will be dealt with seriously.

Any person stealing or secreting any of the ships stores or any other article belonging to the stores in the ship will be severely punished.

The prisoners are on no occasion to hold conversation with the troopers or the ship's company or talk through the bars below once imprisoned.

A trooper has been appointed who will superintend the issue of provisions. A printed copy of the established rations of provisions will be posted. The troopers will put a roster of duties and chores for convicts and they must be followed obediently."

I thought to myself, "That's silly." I doubted if any of these women could read.

"If at any time a prisoner has reason to complain of abusive language or mistreatment by the ship's company or any of the troopers, she is strictly directed not to retaliate but to make the same known to me for the complaint to be investigated.

The night watch will be set at eight o'clock and they will be held responsible for the peace and good order of the prison during the night. It will be the duty of the troopers during daylight hours to see that no more than two to four people at a time use the lavatory.

Prisoners are warned that if found congregating in groups anywhere on the ship, other than their sleeping area, they will be punished in a manner which I shall determine based on the offense.

There is a surgeon aboard ship. If a prisoner becomes ill, the troopers must be notified, and they will report your condition to the surgeon. He, in turn, will see to it that your condition is addressed.

Most importantly, all prisoners are to be accompanied by a trooper when the need arises to visit the lavatory area on the top deck during the day. There is to be no inappropriate behavior from prisoners towards the troopers.

All prisoners will gather together for morning prayer. While the weather holds, such prayers will be held up on deck. In bad weather, prayers are to be said inwardly.

No doubt some of you may experience seasickness. We have allowed for this. You will see buckets in various areas of the ship. If you are not standing near the rails of the ship you are to vomit using the buckets but make sure you empty the buckets into the sea and wash them out.

You will find that the bell in the forecastle will be rung to notify you where you should be. It is likely that those confined below deck will not hear these bells, so a trooper will ring a bell just above the hatch for those who are confined."

As Mr. Tottenham finished, he repeated the trooper's words of last night, "Meals will no longer be provided for you. From now on convicts will be assigned the duty to prepare meals for the convicts, troopers, free men and crew."

We were told we could spend the next hour up on deck as we liked, but we weren't to speak to the ship's company at any time.

Some of the women took little heed to the warnings. I heard a tall and a buxom woman saying to one of the crew, "When are you gunna' be seeking me out then? Ya' surely can't be having much fun pulling on them there ropes."

The crewman seemed taken aback by her brazen words. He flushed a bit and said, "There will be time enough for that."

He quietly told her. "Move along now or else I'll have to be reporting ya' to Head Trooper Tottenham.

A few days later I saw them together in the guard's area on our deck. During the weeks that followed, from time to time I often saw them together. I concluded that perhaps they had formed a relationship and supposed that would be a good thing for the convict.

By that time, we were far out to sea. When opportunity allowed, I sometimes stood at the ship's rail, my eyes drifting towards where I thought my dear homeland might be. At those times tears would often well in my eyes. I wondered if I would ever see my parents, my friends and, of course, dear Edward.

How I longed to see my dear mother and father! How I loved them! Thoughts went around and around in my mind. Thoughts of my dear Edward were paramount. "Please, my darling, please find me!"

Another convict whom I'd seen before, must have seen my distress. She came and stood by my side. I had heard other prisoners call her Angela, but I knew nothing more about her.

"It ain't all that bad ya know. We'll be seeing a bit more of the world than most."

I just nodded, knowing full well that if I spoke too much, I might make another enemy.

"Ya know the food they give us now is better for the most part than what I 'ad used to be 'avin. It was a real 'ard thing to find food for my little-un and me."

My natural curiosity took over. I tried to speak as Betsy had told me. "Where is ya' little one now then?"

"She's below sleepin'. I 'ad a mind to be leavin' 'er with me ma back in England, but some 'ave been sayin' Van Diemen's Land is a place to grow and a good sight better than the streets of London. I was 'avin a right battle to get food and stuff. It was such a 'eart ache. Look forward to it lovey. No more tears. Its gunner work out. Y'll' see."

While Angela had no understanding of my plight, I could see that she meant well and thanked her with a smile.

She asked, "So, where you be from then?"

"London," I replied. "I had a good life. I was falsely accused. It's been a hellish muddle."

"So, you be the one they say is mad?" she asked.

"That's what they say. Only my friend Betsy knows differently. She is the one who keeps me sane. Her presence is reassurance of my past life."

"Be that there as it may, ya don't seem like a mad-un to me. I'll 'ave to be seek'n you out, so you can meet me youngun.' She's only three years. Don't you be grievin' so. It's all gunner work out. Y'll' be seeing that I'm sure. I better go. She sure as 'ell will be awake now. I dunna' want those guards to be givin' her a bad time. See ya later."

I thought she seemed friendly enough. I hoped I would talk to her again.

When she left, I continued looking out toward where I thought England was. Betsy came to my side and noticed I was teary-eyed. She put her arm around me and said, "Don't you worry, the day will come when we shall return."

I doubted that very much but did not say so.

To change the conversation, Betsy remarked, "I haven't seen that evil woman who shaved our heads. I wonder where she is?"

"Who knows?" I replied. "Perhaps she was on the ship to scare us and now she remains back in England. Who knows how they justify the way we are treated and the actions of those who treated us so badly?"

"Don't be so cynical," Betsy responded. "There's bound to be good times. We are together. That's the main thing."

Despite such kindness, I still felt wretched, totally drained both physically and mentally. I feel sure she also must have wondered how we would survive. Some of the other prisoners spoke of barbaric conditions when we reached Australia. I suppose I feared they were right. Nothing good had happened since we left Blakehouse these months past. Still, Angela had different views. I wondered how it could be any worse than what we had experienced.

Betsy noticed Elizabeth stirring uncomfortably and closed Catherine's journal.

"I think that might be enough for today, Elizabeth. Perhaps I should call for lunch?"

"Yes, that would be nice dear. I am feeling a bit peckish."

As I went to sound the bell to alert Woods to bring up lunch, Elizabeth said, "My dear child, what a struggle it must have been for you. I can understand the respect Edward has for you."

I replied sincerely, "In my mind, I really didn't feel as though I did very much. I sometimes think that Edward thinks too highly of me. I am just an ordinary person who loves Catherine. By some miracle, we survived the voyage and were able to remain together during our time in Australia. That was indeed a blessing."

Elizabeth shared an understanding look and asked, "And, how, how did you really feel Betsy?"

"Many times I felt desperate on that voyage." I replied. "But I knew that if I had shown any type of weakness, Catherine would have fallen more deeply into despair."

There was a knock on the door, and I called out to Woods to enter. He carried a large silver tray and placed it on the little table between Elizabeth and me. There were different types of sandwiches, egg, ham, pickles. They looked quite tempting. Woods poured out our tea. He knew I liked mine strong but had to ask Elizabeth her preference. I had never been in this situation before, having a guest and being treated with such respect. I decided it felt "unsettling."

"Thank you, Woods," I said. "Our lunch looks so delicious!"

His usual reply "It's a pleasure to be of service to you, Madam."

Apart from the sandwiches, there were slices of cakes and little coconut and jam pies.

When Woods had left, Elizabeth and I enjoyed our lunch. I imagined Elizabeth could see how awkward I felt being waited upon. Elizabeth and I continued our conversation as we ate.

Elizabeth asked amiably, "I wonder what you might be feeling now that you are no longer in service. Do you have any plans for the future?"

"Not really," I replied. "I did have one idea though. When Lord Edward and Catherine find me a little place, I might try to be a teacher. Lord Kensington permitted me to have a good education and I thought I might be able to work with the children of the servants nearby, teaching them how to read and write. I don't know if Lord Edward would think it appropriate. I cannot go against his views as he is so generous with me."

"Why Betsy, that's a most commendable thing to do. How much would you charge for each child?"

I answered, "My goodness, not a penny. How indebted I feel to Catherine's parents! They allowed my brother and sister and me to join in when Catherine had a governess. That's how we learned to read and write. Anyway, there wouldn't be enough in servant's pay to take on any extra expense. Edward has told me he would provide me with a stipend to pay for my expenses. I also think I could take in a little sewing to put some money away should I be needing it."

As I poured another cup of tea for Elizabeth I asked, "What might you do to keep busy?"

She replied, "I am ashamed to say, very little. In my younger days, I loved to ride horses, but now my old bones won't allow me to do that. I also liked to read and still do when my eyes will let me. I have spectacles, but I find print tiring to read. In the past, I liked to travel, but nowadays it makes me too tired. Nevertheless, I still enjoy shopping and manage to knit a little."

"Yes, I know what it is like to be idle. I started to do a few chores yesterday, but Lord Edward must have told the servants I wasn't allowed to do those sorts of things. If I even attempt to pick up a duster or wash a dish, they strictly forbid it."

"Yesterday I wrote several letters to my old friends sharing a little of what happened over the past months. I need to be careful about what I say about this. I am concerned about Catherine's reputation. I am so relieved that it is all over for both Catherine and me."

"Indeed, as I hear Catherine's story, I marvel how you both dealt with such a hard life," Elizabeth said. "It really is barbaric to think you had to go through this."

I responded passionately, as I felt deeply angered by the past months and it was good to have a friend to share my thoughts with. "It was horrid! Those experiences will stay with me to my deathbed. If only poor Catherine hadn't been so ill during those last few months. I hope she will return to her old self again."

Finishing the last of her tea, Elizabeth stood saying, "I imagine Catherine is enjoying her time with her parents and Edward. Don't you fret, dear. Everything will work out. Most truly, when I heard that you and Catherine were missing, I was distraught. But it just goes to show, everything does work out."

I responded quietly, not fully agreeing with her, "Perhaps."

Elizabeth took little notice of my comment.

Walking towards the door of the parlor, Elizabeth told me, "I will come again on Friday if that is all right. Would you be kind enough to ask Woods to tell my driver to bring my coach around for me? I half imagine he'll be waiting in the servant's kitchen."

As I bid her farewell, I thought to myself, "What a nice soul!" I was pleased to have her as a new friend. After my mother had died, Mrs. Mclintoch had become a mother figure in my life. I thought to myself that perhaps I had taken the care she had shown me for granted. I decided that making a visit to the country to visit with her would have to be a priority once I had moved into my own little home.

Friday morning, at exactly ten thirty, Elizabeth knocked on the door. Although I wasn't really supposed to answer the door, I got to it faster than Woods. When he did come, he gave me a stern look. He then accompanied us to the parlor and put another log on the fire.

"Elizabeth," I said. "I have been looking forward to your visit."

"And I too, dear one," she replied.

I smiled and remarked, "It's such a cold day! Woods has a good fire burning to warm us."

"Yes, as I was coming over the rain was pouring down. We also had a bit of hail. Thank goodness for warm coaches and warm fires. Tell me what the weather was like in Australia."

"It was very warm when we first arrived," I said. "Much warmer than our summers. I didn't much care for the heat. Catherine also found it hard to deal with. But, fortunately, Autumn was a cooler time. Winter was certainly not as bitter where we were as it is here. There was no snow, just rainy windy days. Poor Catherine had to bring in the wood for the kitchen stove no matter what the temperature outdoors was like."

As we were about to take our seats, I told Woods, "I will ring the bell when we are ready for lunch."

"Very good, Ma'am," he replied.

I picked up Catherine's journal murmuring, "Now, where were we?"

"I think Catherine was talking to another prisoner named Angela," Elizabeth prompted.

"Yes, I remember now." I flipped the pages over. "Here we are after Angela left to see to her daughter."

Betsy began to read.

Watching the motion of the sea I started to feel nauseous. According to Betsy, I was even more ashen in color than normal. In a way, it was good that I was standing by the ship's rail overlooking the sea. What food I had in my stomach went into the sea. I heard Betsy asking one of the guards.

"Can I take Catherine back to our quarters? She is not well."

He answered, "Yes, she doesn't look too good. Go ahead. Take her. But there will be no coming back on deck."

As Betsy whisked me back to the prison deck, she grabbed a small wooden bucket as we went down the stairs.

"I have heard that rolling waves can make you seasick."

Betsy was far more knowledgeable than I had ever given her credit for. As I sat on my bench for a while, Betsy put her arm around me.

I assured her, "I feel a lot better now. I'll have no need of the bucket. You know when I was traveling with the other Mrs. Kensington and with Edward, I didn't get seasick. I wonder why now and not then?"

"I expect it could be our diet. I can well imagine you ate much better fare. Did you ever stand to look out over the sea?"

"Yes, at times, but the ship's deck seemed more stable."

About an hour later most of the other convicts came down the ladder. We noticed that several of the prisoners were suffering the same as I. Some were carrying buckets. Like us, they headed straight for their benches.

Benches, that's truly what they were. We would put one blanket folded on the bottom to act as a type of mattress and then used the other blanket to keep warm. Well, to try and keep warm. Those first few days after leaving England the weather was cold and bitter. It penetrated our very bones even though the hatch above us was closed at night. It makes me shudder to even think of it.

I tried not to think of my eiderdown bed back in England. I wanted to remember, but I recognized I could not deal with the memories of better times. My life had been filled with such luxuries, and I had taken them all for granted. I tried to discipline myself. I tried not to think of any joy or happiness. I remember Betsy saying that such thoughts only bought more sorrow and heartache.

8

Life on board ship

The food on the Barringer was better than the food we had on the hulk, particularly the porridge and meat. The porridge was much thicker and seemed less gooey. Of course, having a little sugar on it made it much more palatable.

The meat was somewhat tastier. Although it was still dried, the better cuts made it more palatable.

While I was one of many who suffered from seasickness, I discovered that was just the beginning. There wasn't one part of my body which didn't experience pain of one type or another. The causes were many and varied. Heat and cold, thirst and hunger, frost or dampness, filthy inhuman conditions, and just plain misery and frustration. I sound like I'm complaining, but these things were all true. Betsy never complained to me. But I did to myself and sometimes to Betsy. Betsy was very patient with me.

Head Trooper Tottenham always looked crisp and clean. Perhaps, I thought to myself, he was trying to direct attention away from his other odd features. He came down the ladder with a woman of no tiny proportion.

He called out, "All of you listen to Bertha."

Bertha was a large woman both in width and height. Her dark long hair looked scruffy, as if she had never washed it.

She told us, "I am one of the five free women that are on board this ship. Head trooper Tottenham has put me in charge of the foodstuffs. You all have been allotted rations for the trip, but the captain has chosen me to combine all the rations to make meals for everyone. There will be a guard to watch you as we get the food ready each day, so don't you be think'n you can be takin' food just as you fancy. We'll be fixing porridge of a morning and then a soupy stew for the main meal at midday and then we'll be seeing to something for the evening meal. Those convicts assigned to the cooking detail will prepare food for the crew, the troopers and some of us free folks as well as a meal for all of you. You are all to remember; just like when the captain spoke to you, you are all to obey me as well. The troopers will bring twenty of you to the ship's galley in thirty minutes."

After she climbed that ladder with some degree of effort, I overheard one of my fellow prisoners say, "Who in the 'ell does she think she be… talkin' like she's the Captain? She's probably a wife of one of them guards or somethin' and she's all uppity with 'erself cos she's over us. We'll be waitin'. She'll be eatin' her words."

I shared a knowing look with Betsy. "Nothing good will come of this."

Betsy nodded in agreement.

About twenty minutes later the troopers chose twenty women and led them to the galley. Upon their return, we were surprised to learn that the galley was on the quarterdeck, the same deck as the prison.

Betsy murmured quietly, "Mmm, somehow I thought the galley would be on a different deck. Life is full of surprises, one way or another."

I replied just as quietly, "Agreed. And sometimes those surprises can be ghastly. I hope I'm not chosen for kitchen duty. What would I do? I have never worked in a kitchen. I will be asked to do things I have never done before. The other women will ridicule me."

In a matter-of-fact tone, Betsy's reply mirrored my thoughts, "I think we all will be required to do it sometime. I think you'll be able to manage. If you don't know what to do, you'll just have to ask. But please do not explain your lack of experience by saying who you are."

I replied sulkily. "Yes, I have learned my lesson and remember my promise to you. I will try not to bring any attention to us."

Around mid-day, a bell sounded. We thought that we might be getting our mid-day meal.

A convict called out, "Is that for us?"

A trooper called back, "The first bell is for the troopers, freemen and the crew, two bells for the convicts."

Sometime later, when the bell rang twice, a trooper who both Betsy and I had come to like called out as he was unlocking the prison gate. "You all, be ready to come out and go to the galley. There are several troopers here, so no silly business."

This became our daily routine. We were led by troopers to the ship's galley to eat our food. Other times, when we weren't behind bars, we needed to listen for the second bell which meant lunch. We all were generally back to the prison area after doing our chores before the sixth bell rang. That was our call for the evening meal. It meant more scanty soup and two slices of bread or moldy biscuits.

The galley was larger than I envisioned. There was a cooking area and large tubs for washing dishes. There were long columns of seating and tables in between them. We had to stand in line to get a plate and a mug and then stand in line to get our food. And, if we were lucky, we'd get a seat as well. Often, we had to eat our food standing. That happened to me on several occasions.

After that first scanty meal of a soupy stew, Bertha made it very clear to the convicts, "You are to wash and dry the dishes."

This not only included our own dishes, but also the crew's, trooper's and free men's dishes. It also included the dishes used in the dining area where the Master and his officers and Head Trooper Tottenham and the ship's surgeon ate.

A few of the women were assigned to see to their food. While doing so they were strictly guarded and there was very little chance for them to hide any of the food on their person.

It didn't take all of us to see to the dishes. Bertha chose the ones she wanted to stay back. Often both Betsy and I were chosen. I wasn't fussed about it. When the galley was clean, and all the dishes were washed, dried and put away, we were sent back to our quarters.

As we were confined back in our area after the mid-day meal I commented, "My...She said stew didn't she, Betsy?"

"Yes, how silly that turned out to be!" Betsy replied. "Salty meat, a few scant potatoes, and a few peas. I don't know how the poor women without teeth could eat that meat."

"Why was it so tough?" I asked.

"They salt the meat so that it keeps. It is salted and dried and that makes it harder and tougher. Nonetheless it still isn't as hard as it was on the Hulk."

Head Trooper Tottenham was waiting for us. He watched us as we were coming from the galley and said, "Hurry up now, I want to speak to all of you."

He shifted his weight from one foot to the other as he eyed us convicts making our way to the prison area. Apart from those of us who were just returning from the ship's galley, all the convicts were gathered together. He spoke with pomp and ceremony, puffing out his chest.

"Now that you are all here, I want you to know what you must do. I doubt many of you can read the notices we have put up, so before the night bell sounds a trooper will call out your orders for the following day. Make sure you listen. Days are set aside for you to wash clothes and clean your deck; ship's galley duty; cleaning duty and food preparation both for the captain's table and for the rest of the ship's company. No one is to shirk their duties.

We shall start morning prayers beginning tomorrow. When the first bell rings, all convicts are to join the ship's company on the main deck to thank the Lord for keeping us alive and to keep us from evil.

After prayers have been said, twenty of you will need to go to the galley to prepare breakfast.

Convicts can choose if they want to stay up on the main deck or not, but convict's breakfast won't be until the third bell.

I will take my leave now, but make sure you do your assigned duties well or you will be disciplined."

When he was out of earshot Betsy laughed and called him a pompous ass. I agreed and silently thought to myself that most of the troopers were the same; arrogant and with no sensitivity at all.

Apart from the duties the head trooper mentioned, some prisoners were assigned duties at various times for a multitude of reasons. Sometimes the reasons were not so honorable.

I have always been a late riser of a morning, but after months of captivity, I found that I always woke early. Perhaps it was the discomfort of sleeping on the floor or the noises and smells that were around me that woke me.

Betsy shook me gently. "Catherine wake up, we have to go on deck"

I muttered grumpily, "Alright, alright, it seems like we have just gone to sleep."

I looked around and other prisoners were up making their way to the steps.

"No," Betsy replied. "You just didn't get to sleep until late. Hurry follow me."

I felt very sleepy but did as Betsy bid. I heard others yawning, but we all made it on to the deck on time. The ship's company were all gathered together.

The captain addressed us. "This is a fine morning. I hope you all slept well. There will be duties to be done today and so we should offer thanks for our blessings and praise to our maker for keeping us alive. We should ask for strength in all the duties that we do this day. Mr. Tottenham would you lead us in prayer please."

I don't know if Head Trooper Tottenham was expecting to say the prayer or not, but he stood in front of us and offered thanks and asked for the good Lord to keep all the convicts submissive and willing to do their chores and for the ship's company to be safe on the sea.

Throughout the voyage, the ship's captain, his officers, and one or two of the troopers would offer morning prayers. When the weather was too inclement to go on deck, we were told to say prayers in our hearts. I doubt very much that many convicts heeded that advice.

Each day seemed to roll over into the next. There were often times when convicts disagreed one with another. Some didn't care for the work they were required to do. There were squabbles over food and numerous incidentals.

After a month or so at sea, we felt growing pangs of hunger. In the beginning, it seemed that we would have plenty of food, but our rations seemed to dwindle as time went on. As convicts were the last to eat, we were also the ones who ate the least. Those who worked preparing food often tried to conceal some on their person. But it seldom worked as they were often caught and disciplined by having their heads shaved.

Head Trooper Tottenham was true to his word. Wrongdoing amongst us, no matter how petty, was always penalized.

In the beginning, I felt that I truly had very little in common with the other prisoners. Yet even though they were coarse in manner, little by little, our common destitution made me feel some compassion for them when they were caught.

I said, "I don't understand why they keep on trying, but I do sympathize with them."

Betsy disagreed with me and said bluntly, "Not me. They always get caught and are punished.

They should have learned their lesson."

The sting of my own punishment still fresh, I was equally blunt. "Well, I know what it is like to have your head shaved. It's mortifying. Surely you must feel the same way."

She nodded her understanding but defended her view anyway. "You were trying to save us from this plight. Their crimes can hardly be likened to being truthful. I feel hungry, but I wouldn't try to steal food. I think some of the convicts are planning something big. I've heard talk of roughing up Bertha and stealing the key to the storehouse where the food is kept."

This was news I hadn't heard, and I was concerned. "I hope they don't bring more trouble on us. I can understand to a point. We must have food to eat. What we're allowed isn't enough, even for a wee child. We all look gaunt and emaciated."

Betsy responded grimly. "I don't fancy their chances. Bertha always has a trooper with her who is a six-foot giant."

I quickly agreed, "Yes, I noticed. He has a pistol tucked in his belt and looks very menacing with that huge scar across the right side of his face."

Betsy remarked, "I've heard some prisoners call him Scarface. Some said that he committed a murder and the scar on his face was the doings of a jailer who caught him trying to escape. They said he had served twenty years for his crime and would be a free man when he reached Australia. It was even rumored that he would be given a few acres of land."

I was amazed. I had no idea where she came across this bit of gossip. I spent much of my time in her company and this was something I had never heard. Finally, putting this aside, I offered my own assessment.

"Then I imagine there will be good things for some. But what for you and me? Who knows? I doubt if it could be as bad as our time on the old hulk. You know, Betsy, I am deathly afraid of so many things. You continue to be my joy and my lifesaver. Never forget that!"

Betsy blushed and said, "We are friends and do for each other, even in the dark times. Surely that is what true friendship is. Anyway, last night I heard more talk. Occasionally that smaller trooper is with Bertha. You remember him, Catherine?"

Betsy continued, "He is much friendlier with the convicts than other troopers, but he also has a pistol tucked in his belt."

I agreed with her assessment. "Yes, he seems to be a gentleman, if there can be such a thing on this ship. Only the other day he was pretending to act like Head Trooper Tottenham. Standing on his tippy toes and puffing out his chest and making himself look cross-eyed. Often when he is about, you can hear laughter."

Betsy continued, "It is rumored that he has taken a real liking to one of the women prisoners. You know her. Her name is Emily."

I agreed. "Yes, I have seen them together."

Betsy continued, "Anyway, I heard whisperings last night. Some of the women are trying to plot a way to get to the ship's foodstuffs. I think they have worked out a plan. The next time the guard is on duty who has an eye for Emily, she will try to distract him while several women will overpower Bertha to take the key. They intend to tie Bertha up and gag her and hide her in a storage cabin which they have found to be unlocked. It is somewhere near the galley. That storage cabin is where they keep our shackles, some maps and shipping gear and there is easy access to it."

I knew in my heart that the plan would fail and that those who participated would wind up being killed or hurt badly. I couldn't help but express this to Betsy. "This will be a disaster. Even if they succeed, that weasel of a man, Head Trooper Tottenham will soon discover their plot."

Betsy nodded knowingly, saying, "Yes, I agree. The ringleaders of the plan are those who have already been penalized for trying to steal."

In response, I replied, "Their hair has hardly grown at all, yours and mine are starting to be acceptable but raggedy. I expect trouble will be brewing for all of us. My goodness, Betsy, how do you find out all these things?"

Betsy answered, "I hear them jabbering of a morning, most times before you wake up. And don't forget my bed is nearer to theirs than yours. I pretend to sleep while I listen. I'm not sure we would be safe if they knew we were aware of their plans."

Betsy continued. "They will make their way to the ship's store to steal biscuits and any other foodstuffs they can find and carry. I believe someone has donated their spare clothing, to fashion bags to carry the food in. There is a large group who are in cahoots with each other. I heard several were going to find a place to store the food. Now, it's rumored they have found an area at the rear of our deck to store the food, but the exact location is a secret."

I knew the plot was going to fail. I was certain.

I whispered, "Well, when is all this going to take place?"

Betsy stated, "They are waiting for the right guard to accompany Bertha and then they'll put their plan into action. I think most of the women are excited with the thought of more food. Obviously, they are not thinking of the consequences."

I said, "What foolishness! You would think they would know better."

Betsy agreed with me, "Yes, it's a stupid plan, and doomed to fail. But we can't say anything. We are stuck with these women and, when the plan fails, we don't want to be thought of as traitors who betrayed them. There is much more to fear than just their bad opinion. If we inform on them, and they discover we did, they would likely kill us both."

We watched expectantly and, eventually, the day came when they made their move. It happened after morning prayers. The women chosen for galley duty had already made their way there. Bertha started to go to the galley with the friendly little trooper by her side.

"Did you see Betsy? It's happening as planned. Emily just asked the friendly little trooper to use the lavatory."

The trooper blushed a little as he said, "You know the rules, no convicts are allowed out of a trooper's sight."

"You're the only guard around. What am I to do?" Emily asked.

"Will it be alright then, Bertha? We won't be but a minute," the trooper said.

Bertha nodded, unconcerned, "Yes."

Poor Bertha, little did she know what the next few moments would hold.

As the conspiracy unfolded before us, I remarked quietly, "Did you see Betsy? Three of those women grabbed Bertha."

Betsy stated, "They must be the ringleaders. I think they have stolen the key out of Bertha's pocket and gagged her."

Betsy asked, "Do you know their names?"

I had to think because I had never shared words with any of them. "Yes, I think I recognize them. One of them was Elsie. She was caught stealing down on the London wharves. And Mavis, you know, the one who told us all to stand up for each other. She is the one who pretended to be a nurse and stole money from the patients. I think the last woman was Abby, but I don't know anything about her."

Although poor Bertha let out a stifled squeal, all was done quietly. We no longer saw Bertha, and both Betsy and I shook our heads sadly. We were both of the same opinion, "This will become a problem for everyone."

Later in the day, when Betsy and I and a few others were involved with the clothing detail, it was whispered that the three ringleaders had released Bertha from the storage cabin. From what I could tell most of the convicts knew about it. But perhaps not to the extent we did.

Women who had been assigned to work in the galley that day had already begun their work and looked at each other as Bertha stumbled into the Galley. Her face was very red, and she looked very flustered, as if she had been crying.

Betsy whispered to me, "I heard they gave her back the key and told her that they would slit her throat if she told anyone.".

The following morning Betsy told me, "They were talking last night. I heard they didn't get that much food. But they had a side of dried beef, a side of dried pork, some cheese and several pounds of biscuits."

A day passed. Nothing had been said by anyone and we were given a few biscuits and cheese by the ringleaders.

I told Betsy. "I expect they are giving us food so that we won't turn them in."

We were agreed. Under no circumstances would we say anything. For if we did, they would probably toss us into the sea or some such thing.

Several days later, after morning prayer, when everyone was assembled together, Head Trooper spoke out and said, "The ship's surgeon, Dr. Forbes has asked to see the ship's store. He will go with you, Bertha, when you and your rostered convicts go to prepare the food."

There was a sense of panic amongst the prisoners who had been involved in the plot. I suspect they were fearful of being discovered. I was thankful we weren't involved. I didn't want to think about what was going to happen.

It was all too predictable. The surgeon discovered that some of the supplies were missing. Bertha was summoned by the Head Trooper and I imagine she reported how the theft was carried out. A few hours later all the convicts were summoned to the main deck. All the guards and ship's company, apart from the captain, were present when Head Trooper Tottenham stood before us.

Bertha stood near him.

He puffed out his little chest yet again as he had done numerous times before. As he spoke to us, he straightened himself up as high as his five-foot six-inch stature would allow.

He looked grave, yet pompous at the same time, when he told us, "Bertha has been badly mistreated and you convicts will pay. Bertha was able to recognize two of the women who treated her badly and they have already been shackled, beaten, and put in solitary confinement for ten days. They will be on half rations."

He asked, "Who else among you is responsible for this theft?"

We all bowed our heads. I think most of us were afraid to respond. There were evil persons amongst us. Even though I felt a duty to speak up, I feared that nothing good would come of it. We had spoken up before and told the truth to that evil little man and were abused and treated contemptuously for it. If we told the truth now, he would still punish us along with the rest of the convicts. I can only imagine the threats the conspirators would make against Betsy and me and how our fate would be very clear. I was very much afraid. I still valued my life and instinct told me, be still.

After a marked silence except for the creaking of the ships masts and sounds of the ocean, Trooper Tottenham told us, "We will conduct a thorough search of the ship for the missing supplies. All rations to convicts will be reduced by half for seven days."

That statement drew a troubled murmur amongst us.

He continued, "If anyone is willing to share information about this matter, please come forward and your full rations will be restored."

I thought to myself, what a silly thing to say! Anyone who informed on the others would die at the hands of their fellow convicts. He must know that.

I, who had only a limited grasp of our ship's society, had quickly come to know that you did not turn on your fellow prisoners. Anyone who did could very well fall victim to an accident and wind up being thrown overboard. Also, there was a certain camaraderie about us. While I think most of the women thought of me as a mad woman, a few had begun to trust me. There were some who showed compassion for us, especially after Betsy and I were disciplined on the first night.

Head Trooper Tottenham spoke out, "You will stay behind bars until full rations are restored. Prayers won't be said. You are to plead for forgiveness and beg for a submissive heart as we continue our voyage. For your sakes, I hope the Lord God Almighty will hear your prayers."

And so it was. I had never felt hunger like that before. Before it was over, the remaining convict involved in the theft who had not yet been identified to our jailors passed out the food they had stolen to all of us. I wondered to myself if they believed their crime was worth it.

Betsy looked up from her narration, saying to Elizabeth, "And so there is more drama. But I think we had better stop there for now Elizabeth. Time is getting on. They'll probably have our lunch ready by now. I'll ring for Woods to bring it. As you will see, I asked him to set the larger table by the window. It's too hard to eat soup on one's knee."

Nodding in the direction of the table, Betsy suggested, "Let's take a seat."

As we were about to sit down, Woods knocked on the door. I opened the door for him knowing full well what it was like to carry a silver tureen of soup on a tray along with several other dishes. Not that Woods wasn't skilled when it came to carrying large trays of food. I expect it was probably instinct on my behalf. I still couldn't come to terms with the idea of being waited upon. Elizabeth took a seat at the table and I thanked Woods as I sat down.

Elizabeth remarked, "Soup, it's a soup type of day. How delightful! What type of soup is it, Woods?"

Woods politely said, "I believe it's potato soup, Ma'am. Mrs. Featherstone has had it simmering on the stove all morning."

Elizabeth looked delighted as she looked at Woods and said, "Please tell Mrs. Featherstone we are grateful for her efforts, won't you?"

Woods agreed. "Indeed, Ma'am."

Woods then looked at me. "Will that be all, Ma'am?"

"Yes, thank you, Woods," I replied. "I will serve."

Elizabeth said, "I can't wait to taste it."

When Woods left, I ladled the soup into our bowls. We also had two fresh warm rolls each which Mrs. Featherstone had made. Woods left a teapot, milk, and sugar for us. There was a plate filled with delicate little cakes like those we had enjoyed the last time Elizabeth had come. I felt pleased to be able to share such a nice lunch with her.

"It must have been most unpleasant being on, what was it? 'half rations'?" Elizabeth said as she was eating.

I replied, "Yes, it was."

Between spoonsful of soup, I told her, "A few of the women died. Mind you, Catherine and I were in better health before the whole ordeal began. Most of the convicts were thin and emaciated. Catherine spent most of the time sleeping. I stayed near her all the time. Once or twice I thought she might die in her sleep. But, fortunately, each time when I checked on her, she was still breathing.

Elizabeth ventured, "I imagine you must have felt relieved when you were back on full rations."

I replied, "Yes, Bertha had us make loaves of bread. You can't imagine how delicious they tasted. Not that there was anything to go on the bread, but they still tasted wonderful. What little amount of butter had been bought on board was gone after just a few weeks at sea."

Elizabeth said, "These rolls taste marvelous. I wish my cook over at the manor was as skilled as yours."

"Woods hired her when Mrs. Mclintoch had to leave," I replied. "Lord Edward was about to leave for Australia and left the matter in his hands. He has since told me she had excellent references and he hoped we would be returning sooner. I don't think he realized we would be so long in returning.

But, returning to your question, Elizabeth, I am sure no one who hasn't endured such hardships can really understand the trials we faced. I think the reason Catherine was so determined to see her parents is that she felt disconnected from the life we had before we became convicts." I said thoughtfully. "Edward tried very hard to persuade her that everything will soon be as it was before. Still, no matter how hard Lord Edward tried to persuade her, Catherine still felt estranged from the people and places she knew before all this happened, even to Blakewood House. Can you imagine that? Catherine has always loved it here."

I waited as Elizabeth considered this. After a minute or two, she said, "Perhaps her visit with her parents will help her regain her sense of belonging. Also, a few weeks in the country air might strengthen her. That is what Edward said when he spoke to me."

"What a blessing it was that Lord Edward came when he did!" I said. "Despite her memory loss, I believe that is what gave Catherine the will to live."

Elizabeth said thoughtfully, "It's a good thing the Almighty kept her alive. It is remarkable that anybody could go through the things you did and still be alive."

I had to agree and said, "It's true what you say. I thought Catherine would die before Lord Edward came. She was failing before my eyes. She was mistreated by the housekeeper where we were in service. It wasn't until Catherine learned that Edward was coming that her spirits finally lifted, and she started to eat a little more but then she had a relapse and she lost her memory. She had several more weeks of rest before Edward arranged for our return. I was overjoyed when Catherine was able to go for walks with Edward as she was recovering!"

As Elizabeth looked up at a clock on the wall, she jumped up quickly. "Where has the time gone? I have an appointment with my physician, I should be there now. I told my driver that he needed to take me. I expect he is waiting in your kitchen."

I called for Woods and asked, "Would you tell Elizabeth's coachman that she is ready to leave?"

I walked with Elizabeth to the door and helped her as she put her coat on. I couldn't help note all of her clothes were of such fine quality. Catherine had told me that Elizabeth had a large income owing to the fact that Lord Edward had shared much of his inheritance with his siblings.

I hugged Elizabeth goodbye as her coach pulled up. Wood assisted her as she stepped into it. I returned to the parlor and picked up the book I was reading. Since I had returned to Blakewood House I spent much of my time reading. That was a luxury to me. Catherine and I enjoyed reading before we became convicts. Now I was able to read as much as I wanted and when I wanted. My latest choice was "The Vicar of Wakefield". I hadn't read much of it and was looking forward to it. The novel was written by an Irish writer, Oliver Goldsmith. The storyline, so far, a Vicar lives an idyllic life in a country parish with his wife and children. He had acquired a certain amount of wealth by investing an inheritance he received from a deceased relative and he donates the thirty-five pound that his church position pays annually to local orphans and war veterans.

Most nights I would dine with the servants. Lord Edward told me I could dine in the great dining hall, but it seemed silly for me to be sitting there all alone being waited on by Woods. I enjoyed being with the servants. Mrs. Featherstone continued to tell me, "You are way too scrawny. Give me a few more weeks and I'll put some padding on ya'."

And then, at mealtime, she would say, "Make sure you clean your plate. The dogs have plenty. They'll not be wanting our scraps."

While Elizabeth and I had not set up a time for a further visit, when the doorbell rang the following Monday morning at ten thirty, I hoped it was her. Woods answered the door and escorted her into the parlor.

"Elizabeth!" I greeted her warmly. "I was hoping you might come today. I bought Catherine's journal down from upstairs."

As she walked over to the fire, Elizabeth said, "I nearly didn't make it. I had forgotten to tell James, my coachman, I would need to be leaving by ten-fifteen. Thank goodness it didn't take him long to get the horses ready. It's so cold outside! I am thankful for your warm fire."

Woods had already taken Elizabeth's wet coat off, but she looked very cold. "Pull your chair nearer the fire, Elizabeth," I suggested.

Before he left the room, Woods put another log on the fire. Pulling my own chair nearer to the fire also, I told Woods, "I'll ring the bell when we are ready for lunch."

He replied, smiling slightly, "Very well, madam.".

Seeing his tiny smile made me blush. I smiled, and I think he understood why. If Elizabeth noticed, she didn't say anything.

After a moment she spoke tentatively, "I know we didn't arrange a time for my visit, so I hope it is convenient for you Betsy. Otherwise, I can make this a very short visit."

I immediately tried to reassure her, "I was hoping you might visit today."

Elizabeth replied with apparent relief, "Thank you, dear."

As she sat down on her usual seat, she asked, "I keep thinking of the trials you went through. I know Edward was deeply upset by the circumstances. What was his first reaction to your plight?"

"It troubled him sorely." I began. "The first time Edward read Catherine's journal back in Australia he was quite shocked. I don't think he realized convicts experienced conditions that were so poor and degrading. I overheard him asking the master we served in Australia if he knew how badly convicts were treated. Lord Mars denied any personal knowledge of unwarranted bad treatment. As everyone knew that the men and women sent for resettlement were convicts, he presumed harsh treatment might be required to maintain discipline and prevent further crimes from being committed. When Lord Edward shared some of Catherine's writings with him, both he and Lord Edward were deeply saddened by it all.

On the ship coming home, I noticed, that when Edward was not in Catherine's company, he was very somber; most unlike the Lord Edward I had known in times past. He often came up on deck when Catherine was sleeping and joined me as we both stood looking out to sea. He shared a few of his thoughts with me.

He told me sadly, "I've read Catherine's journal again. I had no idea that people could treat their countrymen as badly as they treated you. How can my country allow such inhuman conditions? Where is our God? How could he allow such intolerable conditions to exist?"

I spoke quietly. "Lord Edward, you certainly know that many people have similar trials to bear. We are but mortals. We can't always understand the whys and the wherefores."

His countenance darkened as he said with grim determination, "When I get back to London, after our visit to Catherine's parents, I will certainly stir things up. But I need to think about it. I don't want to make life more difficult for Catherine. You know, when I was searching for you, I checked one of those hulks, not that I saw anything. There were a few rumors I was checking on at the time. The troopers on the hulk were wary of talking to me and I never made any headway there. The one clue I learned from them is that the majority of the convicts on the hulks had been sentenced by a judge 'Wilkens." The moment I heard that I knew something was off. That man is indeed a devil."

I said earnestly, "It was wonderful that you were able to determine where we were."

Edward declared grimly, "It was through the intervention of Henry, who was in the good graces of the Chancellor, that I was allowed access to the criminal court logs. It was good fortune that the Chancellor was in London at the time I was looking. Fortunately, when he understood the circumstances, he made sure that the records were made available. Without his help, I doubt if I would have been successful. I found out when you were sentenced and where you were sentenced to."

He continued, "Even so, it was tedious work, searching for clues without any knowledge of what to look for. While going through the register I saw your fictitious surnames and I knew it could not be a coincidence. Thank goodness you didn't use fictitious Christian names. That was about the same time Henry brought me a scribbled note written by Catherine. He said a trooper bought it to his office saying it was among the belongings of a trooper who had been killed in Sydney, Australia."

Betsy acknowledged that he was correct. "That was our last plea for help. We had sent out several pleas for help."

Edward raised his eyebrow in question, "What do you mean?"

I replied, "After our first night in confinement we gave a young girl a note to notify your brother. We also gave her Catherine's lucky sovereign in the hope she would deliver the message. Obviously, she never did. We also sent out notes while we were on the hulk, but we found out we were being watched. Those messages were intercepted, and I think the rumor that Catherine was a "mad woman" began being reinforced by the guards and the troopers. I overheard that evil judge tell the policeman who arrested us to 'spread lies about them if need be'."

Edward replied thoughtfully, "So then, it seems that Wilkens was covering his tracks. All the more reason for me to see that he is punished for his crimes against you and Catherine. How he ever got to the position he was in is beyond me. You can be sure I will pursue it.

Every time I think of Wilkens, it makes my blood boil. It's perhaps a good job we are going up to Sheffield. I need to think things through. I will want to talk to you more about it, Betsy, but at a later time."

Edward changed the subject, "Catherine is intent on seeing her parents, and I am sure she will welcome the English sun. Will you be coming with us to Sheffield?"

"It's kind of you to ask, Lord Edward, but I have some friends and family I want to contact."

I thought it far better for Catherine to be with her family, and after a moment I added, "I will still be here when you return."

"Yes, of course. Whatever suits you. Anyway, Betsy, I must get back to Catherine. She will probably be awake now."

Home

I was pleased to tell Elizabeth, "Since we first saw Edward in Australia, he has been at Catherine's side as much as humanly possible. You can see the pure joy he has when he is with her."

Elizabeth responded thoughtfully, "How such a thing could have happened, I don't know."

Gesturing to the book in her lap I asked, "I have forgotten where we were in the journal. I should have marked it. Do you remember, Elizabeth?"

"The last time we read I think it was just after there had been theft on the Barringer. Is that right, Betsy?"

"Yes, you have a good memory," I replied. "Sometimes I feel as though I have read it so many times that now I can almost recite it word for word."

"You do know dear, I appreciate the time you have taken to share Catherine's story with me."

"It's a joy for me, Elizabeth. You have no idea how delighted I feel to be able to share Catherine's tale with a true friend."

Elizabeth responded, "You know it's not just Catherine's story. It's very much your story as well."

I remarked distantly, "Yes, perhaps,"

Turning the pages, I said. "Yes, here we are, Catherine writes"

I was glad, in a way, that we were confined to our quarters. I lay on my bench most of the time. The days seemed to drift by. Betsy occasionally roused me gently to ask how I was feeling. And when the guards came to distribute what little food we were allowed, Betsy was there to help me get up and walk. She made sure I took some nourishment. She seemed to be coping better than most. I was certainly not the only person suffering from privation. Many of the convicts were too weak to get up from their benches, even when it meant the difference between life and death.

The troopers never found the stolen food. It struck me as somewhat ironic. The theft of the food resulted in reduced rations. The one remaining conspirator who had stolen the food was then obliged to share the food they had, lest someone betray her secret. Nothing good had come of it and all of us suffered from their stupidity.

When we were finally allowed up on the main deck, our days of rationing and privation had taken their toll. There were many who were not strong enough to climb the stairs unassisted. Some stumbled and fell as we were ordered to stand before the captain. Indeed, we were in a pitiful state. He looked very serious as he stood on the forecastle and addressed us. He was in full uniform. Abby, the third woman who hadn't been identified earlier, was strung up facing some type of board, her back towards us. I wondered how they found out she was involved.

The captain commenced by saying, "When you came on board, Head Trooper Tottenham gave you all explicit instructions. Any person stealing or secreting any of the ship's stores or any other article belonging to the stores in the ship will be severely punished."

He continued, "We have limited supplies. We cannot allow this foolery to go on. I hope you all have felt the sting of hunger during these past few days. You must understand that we are your masters. We are to order, and you are to obey."

"We have established who the third woman was who grabbed Bertha and treated her badly. She will be caned for her role in the crime. I want you all to witness this so it will be ingrained in your minds. All the ship's company and troopers on this ship are your superiors. We will not put up with your foolish behavior."

The captain motioned to one of the guards who stood in front of the convict. He lifted his arm and we could see he had a long cane. Thank goodness it wasn't the cat of nine tails which we had been threatened with when we first came onboard. He swung the lash in the air and Abby shrieked as it struck. With the second strike, she shrieked again as it struck, the sound fading to a moan as the seconds passed. After the third stroke, she shuddered and moaned plaintively. Spots of blood began to seep through her smock. My heart went out to her. By the time the cane struck again, the poor woman was only hanging there by the heavy ropes that had been tied around her wrists. Her back was a mass of blood and her body was completely slumped.

I watched the captain as the flogging took place. He did not seem in the slightest way perturbed. Head Trooper Tottenham had a satisfied look on his face. He reminded me of a child with a new toy. Abby was almost unconscious by the time the fifth blow was struck. When she was cut down, she fell in a heap. The captain ordered her taken below.

A few of our number went to her. There were tears in their eyes. Indeed, there were tears in all our eyes.

With callous contempt for all of us, the captain continued, "Let it be a lesson to all of you convicts. May this deter you from any further stupidity that your evil minds might consider. I will not have insubordination on my ship."

He left us standing there as he returned to his cabin.

Head Trooper Tottenham came forward and told us, "Bertha has been restored to her rightful place. If any harm befalls her; ten convicts will have their heads shaved and will then be thrown into the coal room for several days without food."

"You are to return to your prison on the quarterdeck below, but twenty of you are to follow Bertha to the galley."

As we made our way back to our prison, we were all distraught. Speaking for myself only, I had no desire to eat. What we saw made my heart ache. I looked at Betsy. She shut her eyes and moved her head side to side in disgust.

Bertha had a few of the guard's fetch supplies. Amongst other things, they carried large bags of flour to the galley. Flour meant bread. The thought of food did not take the beating and horror we had just witnessed away, but it disturbed me how quickly compassion for poor Abby was forgotten. Truth be known, I was not immune, When I thought of fresh bread, my nagging hunger returned.

I berated myself for my weakness. I had little thought for the poor woman's stupidity, or the horror of how she had been treated. Her blood was yet fresh on the deck, drops of it splattered only inches from my feet, and my heart was heavy. During that wicked ordeal, there were outcries amongst the women convicts and I feel sure there was not a dry eye amongst us. Yet, when we saw that bread was being made, it was difficult to hold thoughts of indignation for that poor woman. My own hunger was such that I forgot my sense of right and wrong and could hardly think of anything but my own need.

"Betsy put her arm around me and said, "It is so evil and wicked. How the captain or Head Trooper Tottenham could order that poor woman's beating is beyond me. I watched their faces. They seemed to take delight in the savage way she was treated. And now they give us bread and we have little choice. We must eat now or else we'll die."

I replied slowly, "My thoughts are all over the place. But I must agree those over us found satisfaction in belittling us. Perhaps they think by giving us bread we will just forget it. Yes, I know I will have to eat. Part of me says 'no', but reason tells me I must eat. So, don't go telling me off, I will eat."

It seemed like forever since we'd had bread. I didn't even mind the thought of weevils.

No one, to my knowledge, ever stole food again.

Full rations were returned, and life continued to be an existence of a very meager kind. More of our number took sick and their condition was reported to the surgeon. They were instructed to have a little more time on deck, but they were given little relief from their daily chores. We all had chores of varying types. Betsy would cover for me when I didn't have the energy required to scrub and clean.

Before morning prayers, Mr. Tottenham would often address us.

"While the Almighty might forgive you of your contemptible sins, I must remind you, you are all low, despicable people."

I was beginning to believe it. There were times when I couldn't quite remember who I was. The nightmare just went on and on. I had trouble determining time; the days and nights drifted one into another. If I had been left in these circumstances on my own I would have really become the "mad" women who they said I was. Betsy, oh, how I continued to thank my maker for having Betsy as my friend.

One morning, while up on deck after morning prayer, Angela approached me. She had her little girl with her and said to the little girl, "This is the nice lady I was telling you about."

Looking at me, she continued, "I don't know your right name Mrs, but want ya to be meeting my little'n."

I answered, "Please call me Catherine, Angela."

I knelt so that our faces met. "What a dear little child! You can call me Catherine. What can I call you?"

Looking at her feet she shyly answered, "Daisy, me Ma calls me Daisy."

I asked, "And tell me, Daisy, do you have any other friends on the ship?"

"Na, me Ma says I better no' be 'avin friends." And then she whispered, "I plays with Toby, but don't tell me Ma."

I whispered back, "Your secret is safe with me."

I looked at Angela and suspected she knew what the whispering was about.

Rising to my feet, I told her, "You have a lovely daughter."

Angela agreed, "Yes, I be thinkin' the same."

She continued, "I told me Daisy 'ere if ever we get separated on the ship, she's bound to be comin' to you. May that be right with you then, Catherine?"

To be fair, I thought I would not be much help to the little girl if anything happened to Angela. But I could not help the impulse I felt to try. I replied, "Assuredly, dear little Daisy has won my heart. She's such a sweet little girl."

"That's not always. She gets to be 'ungry just like you and me. And at times, she screams the place down."

Daisy frowned. She knew her behavior was being discussed.

"You must 'ave 'eard 'er."

Daisy continued to look downcast, her chin folded close to her chest and tiny tears beginning to glisten at the corners of her eyes.

"When that there 'appens I just don't know what to be doin'. I just hold n rock 'er. What else can I be doin'?"

She looked at me as though I might have some bit of advice to offer and, sensing I could give none, she continued thoughtfully, "Things will bound to get better. We'll just 'ave to 'ope it might be right soon. I 'ope we'll be getting to Botany Bay. I've no care for this ship life."

When the ship's bell rang, we separated. It was time to begin our daily duties. I was often assigned to washing clothes and hanging them out to dry. We had to use seawater and had bars of coarse soap which made my hands raw after scrubbing for several hours. We had the crew's clothes and bedding as well as the troopers and our own. We would drape the clothes over lines which the crew put up for that very purpose. Prisoners were assigned to attend to the washing every other day. It largely depended on the weather. On rainy days there was no going up on deck. But work below decks continued. However, when there were squalls no one could work except the crew, who were entirely occupied with managing the sails and ensuring the ship didn't founder in the swells.

My first interaction with Bertha came when it was my duty to help in preparing meals for the week. Betsy and I had played no part in her earlier problems with the convicts, but I was uncertain whether she knew the difference. I was also uncertain if she knew that I had been labeled as the 'mad woman.'

She addressed several of us saying, "There's oats and fresh water in them barrels. You are to be makin' porridge and tea of a morning." And, pointing to another row of barrels, she gave additional instructions. "There is salted beef and pork to be mixed in a mash of peas and any other vegetable we can find for the mid-day meal. As our rations allow, I'll be needing you to make bread, but there isn't any butter to be had on the bread. There is cheese to be had also. Get to be knowin' your duties and do them well. No stealing or silliness among you. The troopers will be watching you."

She pointed to me. "You will be keeping the coals in the stove hot and ready for cookin'. Mind you do it well!"

One of my fellow prisoners let out a contemptuous comment. "You can be sure that there mad woman will do it just like old Nick, with flames in her nose."

That bought a laugh among the other prisoners.

"We don't have mad souls on this ship," responded Bertha.

One of the convicts, a bedraggled looking soul, scowled, "She thinks she's miss elegance herself."

Bertha took little notice but said firmly, "Well get on...we've no time for wasting."

She looked at me, "An what be your name then?"

I spoke quietly just as Betsy had advised, "Catherine, they call me Catherine."

Bertha responded, "Alright Catherine, as long as you do as I say, there won't be any trouble."

I nodded. I didn't think there would be much trouble in keeping the coals hot. Little did I know about such things. Bertha already had a good fire burning in the stove. I couldn't see where she got the coal from. As she was instructing the other prisoners, I didn't want to interrupt but knew if I didn't her nice bright fire would go out.

"Excuse me, Miss Bertha, I'm not sure where to get the coal from."

She remarked scornfully, "My, glory be. Don't you know nothin'?"

That caused another titter amongst the other prisoners. I felt humiliated.

A smile tugged briefly at the corners of her mouth which settled quickly back into a thin plain line. Pointing to a large bucket standing by the stove, she said, "Ya get that there bucket, take it to the coal room below, fill it up high and bring it back. Do you understand that? That will be your duty every day this week."

There was contempt in her tone, and I was stung by it. I bit back the sharp rebuke that came instantly to mind. Nothing good would come of making a scene. My embarrassment was growing as I felt the amused scorn of my fellow prisoners. I attempted to comply with her instructions. I lifted the empty bucket, awkwardly swaying with its unexpected weight. This bought another sniggering laugh from the other convicts.

The bucket was much heavier than I had imagined. It was awkward to manage as I climbed down the stairs to the lower deck. As I staggered along, I wondered what it would be like with coal in it. Something told me that I was in danger. Perhaps I was being set up to fail and that failure would bring horrible consequences. I was determined not to let that happen.

My first problem was that though I knew that the coal room was below the quarterdeck, its exact location eluded me.

Thank goodness I encountered a trooper on the lower deck who took pity on me. He looked at me with a flicker of benevolence in his eyes. I imagine I looked very scrawny and unkempt.

Swallowing what little pride I had, I asked, "Excuse me, sir, would you be kind enough to tell me where the coal cabin is?"

A flicker of amusement danced across his face.

"So, what do ya need to be going there for? Are they going to throw you in? What have you been up to?"

A fresh sense of embarrassment caught me. "It's nothing like that, sir. Miss Bertha has told me to fill this bucket with coal and take it back to the galley so we can keep the stove burning."

His amusement was replaced by a solemn scowl and the trooper muttered quietly, "Has she now? I wonder has she thought how you might be carrying it? You being such a slight thing."

His kindness was so unexpected, "Come on I'll git' it for ya. Follow me."

I followed him half the length of the lower deck to a lightless room deep within the ship. I realized that I would probably have spent a long time searching on my own before I would have discovered it. I felt so thankful. To my surprise, he didn't simply stand aside. Speaking bluntly, he said, "Here," handing me his musket. "You hold this for me while I shovel coal into the bucket."

I had never held a musket before. I was surprised at how heavy it was. In minutes the trooper filled the bucket to the top.

"Now I'll carry it up to the galley for ya, but don't be telling Miss Bertha I helped ya. Alright?"

I replied, "Oh no, I'm so grateful to find a kind sir like yourself."

We talked as we made our way back to the galley.

He asked, "How often do ya gotta be gettin' the coal then?"

I replied. "I have been assigned to do it every day this week."

His expression darkened, and for a moment I worried that I must have said something wrong. I bowed my head. I think he noticed my discomfort and said with determination.

"Ya' can't be doin' it. Ya' lucky ya' can be carrying the bucket at all, let alone coal in it. If ya come down every day about the same time, I'll be helpin' ya. But yer' not to be tellin' anyone."

I wasn't sure why he asked that of me, but it felt right. Seeing the trooper labor under the weight of the filled bucket, strong arms straining, I knew that Bertha had intended for me to fail. I quickly thanked the trooper. "How I thank you, good sir! May you be blessed for your kindness!"

He replied, smiling, "I dunna' know about that. I reckon you've 'ad a bad time here being a convict an all. It's not the kind of life you need to be 'avin. You've struck me as a real lady, but I can't say that for some of that other riff-raff who are onboard."

I said sadly, "Oh, I have my story,"

I was thankful he didn't ask me to elaborate further. I didn't want to share my troubles with him. He might suppose me "mad' also.

He asked, "What be your name then?"

"I'm Catherine. And you sir? What name can I call you?"

He stepped into the hallway leading along the quarterdeck, glancing in both directions. No one else was present. I could clearly tell he had some concern about being discovered.

"Officially, I'm Trooper Westward. But you can call me Ned," he said, leading the way back towards the galley, "but only when we's alone ya' hear."

I smiled reassuringly. "Yes, of course. Thank you for helping me, Ned."

Bertha made an appearance in the galley about thirty minutes after I had staggered into the galley with the bucket. She quickly surveyed the room, eyes lingering on the full bucket of coal next to the oven. Her eyes drifted briefly to me. I couldn't fully understand what she was thinking. I wondered why her eyes reflected doubt and malice. Saying nothing either to me or to the other convicts, she then turned and left the galley wordlessly. I was concerned that I had not escaped, but only delayed whatever she might have planned for me.

Watching her leave the galley, I felt a sense of relief. I also felt thankful. Trouper Ned Westward was another friend I now had onboard ship. I added coal to the fire to ensure it burned brightly.

I had a sense of satisfaction as I went to get the coal every day that week. I made sure I went at the exact time. Ned was true to his word. He stood in the same place every day waiting for me. He always had a smile for me and would fill the bucket with coal and then carry the coal up to the galley door and then disappear quickly. Despite their sniggers, the other women who were on kitchen duty that week also showed mercy to me. One of them would come to my aid as I opened the galley door and would help me carry my load over to the oven.

Upon reflection, it seemed strange that they helped me. Perhaps, seeing I was very slight to carry a big load, they set themselves to counter Bertha's attempt to make trouble for me. Not for my sake specifically, but as a small act of rebellion against an obvious bully.

It was a dirty job. My hands were always black, but thank goodness I didn't burn myself. That was another fear among many I had whilst on that ship.

Several other times I was chosen for kitchen duty, but I never carried coal again. I had duties of washing and drying dishes or cutting up slices of cheese and salted meat. All such things were foreign to me and I often panicked when I was given a chore which I had never done before. I learned to swallow my pride and ask for guidance knowing full well that I would be mocked for not knowing how to do such things.

Looking at Betsy that night, I told her, "While I was in the galley today, there was a woman there who threw up and one or two said they had diarrhea."

Even though there has been no official declaration that smallpox was amongst us, the women there talked about it. I expect they would know.

Betsy looked puzzled. "For the first time, you are telling me something I don't know."

Betsy spoke angrily, "My goodness! Smallpox is contagious. They shouldn't be preparing our food. I think that is how smallpox is spread. The surgeon should be notified immediately. I think the disease is characterized by fever, chills, weakness, pain, headache, vomiting and maybe diarrhea.

She continued, "Come to think of it, I have seen a few sad cases. A convict keeled over while we were scrubbing the deck earlier, and then while we were standing in line for lunch, another woman collapsed. The sick convicts were ordered to the prison deck. I didn't think much of it as we are all a sorry lot. And now that I think of it, I believe I have heard women using the night bucket more often than usual. I hadn't thought it was anything of any consequence. We are fed so little. I thought that was the reason. I shall report it to the ship's surgeon."

Sure enough, Betsy spoke to a trooper. I don't know what she said, but it looked like the surgeon was notified. He sent for the women who had the symptoms.

Our hearts went out to them. They were required to climb the stairs to consult with the surgeon in a cabin assigned for medical needs.

A little later, one of the troopers informed us that under no circumstances would the surgeon visit the prisoner's quarters. He told us several of the crew members and some of the troopers were also sick. The surgeon told everyone that it wasn't smallpox as there wasn't a rash on any of the victims who were sick.

Buckets were sent to our deck for prisoners to vomit in and the stronger women were told to empty them into the sea each morning and wash them. Whatever they said, we all knew the disease was contagious, so we were cautious about helping those who were seriously afflicted. Most had fevers, sometimes coughing up blood, and some even appeared to be delirious and very dehydrated. When the surgeon diagnosed twenty or more prisoners as being gravely ill, he gave each a shot of alcohol and told them to drink plenty of water.

What good was that? Clean water was scarce. Sick convicts were relieved from their duties and told to stay in their quarters. An area had to be sectioned off within the quarterdeck to quarantine the sick.

The surgeon seemed to be cruel and callous, unwilling to see the sick personally. He sent word that two of the troopers were to report to him on the condition of the sick.

I commented, "Those poor souls! Anyone with common sense knows they should be given good food and a decent bed."

Betsy agreed with me. "Yes, I agree. It's a fate no one would wish on their worst enemy."

The moaning of the ill throughout the night made my heart bleed. Especially knowing that we had nothing to offer as help. Two convicts died the first night. I thought that others would soon share their fate.

I was right. In the following days, more prisoners died. I had very little faith in the ship's surgeon, but I tried not to be judgmental. I knew very little about the disease. Those who were sick were quarantined, and the convicts on galley duty were relieved of their duties. The free women were conscripted to prepare our food. One of the ship's officers supervised. We saw three more deaths and more grief-stricken prisoners as the days went on.

Nothing was said, but every prisoner who hadn't fallen ill realized they could easily face the same type of misery and death.

We went about our tasks in solitude and were kept isolated for the protection of the troopers and crew. Indeed, we were ordered to keep two body lengths away from the guards and troopers.

I could tell Betsy was hiding her concern that we too would become victims.

She commented, "Despite the precautions, more prisoners are dying. One of the troopers told us they had several deaths among their number and two of the crew have died."

We were ordered to scrub the prison deck continually and as we did so more space became available in our prison.

I whispered to Betsy, "What a price to pay for more space."

Four of the stronger prisoners were ordered to take the bodies of the dead up to the main deck. When they returned, we were told Mr. Tottenham said a prayer for each of them as their bodies were thrown overboard.

Even at a young age, I sometimes wondered how I would die. I can't imagine how those poor souls could have ever foreseen the heartache and horror that led them to their deaths on a ship such as this. For the next three days taking the dead to their end became a daily ritual.

Some of the women taken by that horrible disease left little ones. How confused and afraid they were! Betsy and I befriended one such child, Toby, a little boy of five. He was the same little boy that Daisy, Angela's daughter, had spoken of.

He was crying when he asked, "Where's Muma gone?"

Betsy quickly said, "Your dear Muma has gone to a far better place. She no longer has to deal with the unkind and wicked behavior of the masters of this ship."

I felt tears welling in my eyes. Here I was feeling sorry for myself. What of this poor child's fate?

I told him, "We will take care of you just like your muma did. There is a vacant bench near us. Bring your bedding over near us."

Betsy was moved also. She said, "Yes, come and sleep by us, Toby."

"You need to stay with us when we go for our meals and when we go on deck."

I don't know how much Toby understood, but I was overjoyed when he smiled at Betsy and me when we told him he was special, and we loved him dearly. Poor child. I wondered what was in store for him.

Betsy was sure we would all come down with the disease but, by some good fortune, neither of us were afflicted. On the eighth day after the outbreak, there weren't any more deaths. At the surgeon's direction, we were required to go up to the main deck where we were given a shot of brandy and allowed to walk about a bit.

As the crisis began to subside, we were required to scrub everything. All able-bodied prisoners were ordered to scrub the decks with sea water and wash all clothing and bedding with lye soap. This included the trooper's and crewmen's clothes also.

The horizon was blue where the sea met the sky. It evoked feelings of insignificance in me. A ship, encircled by sea, lost in an immense hue of blue. We were lost, totally lost from anything we knew.

I continued with a prayer in my heart, "Please, oh God, may my Edward find me."

My thoughts of Edward were gone momentarily when we heard a cry from a sailor who was secured to the rigging at the top of the main mast.

"Land," he cried. "Land on the starboard side."

His cry was taken up by other crewmen who seemed to pass the information forward.

I thought back to my honeymoon, when I was with dear Edward, and then when I was with Lady Kensington. The sight of land evoked all sorts of wonder and excitement. I had different feelings now. Was this Australia? What trials waited for me here?

I didn't know what 'starboard' meant, but I noticed movement among the convicts who began moving to the right-hand rail of the main deck. I followed them. After searching the horizon for many long moments, I thought it might be possible. Yes, I decided, if I really looked, I could see a speck of land in the distance.

After a few hours up on deck, we were sent back to the quarterdeck. There was talk that we might get to walk on dry land.

Betsy said suddenly, "Catherine it's a good thing you no longer have to deal with being seasick anymore."

I was somewhat confused and wondered why she said that. But, after consideration, I remembered she was one of the healthier convicts chosen to clean the areas where sickness still lingered. Certainly, some of the survivors were still very weak and their symptoms included nausea and vomiting like the seasickness I had experienced.

I responded, "No matter who they are, I believe most of them will be happy to be back on dry land."

I continued. "I have endured some difficulties, but some of the convicts have endured much worse. They must long to stand on dry land, probably a lot more than me."

Betsy smiled and held my hand, "Yes, I am sure you are right."

And so, we emerged from despair and thoughts of death to a time of shared excitement among prisoners, troopers, and crew. Many of the convicts thought we had sighted Australia, but we were later informed the land we sighted was Africa.

The following day, before morning prayer, we looked beyond the ship and took in the sight of land. Not knowing anything about sailing or distance, both Betsy and I guessed we were about ten miles out.

The land appeared much closer than we had seen it before. During prayers, while our eyes were shut, we heard some splashes in the sea. Everyone looked up to see two prisoners swimming toward the shore. How ridiculous! Who could swim that far? Several of the troopers lifted the butt of their muskets to their shoulders to shoot, but there was no need. Within a minute or two both women were dead. We saw their blood in the water and, shortly after, the sea was churning as the blood attracted sharks that began to tear the bodies to pieces. Many of the convicts on the ship cried out in anger and outrage. The deaths of these women were the result of their own stupidity. Didn't they know there were dangers lying below the surface of the sea?

For several moments I pondered; perhaps that is something I should do when I lost hope altogether. It would put me out of this misery. In the end, common sense prevailed. If I did that, I would never see my dear Edward again.

Betsy was standing beside me and held my hand. I marveled yet again. Somehow, she knew what I was thinking.

We were permitted to stay up on deck for an hour, but then the troopers instructed us to return to our prison and we were put in shackles. As the lock was turned on the gate to ensure we couldn't move, Head Trooper Tottenham addressed us through the bars.

"Some of the ship's company are going ashore to obtain fresh food and fresh water supplies. All prisoners are to remain below deck and shackled while the ship is anchored. You will be kept below until we leave Africa and continue our journey to Australia. You will use the buckets as the need arises and a few of you will be assigned to empty them into the sea each day. You will be under strict guard when doing so. Some of you will be assigned to go with Bertha to the ship's galley to prepare our food. Your food will be served in the prison area.

The general feeling amongst the convicts was great disappointment. We had hoped this land was our destination or at least to feel land beneath our feet. It was devastating to be shackled again.

Being completely jailed for several days dampened our spirits. There was little conversation apart from those who continued to complain. Some of the women thought they knew how to sail a ship, offering opinions on what would happen as were came near the coast. As all of us were shackled there was little to do but talk about what was happening.

One of the convicts spoke out, "Once the ship gets nearer land, the crew will be busy. They will have to watch for reefs and rocks in the water."

Another called out, "How do ya be knowing how they sail a ship then?"

And then the first convict, "I've been on a ship before and, besides, me Da was a sailor and he told us all about it."

The same woman continued, "Anyway they take soundings to see if the ship can keep going the same way cos of rocks an reefs around land."

Then another called out, "When we came on board, I 'eard a crewman say 'e 'ad made this trip several times with the very same captain, so I'll be expectin' they know what they're doin'."

The complaints continued, "Why can't we go up on deck to stretch our legs?"

Betsy spoke up, "Then there might be trouble. Being much closer to land, some might try to escape. The ship's crew can't afford for that to happen. Many of us have died. I don't expect the captain would care to lose any more of us or he will not get paid for delivering us to the governor at Botany Bay. Anyway, the crew will be busy and will not want any distraction from us."

There was silence for a while.

A voice called out, "She's right ya know. Them buggers have got us where they want. None of us are treated like human beins'. We're just like pigs to them. They're just delivering the pigs to market."

I heard murmurs and women agreeing.

It was just another bitter experience. The smell and monotony went on and on. I lay on my bench and let my mind drift to better times; but, weak as I was, and amid fresh horrors, my thoughts drifted aimlessly from pathetic self-pity to uncontrollable weeping. I concealed this as best I could, fearing further isolation and abuse. Alone with my pain and fears, I would often cry myself to sleep.

Betsy and little Toby played word games. Sometimes Toby would tug at my smock, "C'mon, play with us.".

His cheerful demeanor in that ugly place brought unexpected pleasure to my heart. To think he wanted me to join in lifted my spirits a little.

I asked smiling, "What game then?"

He looked at Betsy with a smile. "Guess what?" And, seeing I didn't understand, he quickly added, "You think of something you can see. You can say what it looks like, but you can't say what it is."

I didn't find his description very helpful, but after he and Betsy took a turn I caught on. Indeed, it made the time go a little faster.

We were anchored for a period of four days. On the third day, we heard noises on the main deck.

Betsy said, "Can you hear? There's movement on the ship. Perhaps they are bringing on supplies."

I agreed with her saying, "I hope so. It will be wonderful if they were able to get some fruit and vegetables. Dried meat and a few peas have become rather tiresome, to say the least."

I realized, sadly, that my concerns had now become quite primitive. I wasn't much concerned about affairs around me anymore. Aside from food, I didn't care much about what happened on board the ship. My concerns now seemed to revolve around how much food I would get and when I might expect to eat again. I resolved to think no more about this. I despised this kind of weakness. I was a noblewoman. Such pathetic weakness was beneath the standards I imagined for myself.

On reflection, our food didn't really change. We were given oranges for several days, but little else changed. I felt angry that nothing more was done to improve our circumstances.

On the fourth day, we felt movement and presumed that we were at sea again. Our assumptions were confirmed when our shackles were removed, and morning prayer was resumed. We were permitted to spend the morning hours up on deck again, weather permitting.

The rain and squalls seemed more regular during that part of the journey. We often had to remain below.

Toby's games were very well used, and others would sometimes join us. Just another sign of how far I had fallen, I discovered I was pleased that my fellow convicts showed greater acceptance of me because of Toby's games. Still, only those whom I have previously mentioned made any effort to speak to me.

The rough seas caused difficulties for those of us on the quarterdeck. When the seas were high, one moment we would be sitting on our bench and the next minute we would be tossed to the other side of the deck. There were some injuries among the convicts, but none of the crew were affected. Either that or we didn't hear about it. I expect the crew had experienced similar conditions at sea before.

The first time we encountered rough seas, with the ship rolling wildly, Betsy managed to grab Toby, preventing him from being thrown across the deck. With one hand on our bench and the other on Toby, she called out to me, "Hold on to something,"

There was no dignity to be had if one was using the lavatory.

Mealtimes were sometimes difficult, our food occasionally being tossed to the other side of the galley. We would be seated or standing in the galley, trying to eat what little food we were given, when a large swell would cause the ship to roll and our meal would be tossed to the floor. The roll of the ship made it almost impossible to stay seated, much less to hold onto a bowl of porridge, soup or stew. Many of us, Betsy and I included, soon had to choose between holding onto a bench and losing our meal, or be thrown headlong across the deck into a wall. We could not do both, we had to scrape up whatever was left of our food and eat it. There was nothing else, no second servings.

For the first few times when we were caught in a squall little Toby seemed to understand what was happening. However, one night when we were awakened, and the ship was rolling from side to side, Toby became quite distraught.

"Muma, Muma, I want my Muma!"

Betsy and I fumbled in the darkness, not really knowing how we could calm him. I told him. "Your Muma can't come, but she is watching over you to see if you are being a brave boy."

I held him very close and clung to the prison bars to stop us from sliding all over the place. Betsy was there to help me, and we were able to reassure him that all would be well. I secretly wondered if that was true. But providence would have us survive those times.

One morning, while I was up on the main deck with little Toby, another convict, a little older than me, stood a few yards away. I would not ordinarily have worried about this, but she seemed to be paying too much attention to us. I told myself to act as Betsy would.

When she finally approached us, her soft voice, although it was rough, sounded genuine. "I sees' ya as bein' all alone, how's ya liking sailing in this 'ere ship then?"

Before I spoke, I tried ever so hard to mimic Betsy, speaking as roughly I could. "It's an experience I would never want again."

She put her arm around me and said, "Don't fret lovey. I be not carin' for it at all. We got ta be makin' the best of it I reckon. I dunna know how much farther we need to be goin'!"

She touched my hand gently. "There are some good uns amongst us, that's why I be seeking you out. You and ya friend have got a way with that little-un."

She asked him, "What's your name? Is it Toby?"

Toby just laughed and held onto my dress.

I responded carefully, "Yes, his Muma died when we had the sickness on board. It makes me so sad and I wonder where he'll end up."

She leaned closer towards me, as though we had always been friends, and said knowingly, "I right admires' ya for being so kind. I bet ya 'ave got a sad tale."

I thought it best not to reply immediately.

She began smiling and trying to get Toby's attention again. At first, he shyly clung to my skirt, but it didn't take long for his boyish nature had him smiling and being cheerful.

While I have tried not to write of the mockery and ridicule which I faced from some of the convicts since our first day on the Barringer, I must say that by now I had endured much and felt doubtful that she was being sincere, especially as she had never once spoken to me before. I watched her carefully, thinking that she was playing on my weakness. I was so doubtful that I almost turned her away.

Watching her play with Toby, I gave in to my own neediness. I couldn't help myself. It felt good to be accepted, even by a convict on a prison ship. She gave no impression she thought me mad.

I responded to her question, "Ya."

I continued, trying to remain in character, "We all 'ave been dealt badly with, 'ow is it with you then?"

She spoke with little emotion "The judge condemned me to a convict's life for stealing some clothing for me little-uns.".

I realized that her pain and tears were probably kept under close guard.

I looked at her a little closer. She looked so tired, so exhausted. This journey was taking its toll on her I could plainly see.

She said, "There was no justice at all. They took me from me young 'uns. The older one, being fifteen, so I reckon they might get by. I also be 'avin a little un' like Toby."

"I feel sad for you." I said. "It's all very barbaric, our English law. I had no idea it was like this." She looked at me differently then and her face hardened a little. "My that's a big word, 'barbaric' I wonda' what ya be mean-en?"

I suspected I had lost any opportunity for trust and friendship. Without meaning to I had revealed a huge difference between us. I was educated. She was not. I could see in her eyes that she understood what I had done. It could not be helped, and I answered her honestly.

"It means cruel and unjust."

The hardness never left her eyes, though she answered me with conviction, "You be thinkin' the right way then. It's such a 'eart-ache."

Her friendliness seemed to fade a little when she said, "I best be goin'. I gotta' be work'n in the galley today. I'll look for ya agin', What's ya name lovey?"

"Catherine" I replied, wondering if friendship was still a possibility, "and yours?"

"Janey," she said. "Pleased to be knowing ya. See ya ag'in."

I thought she would never seek us out again. I was wrong and pleased to be so. Janey began spending a few minutes each day playing with Toby and chatting with Betsy and me.

Along with Betsy, Angela and, surprisingly, Janey, whom I came to know better, there were a few others who didn't consider me "mad." Janey had a warm heart and a loving nature. Of course, I also have to include the trooper, Ned. I shouldn't forget him. He saved me from ill-treatment by Bertha.

As I write this, I wonder what became of Janey and Angela? Is there justice on this earth? I don't know.

I must admit, I didn't keep track of the days we had been on board, but the other convicts did. Someone had stolen a knife from the galley and made a mark each day in the side wall of our prison.

It was now ninety days since we had left England.

One morning, during a conversation with Janey, another prisoner suddenly intruded on our conversation. It was clear that she was angry, though I had no idea why her anger would be directed at me. She had long straggly unkempt black hair and thick bushy eyebrows. She was much taller than I, towering above me and Janey. She had a dark complexion, as though the sun had aged and darkened her skin. Her facial features looked very coarse. When she spoke, there was scarcely controlled anger behind every word.

She said scornfully, "Who in the 'ell do ya think ya be? Ya just like us lovey, pretending to be some lady? Ha! Putting on airs and graces… All of us on this here ship, be knowin' about ya." And besides, I 'ave been watchin' ya."

She lifted her head and swung it from side to side, as though she were imitating some movement she imagined a lady might make. She spoke menacingly to me, "There's no ladies on these ships. You'll be learnin' that right enough! Ya ain't no better 'an nobody else. So keep ya little comments to ya self 'ya 'ere, an no more look-en' down yer nose. No more walk-in wit' ya 'ead in the air, ya 'ere!" She pointed a long-crooked finger at me. Her anger punctuated each noisy breath.

She continued, "Ya should be knowin' we figure ya to be a mad woman."

I wasn't sure what had provoked this outburst. I had never seen the woman before. Betsy was not around, and I did not know how to defuse the situation.

"We are the same," I said lamely. "I am a convict just like you."

She replied, snarling at me again, "Yer' a convict jus' like the rest of us. Ya ain't nuthin'. Makin' up fancy words and lyin' bout yer past. Ya ain't worth spit."

She appeared to struggle for a moment trying to find words for some deep-seated anger. Her feelings were fuel for more anger and soon she swung her wagging finger back in my face. The pitch of her voice heightened, "Ya ain't nuthin', ya hear!"

She obviously expected some sort of reaction and when I did not cower in the way she expected she closed her hand into a fist.

While I sensed danger, I spoke candidly, "My goodness, we are all the same."

She was determined to find an outlet for her anger, "So you be thinking we all be mad-uns' just like you."

She drew a knife she had hidden in her boot, telling me. 'Ye'll be feeling this in ya guts if ya go on like ya do. Ya be the only mad un' on board this ship. I'm bound for Australia cos me husband felt me knife in his gut, so I'll be 'ave'n no problems seeing the end of the likes of you."

I began to panic then, looking around desperately. I had no way to defend myself, even if I knew how. It was true that she could kill me and probably no one would even note that I had gone. Maybe Betsy would, but no one would believe her. My eyes must have reflected fear, and I began breathing hard.

She saw my fear and smiled grimly. "Tha's right luv. Ya aint nuthin'. Ya mean nuthin'. Ya keep on as ya 'ave an I'll make sure ya never fer'git it."

Having finally achieved the terror she had intended, she turned and walked away.

After watching a woman get thrown overboard and watching women die of sickness and starvation, I thought I wasn't capable of feeling panic anymore. But, to be sure, I felt overwhelmed by it then.

Janey whispered, "Take little kno' of her. They should 'ave 'ung 'er for it to be right. Most of us be stayin' out of 'er way."

When she returned from her duties, I immediately told Betsy.

She responded, "The rumors are true then. That woman killed her husband and it is rumored she killed her own brother as well."

I shook my head in wonder. "How ever do you find these things out?"

"I listen and watch, but just let it pass. Everything will be alright." Waving her hand in the general direction of the other convicts, she told me, "Keep trying to act like the rest of these poor souls."

Later, while standing looking out to sea, I cried to myself, "Oh, dear Edward, find me. Find me!"

I was shaken by the confrontation and, as a result, I silently drew further into my shell and spoke to no one except Betsy and the few friends I had made. As I observed and listened, it was more and more apparent to me that most of our number were sent to Australia for offenses of little consequence. The women-only stole so they could feed or clothe their little ones. The exception was the one who killed her husband. I would have thought she should have been hanged. Not that I approve of killing anybody, but with the fear she had instilled in me, it seemed appropriate in my mind at the time. Silly thoughts, really. I believe those who have murdered someone should be imprisoned for life.

It made me feel sick to my stomach to think that Edward might be part of this ridiculous judicial system. Surely, I persuaded myself, he is unaware of such inhuman cruelty.

Sometime on our ninety-eighth day at sea, land was sighted again.

"Land ahead!" came the cry from a sailor secured to the rigging atop the main mast.

We all wondered, was this Australia?

We heard the voice of Head Trooper Tottenham call out, "All convicts return to the prison deck."

Most of us obeyed but there were some who sauntered. I saw troopers pushing them along.

Once we were behind bars, Head Trooper Tottenham spoke to us as he had done before when land had been sighted, "Some of the ship's company are going ashore to obtain fresh food and fresh water supplies. All prisoners are to remain below deck while the ship is anchored. The port is called Perth. Prisoners will be kept below until we leave Perth and then continue our journey to Sydney or Botany Bay as it has also been called. You know the routine. You will use the buckets as the need arises, and a few of you will take them above to empty them into the sea each day. You will be under strict guard when doing so."

The group of women who are on galley duty this week will be called out and they will continue to prepare meals. The troopers will accompany the women to the galley and will watch over you all so don't be thinkin' you can take advantage now that our voyage is almost at its end.

There were murmurs and grunts amongst the convicts. Someone called out, "Why can't we go up on deck? We ain't gunna' go nowhere."

A terse reply from Head Trooper Tottenham, "It is standard practice when sighting land that all prisoners are put in restraint. You are fortunate in that we have not shackled you. Now be still all of you."

Betsy whispered to me, "We'll get by. Things might get better."

My immediate response, "And how many days of boredom this time?"

"I can't be saying, Catherine. At least we have made it this far."

When it came time for those on galley duty to prepare our evening meal a crewman called out, "All those assigned to prepare breakfast this morning come forward."

I have never felt envy in my life, but this time I had niggly feelings. I wished I could have been on galley duty. It would have relieved the boredom.

Toby said, "We can try and think of a new game."

Betsy's response wasn't very encouraging, "I don't know my little man, I think we have exhausted all ideas."

"We could try a counting game," he said. "I can count."

I replied, "So how high can you count?"

Toby replied shyly, "Five."

Betsy looked at me as she said, "We'll have to do something about that then."

She asked, "What comes after five?"

Toby seemed embarrassed, so I quickly answered, "Six."

And then Toby counted from one to six. Betsy and I both clapped and made a fuss over the dear little boy. During that time, while the ship was anchored, we taught him how to count to ten using his fingers and, by the time we reached Sydney he was able to count to twenty using his fingers and toes.

The dinner bell rang, and we could hear our food being bought to us by a few of the convicts. One of the troopers opened the prison gate and we were required to stand in line to get our food. Betsy, Toby, and I were about twentieth in line, so we couldn't really see very much. Evidently one of the convicts tried to grab a pistol from one of the guards. There was a scuffle and we heard a shot fired. We wondered what happened.

It was passed down the line.

"It's the one who murdered her husband. She's dead."

We also told those behind us what had happened. Two of the troopers took her body up on deck and as we were finishing our food Head Trooper Tottenham stood before us.

"What you have all witnessed is a testimony to what happens to those who disobey. No matter how far we are into our journey, you must obey us. Because this convict tried to defy us, all the rest of you will have to be shackled."

We all looked at each other knowing full well we could not complain. I thought to myself, 'What comes around goes around.'

Betsy muttered, "She got what she deserved. She should have known better with all those troopers around. Stupid woman!"

10

Not far now

Two days later the anchor was raised, and we were rid of those ghastly shackles.

We all wondered how much further to Sydney town. What would happen to us once we left the ship? Many why's and wherefores.

While up on deck a day or two later, a sailor called out from the top of the main mast, "Adelaide on the port side."

We all rushed to see but it was quite some distance away.

Our daily routine continued to be monotonous, but there was a general feeling of anticipation among the convicts.

A day or two later a crewman called out "Melbourne on the port side."

Again we rushed to see. There were two juts of land, but we could not see a settlement. As the ship turned northward, the weather became warmer. I wished we would be able to go up on deck more.

Toby asked, "Will Australia be like London?"

I promptly replied, "No. This is a new colony, so I expect it will be much different. I think there will be more open land than in England. We will have to wait and see."

A few days later we heard, "Sydney on the port side."

We were fortunate to be up on deck the morning the ship turned towards the harbor. Thank goodness they didn't put us in shackles again.

I really don't know how I survived the trip. Call it providence. Call it what you may. Apart from a few coughing fits I had every so often, I felt well enough. I must admit I had mixed feelings of fear and relief; fear - not knowing what was ahead of us and relief - knowing that our dreadful sea journey was just about over.

We were excited to be able to go on dry land, but anxious to know what lay ahead for us.

I guess Betsy must have sensed my worry. Almost as soon as the thought arose, she slipped her hand in mine, murmuring words of reassurance, "Don't worry, things will work out."

Tears came to my eyes as I said, "You know I couldn't have made it thus far if it hadn't been for you. You are strong both emotionally and mentally."

She replied, "Oh, Catherine, you give yourself too little credit."

"Perhaps that's true," I said. "But what can be said of you? You take what is cast your way and deal with it. I have rarely seen you angered or annoyed. I do admire you, Betsy. I suspect I will be dead within just a few weeks once they separate us."

Betsy responded, "You shouldn't think like that."

I continued tearfully, "We need to face it. We may very well be separated."

My thoughts turned to Toby. "I wonder about little Toby. What will become of him? We have been there for him for these past months. I will find it hard to part from him."

Betsy's face lit up. "Perhaps we won't have to."

After a moment or two she said, "We could say he belonged to us. I think I could pose as his muma, rather than you, cos there will be speaking to do."

I was unsure and expressed my doubts. "I don't know. The captain will have a manifest that has the names of all the convicts he was charged to transport here. He will have to give an accounting of those lost at sea."

I continued to consider the matter for several minutes, finally asking Betsy, "What do you think? Do you think we can do it?"

I was pleased to hear her answer. "Hopefully, but we better speak to Toby first."

I nodded in approval and said, "Yes, I hope he will understand. There he is, leaning over the rail looking into the sea."

Betsy called out to him. "Toby come here. We need to talk to you!"

"Yes, I'm comin'," he said. "I was just watchin' for fish."

She told him, "You can do that later. Come now, don't keep us waiting."

We waited as Toby bounced his way across the deck with typical boyish energy. When he was beside us, Betsy knelt to face him.

"You know we will be separated when we get to Sydney."

His eyes widened, a dark scowl formed, and he said firmly, "Na! They better not."

We could see tears in his eyes and Betsy told him, "Catherine and I have been talking. I could pretend to be your muma so they won't make you go away with someone you don't know."

He considered that, frowning. "You're not my real muma."

I expect it was obviously complicated in his way of thinking. He understood the difference between real and pretend, at least enough that he knew he didn't want to trade a real muma for a pretend one.

"But we must pretend," Betsy explained. "If we do, we will be able to stay together. It's what your real muma would want us to do."

He asked, "What about Catherine? She could be my other pretend mother?"

I felt uncomfortable, Toby referring to me as he did. But it was probably my own fault. Betsy and I had never instructed him as to how to address either of us.

Betsy looked into little Toby's eyes and said somewhat tearfully, "We are not sure what will happen, Toby. We must hope we can all stay together. Now, when we leave the ship you must remember that I am your muma if they ask you. Don't say anything about a pretend mother, you and I know it is only pretending. Remember I am your real muma if they ask you."

He said, "Okay," smiling slyly. He obviously considered it like a game. "Ok, Muma, I got it."

Betsy and I both smiled broadly.

Betsy told him, "Go back to watching for fish then. Don't you go and forget. It's very important."

Betsy put her arm around me. "Some of the troopers say we will be allowed to walk around freely once we reach Botany Bay."

I asked her uncertainly, "What does that mean? 'walk around freely'? Won't there be troopers?"

"I am not really sure," she replied. "I just heard a trooper telling one of the women that after we are let off the ship we will be free to walk around as much as we like."

I said hopefully, "Perhaps we will be able to get word to Edward of our whereabouts."

I thought perhaps we could get a free settler to send a note to Henry. I had no idea how we would get the money to send it. I had no idea how we would even get writing materials for a note.

The troopers rounded up all the convicts, ordering all of us to the main deck. When we were assembled, the strutting peacock, Head Trooper Tottenham, stood before us.

"You are to gather your belongings and make your way to the plank where one of the ship's officers will take your name and age. Those of you who have children must keep them close by you, so their names can be recorded also. Once you have disembarked you will be instructed by troopers from the local government."

As he glanced over us, his summary was not a bit surprising, "You all look a sorry lot. I repeat, all of you who have children are to make sure you have them with you."

I thought to myself, we have been so badly treated by you. It is hardly our fault that we look ragged and emaciated. What a wicked little man! I was going to be glad to see the end of him.

As we left the ship, one of the ship's officers recorded our names. I gave my name and Betsy followed me with Toby.

The ship's officer questioned Betsy, "I don't have any record of you with a child. There must be some mistake."

Betsy was quick to reply," Well your record must be wrong. This is my Toby. I am his muma.

The officer looked at Toby, and both Betsy and I held our breath.

He asked Toby, "Is this your muma?"

Toby said with enthusiasm, "Yes, sure is."

The officer said, "Go ahead then. There must be a clerical error. I'll alter the record to read correctly."

When we were about to step onto God's good soil, both Betsy and I whispered to Toby, "You did great."

His quick response, "It's a good game. I am glad we can be together."

Most of us were escorted by a group of troopers to a rough jail. Betsy found out later that the women who had committed serious crimes had been sifted from our group and were sent separately to a place somewhere south.

Betsy slowly closed Emma's journal and said, "And so a new tale begins. But we had better stop now for lunch Elizabeth. I'll put the journal away for now, and next time you will hear a little of our life in Australia."

I rang the bell, and in a few moments Woods arrived and asked, "Is it time for lunch Madam?"

"Yes," I replied. "The time has passed too quickly. I hope Mrs. Featherstone hasn't given up on us. Tell her I'm sorry. The time has just slipped away."

Ever the diplomat, he answered, "I know she has some soup simmering on the stove. I'm sure she doesn't mind at all."

Bowing politely, he excused himself and said, "I'll be back shortly."

After he had gone Elizabeth asked, "Do you know when Catherine and Edward will return?"

I replied, "No, I have no idea. But I expect they may be away for a few more weeks. I think it depends on Catherine's heath. I do hope her memory returns."

Elisabeth responded, "Don't worry too much Betsy. Love and gentle care can work wonders."

"I hope so," I replied.

There was a knock at the door and Woods came in carrying a large tray. He had previously set the small table in the room, so we both stood and took a seat at the table.

As he placed the tureen on the table, Elizabeth remarked, "Pumpkin soup. I just love it. And the whole-meal buns look delicious!"

Addressing me, Woods said, "I'll leave the tea for you to pour Madam. There is a plate of scones with jam and cream also. If you need anything else, please ring the bell."

"Thank you, Woods," I replied. "The food looks wonderful."

He dutifully replied, "I'll tell Mrs. Featherstone. She will be pleased."

As Woods exited the door, Elizabeth exclaimed, "It is such a delight to come over here! I get to enjoy your company, hear Catherine's story, and have delicious food."

I responded, "I hope we might remain friends, after we have read Catherine's journal,"

Elizabeth's reply was encouraging, "Oh yes, Betsy. I was hoping you might come over to the manor and read to me. My eyes won't let me read much and I used to love to read."

I agreed quickly, "Yes, I love to read! Of course, I would love to do it."

Elizabeth smiled, "I am so pleased! Thank you. Now let's enjoy this fine fare."

After the last of the scones were gone, and we had enjoyed a second cup of tea, Elizabeth stood to leave.

"Well, it has been a joy. I'd best be getting back to the manor. Would you ask Woods to notify my coachman, I expect he'll be in your kitchen."

When Elizabeth left that day, she hadn't informed me when her next visit would be. Based on our previous arrangements, I assumed she might come in two days' time. I was not disappointed when, exactly at ten-thirty, there was a familiar rap on the door.

Elizabeth never rang the bell. She always knocked. I thought it a little odd and wondered about it. Perhaps she had missed seeing it. Regardless, her knock had become familiar to me.

I was waiting as Woods escorted her to the parlor. I welcomed her, "So good to see you Elizabeth, I hoped you would come today." Turning, I gave instructions to Woods, "Please tell Mrs. Featherstone we will be needing our lunch at about one o'clock."

He made a courteous reply, "Certainly madam."

I continued to feel awkward, having someone waiting on me, but said, "Thank you, Woods."

He put another log on the fire and left discreetly.

Looking at Elizabeth, I said, "By having lunch a bit later I think we could get more of Catherine's journal read."

"Yes," she said. 'I have been pondering the ordeals you both faced while on that ship."

"Catherine and I need to put it behind us, I know. I suspect that is why Lord Edward didn't take the journal to Sheffield with them."

Picking up the journal from the table, I said, "You'll remember we had just arrived in Sydney, Australia."

Elizabeth responded, "Yes, I do. I am anxious to know what you did there."

I began reading from Catherine's journal.

The jail had been roughly built. It consisted of a row of rough-cut logs made into four walls that were just about the height of a tall man. The roof didn't look very secure, just logs of wood lay across the walls. It looked to have been recently built and formed an irregular enclosure at one edge of Sydney. Even I, who knew very little about building, could see it wasn't structurally sound. We were among the first in the jail. As the day progressed, and more convicts arrived to share our lodging, the size proved entirely inadequate.

As we were pushed into an enclosure beside the jail, a tall, lanky, woman with curly black hair instructed us, "You are all to wash yourselves thoroughly. Don't none of ya pretend to be shy. The Good Lord made us all the same. You will see here in the enclosure there are several big tubs of water. Give yourselves a good top to toe. You'll see there are towels, washcloths, and soap near the water tubs. When you are clean and dry, Jessica will give you a fresh change of clothes."

She indicated a woman standing over by the table with several piles of clothing. "She is a convict just like you."

"You can see we have roped off an area where your youngins' can wait for you. We will watch that none run away. You are to return to this area when you are clean and dressed."

Betsy said, "There now Toby, wait with the other children. We won't be long."

"Can't I come with you?" Toby pleaded.

Betsy told him, "Not this time Toby. Catherine and I need to wash. You'll have fun playing with the other children. Mind you stay with them. We won't be very long."

He sauntered off. Toby was a sociable child. We knew he'd be happy playing with the other children.

It didn't matter much that the water was cold. After that bath, appalling as the conditions were, for the first time in many months I felt as if there was something human about me. I think standing on firm ground also had a lot to do with it.

We had to go up to the front to obtain our fresh change of clothes. I followed Betsy's example and wrapped a towel around me.

The woman who handed us our clothing seemed a little nervous as she said, "We have three sizes, small, medium and large. There are undergarments also. You can take what will be fittin' you."

I took a small but as Betsy was much taller, she took the larger size. We went behind the tubs to dress.

I told Betsy, "This clothing is not very becoming at all, I am sick of wearing such ungainly things."

Betsy's good-humored response made me smile, "Why Catherine, you'll have all the troopers turning their heads to get a better look at you."

Yes, I imagined I did look a sorry sight; an emaciated woman with scraggly hair. What did it matter? I had no one to impress. I continued to marvel; Betsy was always able to make a joke at the appropriate time.

I grinned and said, "Indeed."

The convict who handed out our clothing didn't look much better than we did, but at least her hair was long, and it gleamed in the morning sunlight. She wore the same brown cotton smock as that we were instructed to wear.

As we were dressing, I told Betsy, "I think the tall woman is in charge. She has three stripes on her jacket signifying she's a Sargent. I suppose they have police here like they do in England."

When we all returned to the area which had been designated, she spoke loudly, "Now all those of ya who have little ones, you must make sure you wash them in the remaining tubs of water that haven't been used. She pointed to an area to the right, which had been roped off until now. Use soap and scrub them clean."

Little Toby was playing tiggy with some of the other children. I remembered Betsy and I playing tiggy when we were young, chasing each other and our playmates around the manor laughing merrily all the while.

When Betsy took him up in her arms, Toby squealed and squirmed, but within a few moments I heard delighted peals of laughter. Dear little Toby had taken to Betsy as if she were his real muma. Nonetheless, I also felt his love.

After bathing, we all gathered in the enclosure.

The lanky woman who had addressed us earlier said, "It's too late for breakfast, so we will be givin' ya soup and bread for lunch. It will be brought over from the workhouse. You'll have to be waitin' for a bit."

We were used to waiting and being told what we should be doing, I spoke wistfully to Betsy, "I do hope and pray there will be some respite from being told what to do."

I thought to myself, who knows what lies ahead? I was afraid that Betsy and I would be parted. I was afraid of so much.

We continued to be guarded by troopers outside the enclosure.

After a time the woman in charge pointed in the direction of the workhouse. "Here comes your lunch."

Several women, dressed as we were, pulled a cart with several big pots of soup and trays of bread to our enclosure. Another cart followed with dishes and spoons.

The lanky woman told us: "Wait in line, and when it's your turn you may take a dish and a spoon." Then, pointing to the women who had pulled the food cart, she said, "These convicts will serve you. You can take two slices of bread. No more. When you have finished put your dirty dishes and eating utensils back on the cart."

The women serving our food didn't say much. Another guard oversaw their work. From her scowl and harsh demeanor, she seemed a stern and unhappy woman. I resolved to stay away from her.

There were four or five wooden tables with benches, obviously not enough seating for so many women. Betsy, Toby, and I sat on the ground. Having tastier food in our stomachs was a mercy which was appreciated by everyone.

I glanced at the group of women who seemed to be in charge and noticed a buxom woman with tatty brown hair. She was talking to the tall lanky guard.

After we had put our dishes back on the cart, the woman addressed us again. She stood on a raised platform which had been placed in our enclosure by two of the troopers. She spoke with authority in her voice and manner.

"Most of you will be assigned to work as domestic servants with settlers outside the city. This will happen over the next few days. Meanwhile, you are to keep yourselves tidy and clean in preparation to meet the colonists you will work for. You can walk around as far as your prison and the workhouse and then as far as the courthouse." There will be troopers standing guard on each perimeter. We are only allowing this, so you will have a little freedom to exercise and increase your energy.

It was true. We were permitted to walk a little, but only within about five hundred yards. When I had heard we would be free to walk around, I had imagined we could look over the settlement. So as the real limits were made clear, my hopes were dashed. If we couldn't contact someone in the settlement, how would we get a note to anyone for help?

As we were walking, I looked at Betsy. I knew there was something on her mind.

She finally said. "I expect this will be our last chance to get word to Lord Edward. We need to do it quickly. Who knows when we'll be sent further away from Sydney?"

I responded carefully, "I don't see how we'll have time to steal writing materials, but I can't see any other way we can do it. I looked in the guard's office last night and saw there were writing materials, but there were guards present and I had no opportunity to do anything. I looked again this morning. I'm certain there were writing materials. If we can sneak in there tonight without being caught, I might be able to write a note, but I don't like stealing."

Betsy said, "I don't have a problem with that. We have had to deal with a real-life change. Anyway, it will be our only chance to get word to Henry."

I replied, "Perhaps we could persuade one of the troopers to send word to Henry, but you'll have to do the talking or else things might unravel on us as they have before. I suspect some of the locals have already heard about the mad woman from the ship."

As the day moved on, I grew more concerned. What if we were caught? The most likely outcome would be that my sentence would be extended and the accusation that I had attempted to steal something back in England would be validated.

I said as much to Betsy. She looked a little pensive and then responded, "Well I could just do it by myself."

I was quick to say, "A fat lot of good that would do. Then we would be separated if you were caught. No, we shall have to do it together."

Betsy suggested, "Lets walk back to the jail and have another look."

I called to Toby who had scampered ahead of us, "Come now, Toby, we are turning back."

"Oh, I am chasing a stone. Do we have to?" His idea of chasing a stone was kicking it along the path.

"Yes, we do. You can chase a stone as we go back."

Betsy suggested, "We need to make up an excuse why we are looking in the office." She thought for a moment or two. "I think we could ask when our evening meal will be."

I smiled, "You'll get rewards for your creativity."

As we entered our sleeping quarters, we noticed the door to the office was partly open. There was no way to determine if there was a lock on the other side of the door. Nevertheless, we saw a quantity of loose paper and envelopes lying on a desk. As I had noted earlier there were quills and ink as well.

Betsy went into the office and asked the woman guard, the one who was tall and lanky, "Excuse me, can you tell me when we will be fed next?'

The woman replied, "You're keen, aren't you?"

"No, ma'am. I was just thinking for me friend. She wasn't well, so she couldn't be eatin' lunch and now she's feeling a bit light-headed. I meant no harm in asking."

The guard responded, "Well, she'll just have to wait two more hours. But you can get some water from the well across the path near the workhouse if you want."

Betsy replied, "Thank you."

When Betsy joined me, she said, "Good news. There doesn't appear to be a lock on the other side of the door."

I responded smiling, "You're a clever one. Now how do we steal what we need?"

Besty looked contemplative. "Well I definitely saw candles in there, but wonder how we can light one to seal the envelope."

I volunteered, "Perhaps there will be something to light the candle in the office."

Betsy agreed. "Yes, you could be right. Thank goodness I got a good look in the office. It will be harder to navigate at night. It looked like there was a stove and I felt the warmth from it. If they keep it burning overnight, then our worries are over."

That guard was right. Two hours later the dinner bell rang. Most of the woman had returned to the enclosure as there was not a lot to see between our prison and the courthouse.

Our meal was much the same as we had for lunch with exception of the soup. They gave us a mealy stew instead. It had one or two more vegetables than we had been used to on the ship. They also allowed us to have a cup of tea. It was stronger than we had been used to, but there was no milk to be had. Nonetheless, there was sugar.

The plan kept revolving in my head. While eating my meal, I could think of nothing else. I just hoped Betsy and I wouldn't be caught.

I remarked to Betsy, "I am feeling very unsure about stealing things from the office. I wonder if they will notice things missing?"

Betsy quickly responded, "Obviously none of our notes have been received. This could well be our last opportunity to send word to Edward. It's a chance we must take. As for me, I believe we should try."

I agreed nervously. It didn't get dark until after eight. A few candles were issued to those who wanted them and, of course, we snapped them up. Each of us managed to snag one. I was pleased. It was one thing we wouldn't have to steal.

At nine we were told to extinguish our candles and to return to our sleeping area. The tall lanky female guard told us, "There are pillows, blankets and straw on the floor. You are to push in together. It might be a little cramped, but you will just have to make do. There will be troopers stationed around the building all night, so if any of you attempt to escape you are bound to feel the sting of a bullet.

We were all pushed into that shoddily built building. Betsy, Toby and I lagged behind in order to remain near the door of the office. Of course, Toby didn't know about our plans. As we lay down to sleep, Betsy whispered something to him, and they hugged each other. I also got my hug from Toby.

Not really knowing what the time was, we waited for what we thought was an hour. The prison was quite rowdy. So many snorts and snores. I had never heard such a racket before. No, not even on the ship.

Betsy whispered to me, "Its time. Follow me."

We crawled as quietly as we could. Betsy pushed the office door open and it creaked quite loudly so we laid down and waited for another ten minutes or so. Nobody stirred. We crawled into the office in the dark but, once our eyes had adapted, we realized there was enough light to see. A full moon shined brightly into the room. Nonetheless, we had to move in the shadows just in case we might be seen from the open window space.

I looked for the stove, but Betsy had beaten me to it. She quietly opened the handle and sure enough, there were a few red coals. We crept behind the desk and took one envelope and one sheet of paper. We also took a quill and ink.

Betsy urged me, "Write quickly Catherine."

I had already practiced in my mind what I would write:

Dear Henry,

I have no way of contacting Edward. Betsy and I have been convicted as criminals and sent to Australia. We were falsely accused, obviously. We are to be servants in New South Wales in the Australian Colonies. We gave our names as Catherine Lancaster and Betsy Longwood. Please ask Edward to rescue us.

Regards
Catherine Bannister

While we were waiting for the ink to dry, I addressed the envelope.

Betsy returned the ink bottle to its original place. I wiped the nib of the pen on the inside of my dress and Betsy returned it to its original place. We checked to see if we had disturbed anything else. I placed my note in the envelope and Betsy continued crawling as she made her way to the stove to light the candle we had saved for this very purpose. She held her hand around the flame so as not to shed any light on us should a trooper walk in. I was hiding behind the desk, but I had to stand in order to ensure the wax created a good seal. It did.

We began crawling towards the door, thinking we had succeeded but when we saw the door start to open, we quickly returned to a place of concealment under the desk. It was a trooper who had come in to get a light for his pipe. He took a piece of paper from the desk and lit it from the embers in the stove.

I started to shake. Many thoughts ran through my mind. What if we are discovered? What would be our fate? I would never see my darling Edward again. Betsy held me close, sensing my thoughts.

To our surprise, once the trooper lit his pipe, he put some more coal on the fire and went out the door. He would have had to walk in between sleeping bodies to get to the office. Presumably, he must have done the same again when he left. I hoped he hadn't woken anyone. We waited a few more minutes and crawled toward the door. The door hadn't creaked when the trooper used it.

I whispered to Betsy, "Perhaps we need to be standing when we open the door because it didn't creak when the trooper used it."

Betsy whispered, "You crawl, and I'll stand to open the door."

It worked. We opened the door noiselessly and closed it in the same manner. I was still trembling as we lay on the hay to sleep, but felt content knowing that we had succeeded in creating the letter.

I doubted that anyone had noticed that we were missing. I hid the envelope on my person until the following morning, not really knowing how we would be able to get the letter sent.

Most of the convicts were awake before the bell sounded. We all made our way to the outdoor enclosure.

One of the women from the ship came up to me and said, "What are ya plannin'?"

I stammered, "What do you mean/"

Her response, "You and ya friend," pointing to Betsy, "We seen ya last night coming from that little room. Let us in on ya plans."

I had to think quickly. I hated to lie but could see no other avenue, so I said, "Betsy and I were just looking to see if they had more food hidden away."

Her quick response, "An' do they?"

"Not that we could find," I replied.

She said, "If you find any ways we can be escaping, tell us. I am sick of so many folk tellin' us what to do."

As fortune would have it, we had a better breakfast than we were accustomed to on the ship.

We were told by the woman who had given us orders to wash, "You can walk around a little as you did yesterday. When you hear three bells ring you are to return to the enclosure next to the jail. Remember to stay within the boundaries. Troopers are stationed all around and they won't hesitate to shoot."

The thought of troopers and their muskets was irksome. I wondered if anyone would make a run for it and asked myself where could they run to? Most of our number were conspicuous as we all wore similar brown smocks.

My mind went on. I asked Betsy, "And what about the aborigines?"

"Yes, I've heard of them," she said. "I think they are a primitive people who have lived here before the English came."

Betsy always seemed to have the answers to my questions.

"What do you know about these aborigines?" I asked.

She replied, "I've heard tell some of them can be ferocious. They are dark-skinned people."

Betsy, Toby, and I walked toward the courthouse in the faint hope that we would find a way to send the letter. I carried it on my person.

I asked Betsy, "What are we going to do?"

Her reply was encouraging, "Don't give up hope. We must be careful, but somehow we'll find a way." We walked a little farther beyond the courthouse and wondered if we would be punished in some way.

A trooper walked up to us. Angling his musket in our direction he spoke brusquely, "You know you have gone past the boundary. You need to turn around and walk the other way."

He gave us a hard stare, continuing to watch us until he was certain we would comply.

We started back towards the jail but not directly, we walked around the perimeter slowly. We were still in the view of the trooper when we heard a gunshot. We were curious and hurried to see what had happened. To our surprise, we found the same woman I had spoken to earlier lying injured on the ground.

This was not something I thought Toby should see. I quickly gathered him close and told him not to look. He frowned, and I could see he was frightened. I told him, "it's going to be all right, Toby. It's just some people who started a fight with one another. Just look at me. You don't need to worry.

He squirmed a bit but looked mostly at my skirt. It looked as if the woman had been shot in the shoulder. She was bleeding and seemed to be semi-conscious. She held a blood-stained knife.

A pistol lay near the body of a trooper who was lying on his back. He was lying in a spreading pool of blood, though his wound must have been taken in the back because there was no obvious wound on the front of his uniform. I thought he looked dead. I muttered to Betsy, "Looks like she stabbed the poor man, and then he managed to shoot her before he died."

We were alone for a few moments before things started to get frantic. We heard shouts and the sound of men running towards us. I drew Toby closer, anxious about being found close to the two bodies.

Betsy quickly said, "Give me the letter."

She hastily put it in the dead trooper's pocket and rose to her feet, dragging Toby and me away from the trooper's body. A moment passed before the trooper who had spoken to us earlier and several other troopers came rushing up. There was shouting, with the arriving troopers hastily aiming muskets in our direction, yelling at us to lay on the ground. I was afraid we would be shot by someone who mistook our presence to mean we were somehow involved in the gunfire and the death of their comrade.

Fortunately, the trooper who had sent us back to the prison was among the first to arrive. He knew we could not have been involved. With lots more yelling and shouts of "lie down", he assured the others that we didn't have anything to do with the shooting. There was open hostility, and despite the trooper's defense, we were handled roughly and shoved awkwardly to the ground.

Poor Toby, eyes wide, was shoved fifteen feet away and made to face the ground. He was very frightened and anxious and tried manfully to hold back tears.

More convicts and settlers soon arrived on the scene, further unsettling the troopers. Between angry shouts telling us to keep down, and a lot of cursing and threats on our lives, and the brandishing of weapons in both our direction and the gathering crowd, I felt we were in great danger for a time.

Betsy spoke up from where we were laying on the ground, "Look at them. It looks like she stabbed the trooper and he shot her. Look at the knife in her hand and how she was shot in the shoulder."

She would have said more, I think, but one of the troopers angrily told her "Shut your mouth" as he stuck the end of his musket near her mouth "or I will shut it for you."

She looked like she was going to speak up anyway but thought better of it and turned her head away from the trooper. There was a lot of talking back and forth among the troopers as they eventually reached the same conclusion Betsy and I had about how their comrade was killed and who was responsible. The trooper who had seen us near the edge of our permitted walking area continued telling the others that we couldn't have arrived more than fifteen seconds before they did.

Eventually, when our presence in the area was explained, the troopers gradually settled down and we were allowed to get up. The moment we were allowed to get to our feet, Betsy hurried over to collect Toby from where the troopers had pushed him.

It took a while before reason finally reasserted itself and angry voices quietened. A trooper asked, "Can ya be tellin' us what happened?"

Betsy responded, "We came when we heard the shots. We don't know what happened."

This confirmed what the trooper had told them.

One of the troopers said, "There will need be an investigation."

"You convicts," he said pointing to us, "What are your names?"

Betsy spoke, "I am Betsy Longwood, and this is my friend Catherine Lancaster and my son Toby."

The trooper wrote our names in a little book which he took from his pocket and then told us, "Go back to the prison area."

We were pleased to leave. I certainly didn't want to be linked to the trooper's investigation and I didn't think it was good for Toby to see. We were lucky we had been near a trooper when the shooting took place.

After the immediate shock had passed, I asked Betsy why she had placed the letter in the dead trooper's jacket. "Do you think they will send the letter when they take his belongings from his pockets?"

"Yes," she replied. "I think there's a good possibility. It was impulsive I must admit, but I think it's our best chance. Lucky we were in the right place at the right time."

Despite our innocence, the whole experience was unsettling but Betsy and I concluded we shouldn't discuss it in Toby's presence. It took lots of hugs to assure him all was well.

As the day went on, several different troopers came to question us. We were certainly not involved in what happened, thank goodness.

Somehow, word got out and there was talk amongst the prisoners about the incident. When the troopers spoke to us, they were curious about why we were there and expressed doubts about our story. But I didn't care and neither did Betsy. We had no reason to lie and no reason not to tell them what we knew.

I don't know what became of the woman who was wounded. We never saw her again.

During those days in the Sydney prison, Betsy and I remained hopeful. We knew it would take time for my letter to be sent and if it was sent, time for it to reach Henry.

CHAPTER

11

Questions

For the few days we were in Sydney, all the convicts felt anxious, not knowing what our future would bring. We recognized many of the convicts from our shared mealtimes, from our time on the ship, and from meals we had shared over the past few days.

After lunch one day, the tall lanky woman told us to stay in the prisoner's compound. Several troopers gathered together. One of the troopers brought in a desk. He used a tree stump for a chair. Several others loitered nearby just staring at us. A rather plump, ruddy-faced, officer came forward and stood in front of us.

"I am the Lieutenant Governor of New South Wales, here on behalf of the Governor of the colony. For your own good, you should listen to what I have to say."

A murmur of women's voices could be heard as he went on with his speech.

"We are building up a new country here and, if you do what's right, nobody needs to get into trouble. You'll all be assigned to work in households throughout the colony. It's up to you to see that you do a good job. If you get into trouble, you'll be sent to the workhouse for a period.

From there you'll go to another household. If anyone is treated poorly, you can put in a complaint and one of the Governor's representatives will see what can be done. We don't hold with drunkenness or people going missing. It's up to each one of you to make a go of life here in the colony. Once most of you have been in service for two years, you will have earned your freedom. So, do well, all of you! Trooper Hallow here will tell you which households you have been assigned to work in."

The Lieutenant Governor left and then another trooper who was sitting at the desk stood up and told us. "My name is Trooper Hallow. Tomorrow some of you will meet the settlers to whom you have been assigned. Your new masters, or someone in their employ, will pick you up. You must remember the name of the settler to whom you will be assigned. You are to be ready by an hour after breakfast."

Looking at us he said, "Each of you will come forward when your name is called."

He started to name convicts and match them to the names of settlers who had requested convicts to serve in their households.

"Ethel Chibnall and son to serve in the Hamilton residence. Kitchen hand and errand boy.

Mary Lewis to serve in the Bentley residence. Cook and housekeeper.

Betsy Longwood and son Toby, to serve in the Mars residence. Lady's maid and farmer's boy."

I felt my heart leap! How I abhorred the thought of this life without Betsy! She looked at me with such an endearing smile. Most of the women whose names had been called made their way further back towards the jail, but Betsy lingered. I knew she wanted to know what my destiny was.

They continued calling out names

"Lissa McNalley and son Henry to serve in the W.M. Williams residence. Cook and farmer's boy.

Mary McCarthy and Dotty Pincher to serve in the Blaney residence. Cook and kitchen hand.

Martha McLintoch and Lizzy Neeson to serve in the Collins residence. Cook and kitchen hand."

Many more names were called. There were only a few of us left when, finally, he said, "Catherine Lancaster you will go with Betsy Longwood to serve in the Mars residence as a kitchen hand."

At first, I didn't answer to the name. But, after it was repeated and Betsy nudged me, I realized that they were calling my name. After a moment's confusion, I made my way to the officer.

He repeated the assignment. "Catherine Lancaster, you are to serve in the Mars residence along with Betsy Longwood and son. You have been assigned to work as a kitchen hand."

Betsy and I were jubilant, hugging each other during this process. The officer soon scowled in our direction, "You there! Return to the prison. Convicts should return to the prison after their names are called."

When we returned to the jail, I couldn't remember what job I had been assigned. I had to ask Betsy. When she said I was to be a kitchen hand and she a lady's maid, I was pleased for Betsy. I had scant knowledge of what kitchen hands did and that only from my early childhood days when I used to play with the cook's son at Blakewood House.

I wasn't the prim and proper sort my mother hoped I would be. I would sometimes take my lunch with the cook and her son, Toddy. We would sit in the kitchen and eat our lunch together. This was something my mother frowned upon but nonetheless permitted.

Mother also allowed me to befriend Toddy. I guess she felt that we were of a similar station when she was my age. Toddy was going to be a groomsman when he grew up. Toddy's sister was the kitchen hand.

She always seemed to be scrubbing pots. I wondered if that would be my fate.

My thoughts went back to Todd and I thought of what a fine man he had become. He was the head groomsman at Blakewood House and was liked by all.

The following morning, we waited in anticipation. We were instructed to wash and then we were given porridge which tasted like porridge as I knew it to be. There were also pots of tea and slices of bread and butter.

We observed there seemed to be a queue of arriving wagons and coaches. As a coach or wagon would arrive, the trooper in charge spoke to the driver and afterward called out the names of the convicts assigned to go with that driver. The morning passed slowly but eventually, a team of four horses pulling a coach appeared. The young man who drove the team spoke to the trooper and, shortly thereafter, our names were called.

The driver, who was to be our only contact with humanity for the following five hours, introduced himself, "My name is Alf. I left at dawn to get you, so the return journey will take a while. We should reach the property by nightfall."

He seemed to be a nice young man and didn't speak down to us.

"The property is located fifty miles north-west of here. The trip might be a bit longer than you have been used to. These summer days are hotter than you have been used to in England. Make yourself comfortable in the coach."

As we climbed into the coach he pointed to two large bottles of water that were on the floor "There is water to use as you need it. You will get a good meal when we arrive at the property. The place we are going to is called Grangewood. The owner there runs a sheep farm. You both will be under the direction of Miss Beatrice, she is the housekeeper."

Although Alf had told us what to expect, I was somewhat surprised as we made our way over many, many miles of flat dry country. The weather was much hotter than I had ever imagined. Those hours in the coach were very uncomfortable. Betsy, Toby, and I all grumbled about how much hotter it seemed in comparison to anything we had ever felt before. I was grateful we had extra water to drink.

Three hours into our journey we went over some rickety bridges and then Alf stopped the horses near a stream.

"The horses need a rest and a drink," he said. "Come on down by the water, ladies. And you, young'n, cool yourself off."

While we watched the horses drink thirstily, Betsy and I ran down to the stream with Toby and splashed each other with our hands. Toby thought it was great fun.

Alf fetched a wooden box from the back of the coach saying, "Here, you can have some bread and butter."

As we ate the bread and drank more water Betsy asked, "Does the countryside always look so barren and dry all the time?"

Alf answered, "January and February are always the driest part of the year. Come June or July the countryside will take on a new look. These dry fields will be lush green pastures then. That's the time when the master's sheep will start to fatten."

I found myself saying, "I've never seen some of these trees."

He told us, "We call them eucalyptus trees, pretty common in Australia."

He picked up some leaves and encouraged us to smell them.

He said, "They have a distinct odor which feels new and fresh. Eucalyptus trees are very sturdy and can resist drought."

He volunteered more information, but by that time I had lost interest.

Despite his optimism that the color of the countryside would change, I felt nobody in their right mind would want to live here. It seemed like such a desolate and isolated place. The smell of the eucalyptus trees was refreshing, but an oak or an elm suited me far better.

While it was good not to be able to feel the rolling motion of the ship, I viewed my time on this land with apprehension. I roused from my worries as Alf started to hitch up the team.

He told us, "We had best be getting on. If we leave now, we might get to catch a glimpse of a few aborigines."

Personally, I had no desire to see aborigines. All the stories about them made them sound terrifying.

Betsy seemed unfazed by the stories. She commented. "Yes, we haven't heard a lot about them, only that they might be ferocious."

Alf replied. "That's not true. The aborigines have lived in this country for many years, way before any British settlers. The master at Grangewood is not hostile towards them, but there are a lot of settlers and soldiers who hate them."

As we made our way back toward the coach, a herd of animals suddenly ran in front of us. They were just a few tree lengths away. They were brown and seemed to hop. In a moment of panic, I shrieked at Alf and grabbed Betsy by the arm. Betsy started at my touch, and a similar squeak popped quietly from her lips when she caught sight of what had frightened me. We both retreated a few steps back towards the stream.

Alf smiled gleefully, "Don't go worrying about the kangaroos. While it's best not to get too near them, they're not likely to harm anyone."

Despite his reassurances, I was glad to be in the coach again.

After our stop, I felt a little better and I am sure Betsy and Toby did also. After their short respite, the horses settled back into a steady pace.

As the late afternoon hours approached a cool breeze developed. It helped us feel a little refreshed. The countryside continued to look dry and barren. Such a countryside reminded me of its opposite, the lush green meadows of home.

When we were near our destination, Alf called out from his seat in front of the coach, "Look, look to where the sun is setting."

Following his direction, we all looked towards the west. In the fading light we could see the silhouette of people, and then, as the coach drew a little nearer, we could fully see a few dark colored people carrying sticks. I had never seen a colored person before. How strange. But they didn't look ferocious, rather placid I thought. I would have liked to have stopped and spoken with them, but I wasn't in charge of anything anymore.

It was dusk when we arrived at Grangewood. We were able to make out a wide, well-constructed building made of stone. The workmanship was of good quality, leading me to conclude the owner was a man of considerable means. The front entrance was very impressive as we passed, but the coach continued around to the back before coming to a stop.

Alf got down from his perch high on the buckboard of the coach and opened the coach door for us.

"Well, here we are ladies. This square behind the main house is for the servants and some storage areas."

Betsy and I moved stiffly as we climbed down from the coach, but Toby moved much faster.

Toby commented, "It's a real big place!"

Betsy and I nodded in agreement.

Alf seemed to focus back on the task at hand. "I had better take you into the main house. Surely, I'll be in trouble if I don't. Miss Beatrice will want to meet you, you can be sure."

He led us into a room that looked like a kitchen.

As we were walking, Betsy whispered to me. "Let me do most of the talking if possible."

We were met by a woman who had a very coarse countenance. Her dark eyes seemed to peer right through us.

This must be Miss Beatrice, I concluded. She was middle-aged with auburn hair. Her face was somewhat wrinkled. Within moments, by the scowl and sneer that formed and settled on her face, I could see that this was a woman who thought highly of herself and, in contrast, had only thinly veiled contempt for us.

All she said to Alf was, "You're back then."

Alf handed her a paper. I imagined it must have been something about us, because before we left Sydney, he was given some information about us by one of the troopers.

She introduced herself. "My name is Beatrice MacKennery. You will address me as 'Miss Beatrice.' The master and mistress here leave the running of the house to me. They know things get done when I am in charge. You will always do as I say. You must never disobey me, or you will pay. Which one of you is Betsy Longwood?"

Betsy volunteered, "I am Betsy." And pointing to me, she said "This is Catherine."

Miss Beatrice looked at Betsy as she said, "You are to serve the mistress. Make sure you do your work well or you will answer to me. Remember that!"

As she looked at me she said, "Catherine Lancaster you will work in the kitchen." She spoke with no inflection. Just a monotone list of instructions. Nevertheless, her eyes continued to glance first to Betsy and then to me.

She struck us as not having a friendly bone in her body.

She said, "You will do exactly what I tell you and when I tell you. Do you understand?"

We nodded meekly.

She noted our submissiveness as she smiled thinly, "You will share living space with Katty, out in the quadrangle. You'll have one hour's free time per day. Apart from that, and when you are sleeping for eight hours, you will be on duty. You will meet the other servants at meal time. If you do as you are told, we will get along well. Alf will show you to your room."

It appeared that she had a mental checklist, and she moved from one topic to the next. "The master and mistress issue clothing regularly," she said. "I oversee that."

"As you have arrived so late in the day we have already seen to the family's meal. But knowing that you might be hungry after a long day, we servants will eat together now."

She pointed to Alf. "Alf will show you the room where you can wash up if you wish but be sure you are back here in twenty minutes."

We followed Alf out to the quadrangle. We walked past a few doors which were closed but then Alf opened a door. He spoke to Toby. "You can choose for yourself, little fella, you can sleep in here with your mum or ya can share a room with me."

Toby pulled at Betsy's dress and she answered for him. "I think he'd rather be with me until we settle in."

"Okay, I understand. You can change your mind later if ya want," he replied.

He opened the door and pointed to things in the room. "This is your room. Katty's bed is on the right, so you can choose which of the other beds you want. There is a pitcher of water on the table and a bowl to wash your hands. I'll be changing the water every day so you've no need to be worrying about that. Remember, Miss Beatrice said twenty minutes. Take my advice. Do as she tells you. She can be mean when she wants. It's best to start off on the right footing."

Betsy's was quick to thank him saying, "We will hurry. Alf, you are a good man. We appreciate all your help."

"Okay then, I'll see you soon."

We returned to the kitchen just nineteen minutes later. We had no clock, but Betsy and I had learned to gauge time from our past experiences on the Hulk while still in London.

Miss Beatrice stood watching as Katty was laying the table.

"You can take your places. Betsy and Catherine, you will sit on the left side."

Betsy whispered to me, "We have never seen so much food for ever so long."

On the table were slices of cold meat, tomato, lettuce, beetroot, cheese and sliced white bread. There was also a large slab of butter on a dish. To Betsy and I this was a great feast. While they gave us a good breakfast of porridge and bread back in Sydney town that morning, the only food we had eaten since then was the bread and butter Alf had shared with us on our journey to the property. By this time, I was both hungry and tired. Nevertheless, after grace was said by Miss Beatrice, Betsy and I followed the example of the other servants and helped ourselves to a good meal. Indeed, I ate my food somewhat eagerly.

Miss Beatrice told us, "The master here is very generous and has told me to make sure we all get plenty to eat."

There were just six of us sitting at the table: Miss Beatrice, Alf, Kitty, Betsy, myself and, of course, little Toby.

Miss Beatrice announced with obvious pride, "All of the food you are eating has been grown on the property. Beginning tomorrow it will be your duty, Catherine, to make the cheese."

That frightened me. I kept eating my food and tried to put my worries aside as I filled my empty stomach for the first time in months. I said to myself, Betsy will tell me what to do. I must remember to ask her. There was little talk as we were eating. By the time we had finished, I struggled to keep my eyes open and to pay heed to what Miss Beatrice said.

"You will both be relieved of your duties tonight, but you are to start tomorrow at six in the morning."

"Yes, of course," I answered, knowing that I must show that I understood her clearly.

Our mornings had been early ever since we were imprisoned back in London, so arising early was no shock to me.

"Betsy Longwood you are to dress in the clothing suitable for your position as lady's maid. You will see there is a large wardrobe in your sleeping quarters. There are three sizes, choose the one which fits you the best. Make sure you hang the other ones back in the wardrobe. When you have chosen which one fits, you are to tell me and I will order an extra, so you will have a change."

"Catherine Lancaster, I don't want you to wear that convict dress. Wait here and I will find something for you."

While she was gone, I whispered to Betsy. "I can't make cheese, I have no idea where to even start."

Betsy's provided a reassuring answer, "I'll have to tell you later. I did it often at Blakewood House. I can tell you what you have to do."

I muttered, "But I am so tired."

Betsy spoke in her matter of fact way, "We don't have any option."

Miss Beatrice returned.

"Here," she said. "Wear this tomorrow. I will also order you another dress so you can change weekly. The women in the workhouse in Sydney make our clothes and I place orders when required. You should go now. Be on time in the morning or there will be trouble."

As we made our way to our room, Betsy muttered, "We will have to sleep in our underwear I expect. It's all we have."

It didn't matter too much as the evening was still very warm. I had never been able to get my mind in tune. In this country, they had winter in July. I wondered what we would do as the weather got colder.

I told Betsy. "I am so tired! Yet we have done nothing for most of the day."

She replied, "Get a good sleep, Catherine. I think you will need it. I don't like that Miss Beatrice at all. She is like the ship's commander. Who does she think she is?"

After Katty had finished her chores, she came in very quietly. Betsy, Toby, and I were sound asleep. We were awakened the following morning by Alf as he tapped on the door. He called out "You've got half an hour, ladies."

After we had washed, dressed, and exchanged some pleasantries with Katty, we made our way to the kitchen, taking Toby with us. I would have liked to look through the big yard but we hadn't time if we were to follow orders. Miss Beatrice was waiting for us. She had the oven stoked and it made the kitchen area very warm.

"Betsy Longwood you may look around outside, but Catherine and Katty are to prepare breakfast for the servants. In this household, the servants eat first and then the family eats at eight o'clock."

"That boy, Toby, needn't be here. He is to help Alf. Go find Alf, boy. Go now."

Betsy quickly reassured him that he would be all right. and Alf would be along in a moment to go with him. With little effort, Betsy encouraged him to go with her into the yard.

"Betsy," Miss Beatrice continued, "When you hear the bell sound you are to come quickly to the kitchen. Make sure you don't go too far or there will be snakes and lizards chasing ya."

Katty glanced at me when Miss Beatrice spoke. She had a far gentler demeanor than Miss Beatrice. She looked somewhat older than even Miss Beatrice herself.

Miss Beatrice left the kitchen for a few moments and Katty smiled kindly and came up to me.

"I am a convict like you," she said. "I was sentenced to two years of service. I have been here a year already. I'll be here to help you, lovey, if Miss Beatrice gives you a bad time."

Katty became a good ally and was there to help me as I tried to follow Miss Beatrice's orders.

I decided that 'normal' for Miss Beatrice was something between hostile and angry. Before we had been given our orders, she was already scowling.

She returned to the kitchen, already scowling, and glared at Katty and I with her piercing black eyes and said, "You must have everything ready within the hour."

I determined that there must be a pendulum clock somewhere in the house as I heard it chime on the hour just after we had entered the kitchen.

"Katty, it is your duty to show Catherine Lancaster what to do as she sees to the servant's table. Make sure it is set suitably. It is your responsibility, Catherine, to see that the servant's table is cleared, and the dishes are washed, dried, and put away after breakfast."

Her tone of voice made me shiver. She spoke to me as if I was the lowest of the low. I could not understand her demeanor at all. Why was she so bitter?

Miss Beatrice told us: "Make haste and get everything done. I am going up to the family dining room to see if Robert has set the table properly."

I was very anxious about the work I was expected to do. I had gained a little experience on the Barringer, but I was far from being capable. And given the attitude I had seen from Miss Beatrice, I knew I had little time to learn.

As soon as she left the room, I turned to Katty. "I have never been a kitchen hand, I am not sure what I have to do."

Katty smiled and quietly instructed me in the preparation of oatmeal, eggs, bacon, toast and a large pot of tea. I tried as hard as I could, but most of my efforts were clumsy.

As Katty stirred the porridge, she suggested, "Why don't you set the table now. You will find the dishes in that cupboard over there," she said pointing to a cabinet. "And cutlery is in the drawer here. You'll be needing to set the table for eight."

I was relieved. This was something I knew how to do. I had seen a proper table setting at every meal in my life. I smiled inwardly, confident that I could manage this.

During my childhood, I had often assisted the servants with this chore, so I didn't feel so threatened. I didn't think I would have a problem.

I asked Katty, "Does Miss Beatrice have a particular seat where she sits? Because honestly, I can't remember where she was sitting last night. I was so tired."

"Yes," Katty answered. "She sits at the head of the table and Robert sits at the other end."

I glanced at her enquiringly.

"Robert acts as a butler and gentleman's valet to the master. Last night he was called away to help on another farm. Robert has some experience with animals. He is sought after often by the country folks around here."

I thought it strange that he was the butler. Later, I saw his position improve. He was made foreman over the property itself, and another male convict was sent to take over his duties as butler and valet.

Katty told me, "You will need to set extra places for the two farm hands."

"All right, so that makes eight places, is that right?"

She reaffirmed what I said.

I asked her. "What about jam or cream or milk?"

"Yes," she replied. "Get the jam and sugar from the pantry and the milk from the cooling chest. We have three dairy cows on the property and Alf milks them. Make sure you put the jam and sugar in clean bowls. Miss Beatrice likes the table to be just so. She certainly has an attitude problem."

I completed my task as quickly as I could and asked Katty, "Have a quick look for me. See if it's alright?"

As Kitty glanced over the table, she said, "It's just like I would do."

Miss Beatrice appeared and asked, "Have you got everything ready?"

Both Katty and I replied in unison. "Yes, Miss Beatrice."

The scowl never left her face as she gave us her orders, "Serve the food then. I'll sound the bell. Everyone needs to be seated."

When we gathered the food to go on the table, it certainly looked bounteous. As everyone took their places, Miss Beatrice introduced us to Robert and the farm hands, Tom and Bert.

Miss Beatrice told Robert to say grace and afterward reminded us to mind our manners as we ate. Robert poured out our tea and then Miss Beatrice asked for the milk.

There wasn't any milk on the table.

"Catherine Lancaster, why is there no milk?"

Blushing furiously, realizing there was really no excuse, I tried to find the right words for an apology.

Katty intervened and said, "It is my fault. The milk is in a jug in the cooling chest."

I didn't know why she would cover for me but reminded myself to try and do something kind for her.

"Catherine asked me where to get the milk, and I forgot to tell her where it was."

Katty jumped up to get it.

While she was gone Miss Beatrice thoroughly dressed me down in front of the other servants.

"Servants must take their duties seriously. I will not stand for mistakes like this. A good household must be run precisely, and no one is allowed to shirk their duties. Do you understand, Catherine Lancaster? I will not penalize you this time, but if something like this happens again, you'll wish you never came to this household."

Robert looked up as he put two fried eggs on his plate and said, "It is such a trifling matter."

Robert was with the master often and Miss Beatrice couldn't entirely ignore what he said. Still, she was determined that no one was going to interfere with how she ran the house. Miss Beatrice seemed to hold back a little. However, she continued saying, "Servants in this house are under my authority. If you want, you can speak to the master. He will tell you that."

Robert didn't bother to respond. He took another slice of toast from the table.

I kept my head lowered and focused on the meal before me. I wished I could go back six months and find myself mistress of my own household. Oh, how I wished to be in the country which I knew and loved. How I longed to see my dear mother and father and of course dear Edward. I continually asked myself, who am I? Will I continue to live this way until I'm worn down to defeat and death?

Thank Goodness, no more was said about the milk.

As Miss Beatrice ordered, I had to make the cheese. I had forgotten all about it when I saw my bed last night and I think Betsy must have forgotten also. I had never concerned myself or wondered how cheese was made. It was one of those things that was always there.

After we had washed, dried and put the dishes away, I had to humble myself and ask, "Katty, I have no idea how to make cheese. Will you show me?"

"We have six milking cows and from there we make the cheese," she said. I am sure my eyes must have gotten round as saucers. I had no idea how cows were milked. Katty must have reasoned out my thoughts. She quickly said, "You don't have to milk the cows. That's Alf's job. The cows provide milk, cream, and cheese for the entire household."

Katty had a large bowl of milk set out. She must have known I was going to ask her.

"We need to let the milk sour and curdle, then separate the curds from the whey. It should be ready in a couple of hours in this heat."

As she opened a drawer, she showed me, "We have some cloths here to strain the curds. We make butter and cheese during spring and summer. That's when cows produce the most milk and we preserve these products with salt for autumn and winter. But we only need to make cheese today and I'll be showing ya what to do"

"Oh, Katty, thank you," I said.

Katty said confidently, "Mm, I be thinking there'll be a lot ya don't know. I'll help ya, so don't be terrified of that Miss Beatrice. I remember I was at first. Just do what she says and don't bother about it."

I replied, "Oh I wish I could share your attitude. She makes me feel petrified."

After the evening meal, I felt exhausted, but with Katty's help, we managed to get all the dishes washed, dried, and put away. Katty could see my plight and told me to hurry to bed. I felt a little guilty because I imagined there was more to do, but I did as she bid.

The following evening, despite my feelings of fatigue. I stayed back after the dishes were done and asked Katty what I needed to do.

She answered, "Sweep and scrub the floor. I'll do the scrubbing, but ya can sweep before me. We'll keep that as our little secret lovey."

One day ran into another, meal preparations, cleaning, and sleeping. Sometimes Betsy and I would chat of an evening when I didn't feel too exhausted. As colder weather drew near, Betsy looked for dry sticks in the bush to burn in the little fireplace we had in our room.

Often after dinner, Toby would go with Alf to do chores and then we would find him sound asleep when we returned to our room after completing our duties.

As we were washing one morning, Toby asked Betsy, "Would ya mind if I sleep in Alf's room?"

Betsy smiled, "That's a good idea. We won't mind at all will we Catherine?"

"Not at all," I said, smiling at Toby. "We are pleased that you like Alf. He is a good young man."

Toby eagerly said, "He took me on his horse yesterday. It was fun."

I think Betsy shared my opinion. We would miss him, but we were pleased that he and Alf got along so well.

I reflected that two good things had happened since we had arrived in Australia. Toby had found a new home and Betsy and I had remained together.

My duties taught me how the other half lived. I believe I grew humbler, and I expect the things I endured had strengthened me. I completed my duties as well as I could. Katty was my instructor when I didn't know how to perform my duties or lacked the strength to perform them quickly enough to suit Miss Beatrice.

I tried ever so much to complete the duties assigned to me. Katty became my stalwart. I was required to scrub the pots and pans, but she always helped me. Unbeknownst to Miss Beatrice, Katty continued to scrub the floor at night for me, but I was required to do it after breakfast. My knees became badly bruised as a result, my hands raw and painful from the harsh soap.

Betsy tried to help. "Wash your hands at the sink in the kitchen more often and dry them well. Miss Beatrice won't criticize you for that. If I could do it for you I would, and I am sure Katty would too. You should cover your hands at night."

When Katty returned from the kitchen, Betsy asked for her advice. "Katty, what do you think? You see that Catherine's hands are swollen and red. What can she do to relieve the pain?"

In answer to Betsy's question, she said, "What I would tell ya we don't have. Maybe you could try rubbing them with butter."

I asked, "And how can I get any butter? Miss Beatrice watches me like a hawk. She probably knows how much butter is in the kitchen to the very ounce."

Katty said, "I'll get it for ya. Never you mind."

I don't know how she did it, but the following evening I discovered a thin slab of butter on a little plate on the nightstand next to my bed.

I wondered how Katty had managed that. We had been together for most of the day. I could not recall a time when she had been gone.

I had just discovered this act of kindness when a slight noise alerted me that someone was following close behind me. Fearing the worst, expecting Miss Beatrice would discover the butter before I even had a chance to use it, I turned toward the sound. With a huge sigh of relief, I swallowed my fears as Katty slipped quietly into the room behind me.

"Now wash your hands, lovey, and I'll rub the butter into your skin. I found a petticoat in the wardrobe and I tore it up to make bandages for ya hands."

To my surprise, Betsy had somehow slipped in at the same time Katty did. She worried out loud about the use of the petticoat, "I hope Miss Beatrice doesn't go looking in the wardrobe too soon."

"Ah, she'll get over it," Katty replied. "The woman's got no feelings."

I wore my bandages for the next several nights. Betsy would wrap my hands each night with loving care. My hands felt a lot better as we continued this treatment for many days.

One night, when we had some time before we slept, I asked Betsy, "Do you think I should tell Katty of our past and who we really are?"

Betsy's reply was one of caution, "I know that Katty has been of great help to you, but I worry that if you tell her she might turn against you."

I answered, "That very well might be, but I feel I need to be honest with Katty. She has been so kind to me."

Betsy's reply wasn't what I wanted to hear, "I only have your best interests at heart. I don't know if it would be wise. What have you got to gain if you tell her? Why don't you find out more about her? What happened to her in England? Why was she sent to the colonies? Does she have family back in England? Be interested in her story! What is she planning to do when her time here is over?"

I felt regretful and replied, "I know what you say is true. I have felt consumed by my duties and troubles. I should have thought of that already. I have taken no thought to inquire about her life and what her worries and challenges might be. But if I ask her these sorts of questions, I've no doubt she'll ask the same of me."

"Well, that could be true too. If I were you, I'd let some time pass. Let her know that you appreciate all she does for you. When and if you tell her, make sure I am present."

I answered, "Yes, I know you are right of course. I'll continue to think about it."

Some weeks later, we three were in our room earlier than normal. I looked at Betsy and suspected she knew what I was going to say.

I began, "Dear Katty, Betsy and I have been keeping a secret and I feel you should know. I want to tell you the truth about Betsy and me. We are here in this devilishly hot country because I made a terrible mistake."

Realizing that Katty would imagine that I meant some criminal deed. I hurried to explain. "It is nothing criminal, but a terrible mistake and entirely my own fault."

My name is Catherine Bannister. My father is Baron Robert Kensington. He owns lands in Sheffield. My husband is Lord Edward Bannister, Lieutenant-Governor over the North-Western Provinces in India."

Katty's eyes opened in disbelief. She opened her mouth as she was about to protest, but instead nodded slightly at me to continue as she looked on skeptically.

"It's a long story," I said. "And I know it sounds ridiculous, but it is true, Betsy can testify to it.

It began when Betsy and I were fed up with the monotony of our days. It felt like we were locked up in the stuffy confines of Blakewood

House. It felt like we were trapped there, with a butler and maids hovering around us and never a moment to call our own. We just wanted some freedom! We chatted, in jest, about having an adventure and sneaking out of Blakewood House without anyone knowing. We thought we would go over to the East End. We were curious to have a look around and see how the poor folk lived.

I fancied we should disguise ourselves so that no one would know who we were. Betsy argued with me and told me it might turn out badly, but I took no heed to her warnings. Now I berate myself continually because I was so wrong. I threatened to go by myself knowing that if I did Betsy would give in and go with me. And yes, she did.

We knew it would be inappropriate to dress as we normally did, so we found two tatty dresses and soiled and tore them a bit to make them look more worn. We made up names in case we were asked, but truthfully, I didn't think we would have to tell anyone. We made sure not to wear any jewelry or cosmetics and refrained from using any scented waters.

Betsy suggested I try to drop some of my consonants when talking and make my words sound different.

What was it she said? 'Ya otter be 'ore carin' if ya be 'inking it be right.

But all that is trite in comparison to our tale.

We were looking in a store where cloth was being sold. I picked up a bolt of cloth and told Betsy to tell the shopkeeper I was going to buy it. I took it outside into the light to see the color better.

I can still hear the shopkeeper's words: "Excuse me Missus, Where do you think ya be goin' with that bolt of cloth?"

I said, "I am just going out in the light to see if I like the color." I had forgotten my attempt at plain speaking.

He responded, "A likely story that be, who in the 'ell do ya think ya be, talking like that. Do ya think by pretending to be a toff ya gunna make me be thinking, I'm go-in above me station and I'm gunna let ya off? Ya must think I'm a right nit."

"Then he grabbed Betsy and wouldn't let her go despite me trying to pull her away from him. He called to two ruffians who were walking by and had them take us and beat us. When they left us, we searched for a constable and then he wanted to see the shop where we were going to buy the bolt of cloth from."

When I was telling our story to Katty, she could scarcely conceal her disbelief. Listening to the story, and considering how unlikely it sounded, I thought I was going to be called a 'mad woman' again by the end of my tale.

When she didn't stop me, I continued with our story, "As I think back, that was the stupidest thing I have ever done. Betsy had said the east end was full of thieves and vagabonds. We had no idea that some police were just as bad! If only I had listened to Betsy, this would never have happened. I am entirely to blame.

I said earnestly, "The judge who sentenced us to this miserable fate was cold and evil. He refused to even try to check our story. He deliberately ignored me when I told him that it all had been a terrible mistake. I would never commit such an unforgivable act. We had given false names because we didn't want it to be known that I was in that part of the town. I pleaded, 'Please check with your superiors.'"

I described the experience for Katty as if he was there before us, "He became enraged and scowled at us fiercely when I told him who I really was. He didn't seem to be in control of himself. The scorn fairly dribbled from his tongue when he snarled at me.

"You are but a woman of little worth, a street trollop; I don't seek out my superiors for the likes of you. Get them out of here!"

For a moment Katty looked disbelieving, but when Betsy confirmed my words, she looked at me thoughtfully and asked, "Why didn't you report your identity to the authorities?"

Both Betsy and I smiled bitterly. I answered, "We tried that several times, but it didn't work. Twice when we were on the hulk we sent out messages to Edward's brother, Henry, but both were intercepted."

Katty asked, "Where was your husband then?"

I replied, "He was in North-Western India. I had no way of getting word to him."

"On the hulk, where they put us to wait for transportation, I made several attempts to affirm my identity, but no one would listen. I told the policeman who arrested us, the judge, the jailer on the hulk and the head trooper on the ship we came over on. They all agreed that it was unlikely a judge would convict and sentence a lady of nobility without checking her story. It seemed easier for them to believe I was insane than to accept my claim that I am an innocent victim of cruel injustice. I was labeled a 'mad woman.'

Every time I opened my mouth and proclaimed my innocence, the jailers would laugh, and the other convicts mocked and scorned me. Betsy did as much talking for me as possible because we were so tired of rebuke and contempt.

I have always been a great believer in the adage, 'what goes around, comes around.' Although I must admit, I don't know how my tale could be more turned around than it is. I wonder if I will ever be acknowledged for who I really am again. If Edward ever finds us, I will make sure he knows how badly we have been treated, and he will find out why no one would listen to our claims."

Betsy looked up from Catherine's journal and said, "I think we better stop there for today, Elizabeth. I think we will be able to finish Catherine's journal next time you come."

I walked over to the corner of the room and rang the bell for Woods.

Elizabeth had been riveted by the story for several hours. It was clear that she found the narrative moving.

"I consider it an honor that you have taken the time to read dear Catherine's story to me," she said. "I can see how you might fret over such an ordeal, even though it's in the past. Please, dear Betsy, look to the future. No matter what you end up doing, it will be far better."

"Yes," I replied. "My thoughts go back there. I wonder what we could have done differently to have stopped it all. I shouldn't have given in to Catherine's pleas to go to the east end, but after we became convicts there was very little I could do."

Elizabeth said with conviction, "Not very much from what I can see. You made the best of beastly, inhuman conditions. I am moved by your courage in the face of such challenges."

I could see Elizabeth was struggling to find the right words as she was clearly upset.

"I know that you and Catherine have suffered immensely," Elizabeth said. "I want you to know that I recognize that. My heart aches for you. In some ways I blame Edward. If he hadn't spent so much time in India none of this would have happened. Mind you, never speak of this to Edward. I feel sure he already blames himself for dear Catherine's ordeal."

I acknowledged, "Yes, he does. He spoke of it while we were on the ship coming home. I hope being in the country with Catherine will lift his feelings."

Elizabeth turned to face Betsy, "You mustn't allow those trials to overcome you. We need to look forward and get on with our lives. As you have shared dear Catherine's journal with me, Betsy, I feel like I have found a new friend. I am fortunate to have been your new friend over these past weeks. But let's not begin our friendship on your misfortune. Let us rejoice that you are alive and we have come to know each other."

I blushed. The sudden affirmation of Elizabeth's friendship left me feeling tearful. I found myself struggling not to break down. Apart from Catherine, no one else had befriended me as Elizabeth had.

With a quiet knock at the door, Woods arrived at that moment with lunch. The distraction gave me a few moments to compose myself before we resumed our conversation.

As we took our seats at the table, Woods placed the food on the table which he had previously set that morning. I told him the lunch looked wonderful. Potato and leek soup in a soup tureen and delicious warm white rolls. Special little cake delicacies and a pot of tea.

After he placed the food on the table Woods addressed me, "May I pour your tea Ma'am?"

"No, thank you, Woods," I replied. "I'll do it after we have our soup."

When he left the room, Elizabeth picked up our earlier conversation. "Time is yet young for Catherine. She is a strong woman. I feel confident her memory will come back and if not, we can still enjoy time together."

Elizabeth continued, "I don't think many of our countrymen know how badly convicts are treated. When Edward starts to make ripples, he will do a good job I know. I feel confident he will stir things up without allowing anyone to demean Catherine. Surely, as human beings, we should look to the poor and needy with a far greater depth of understanding and benevolence than we do. To be sure, from now on I will."

12

Impressions

After we had poured a second cup of tea Elizabeth asked, "What was your impression of Australia?"

I allowed several moments to pass before responding. "Oh, it was very different from England. From what I could tell, Australia is a very large country. It was much hotter than England, and a somewhat hard and unforgiving place. It was less civilized, though I recognize that the English are trying to build up a new colony there and that will take time. It never got cold as it does here. During the summer it was quite hot, and the days were almost unbearable. They never really had winter like we do, just a rainy season, though at night it could sometimes get very chilly.

We had a fireplace in the room we shared with Katty. I gathered firewood that had fallen from the trees around the station. That was a bit scary because when Alf noticed me searching for wood, he warned me to watch out for snakes. I didn't want to accidentally pick one up."

Elizabeth remarked, "Mmm, I've heard about snakes, but I have never seen one. What a brave soul you are Betsy!"

"Maybe. After Alf saw my miserable attempt to collect wood and make a fire, he surprised us. One evening when we returned to our room, we discovered he had collected wood for us and arranged the kindling and paper in the fireplace. All we had to do was to light the fire. Thereafter, he often set a fire for us and put a stack of wood near the fireplace.

"You were fortunate to have Alf as your friend. But you, Betsy, you stood by Catherine. You are to be commended highly for staying faithful to her throughout the whole ordeal."

"I suppose so. I don't know. I didn't do any more than anybody else would under the circumstances."

Elizabeth raised an eyebrow, "No, Betsy, I don't believe that. Think about it. You were following Catherine, doing your duty. You could have very well blamed Catherine for putting you in such a difficult situation. No one would blame you for disliking Catherine after she put you in such hellish circumstances."

"Not likely, Elizabeth," I replied. "Catherine and I have been best friends for as long as I can remember. My dear muma taught me loyalty is a blessing to be cherished."

Elizabeth replied, "Maybe so. The Almighty will bless you for your loyalty to Catherine. Don't forget that!"

As Elizabeth stood to leave, she asked, "Would you mind getting Woods to tell my driver I am ready to go home now?

I rang the bell and almost immediately Woods appeared. He asked, "Can I be of assistance?"

"Would you tell Miss Banisters coachman she is ready to leave now?" I asked.

Woods, always agreeable, replied, "Certainly Ma'am."

While we were waiting, after Elizabeth had put on her coat, she told me, "Henry, Edward's brother, visited me last night and was asking about Catherine's situation. He asked if he might join us next time I come. His schedule will not permit a daytime visit. Would an evening visit be possible?"

"Certainly," I replied. "Edward made me promise that I would never take Catherine's journal out of Blakewood House. If you think it would be appropriate, why don't you both come here for dinner? I feel sure Mrs. Featherstone wants to show off her skills as a cook."

Elizabeth smiled saying, "Of course, it is appropriate. We can eat dinner at our brother's house without drawing unwanted attention. Think nothing of it."

"I am just a servant," I said. "I would hate for others to be critical of you for befriending me."

Elizabeth chuckled, "Didn't Edward direct me to you so you would share your experiences with me? Have you not been my friend? Were you not schooled alongside my sister-in-law? You are certainly no longer a servant. In my opinion, you should get the Most Distinguished Order of Saint Michael and Saint George award. Besides I couldn't care less what people think. For the few years I have left on this earth, I shall continue to do as I want. Henry and I will look forward to it. Friday then? I shall tell Henry, not just ask. Nonetheless, I am confident he will welcome the opportunity."

I was thankful Elizabeth explained her feelings, because inwardly I struggled, thinking that our friendship might hurt Elizabeth's social standing.

After considering things, I replied, "Yes, Friday about six. I shall look forward to it."

At that moment Woods arrived, "The coach is here," he said.

Elizabeth gave me a hug and was gone. I knew Woods would assist her as she stepped into the coach.

After Elizabeth left, I made my way to the kitchen and spoke to Mrs. Featherstone. "I am having company for dinner on Friday. Lord

Edward's sister, Miss. Elizabeth Bannister, and his brother, Mr. Henry Bannister."

Mrs. Featherstone replied, "Well there you are, Miss Betsy, now you will see how a real meal should be cooked."

"I thought we might have three courses; soup and one of your roasts, followed by a desert, perhaps apple pie? Does that suit?" I asked.

Mrs. Featherstone nodded genially, "Just as you want, Miss Betsy. What time would you be havin' the meal then?"

I considered it thoughtfully, "They are coming at six, but we won't want to eat until six-thirty. I was hoping you might make some hors-d'oeuvres for us to have prior to dining."

Mrs. Featherstone replied confidently, "You are not to be worried, Miss Betsy. It will be just as you hope. We've never had real dinner guests since I started workin' 'ere."

Later that day I spoke to Woods, "I've told Mrs. Featherstone we are having dinner guests on Friday, I'd appreciate it if you would see that it runs smoothly."

Woods bowed slightly, "Of course, Miss Betsy, you have no need to worry. Might I ask what time your guests are coming?"

"They should arrive at six, but we won't sit down to eat until six-thirty," I replied. "I have asked Mrs. Featherstone to make some hors-d'oeuvres."

I was excited as I dressed to dine for the evening. I was dabbing on a little rouge when I heard the bell ring. That would be Mr. Bannister I thought. Elizabeth would have knocked. In either case, I knew that Woods would answer it. I had told him to take them into the drawing room, so I hurried to make my way there. I slipped into the room and was ready to welcome them.

Woods took their coats and escorted them to meet me. I felt flush as I welcomed them. I felt very inadequate, but, having served at tables many times, I took comfort in the knowledge that I knew how to conduct the evening as any lady should.

As they walked into the room, I welcomed them, "I am so pleased to see you Elizabeth and Mr. Bannister. I am sure if Lord Edward were here, he would be most pleased. It's wonderful to have you here."

I hadn't seen Mr. Bannister since returning to London.

Elizabeth sat down and Mr Bannister came up to me, smiling. "It's so good to see you, Betsy," he said. "I've heard you have been a lifesaver to Catherine."

"I don't know about that," I replied, embarrassed by the familiarity.

Elizabeth's remark deepened my embarrassment, "She is far too humble. Our dear Betsy won't admit to any benignity."

I shared a smile and a slight hug with Henry, surprised that Henry didn't have some noble floozy with him. He was a well-known lady's man. I half imagined Elizabeth had foreseen the possibility and told him to come alone.

I spoke to Woods, who was standing by the door, "Get a drink for our guests please, Woods."

His reply was gracious, "Certainly Ma'am."

He turned to Elizabeth, "What can I get for you, Miss Banister?"

"Oh, I don't care too much for alcohol these days, but perhaps I will have just one. I'll have a sweet sherry, thank you."

Turning to Mr. Banister, Woods asked, "And you sir? What would you like?"

Henry looked briefly in his direction, "I'll have a whiskey and water, thank you."

Woods caught my eye and asked, "And for you Miss Betsy?"

I thought briefly, "I would like a sherry," but thought better of it and said instead, "I'll have a lemonade."

Henry began speaking to me as though I was the entire reason he had come. "There is so much I want to know, Betsy. Elizabeth tells me you have been reading Catherine's journal to her. Perhaps I could also read it sometime?"

"I suppose you could, sir, but Lord Edward gave me strict instructions not to let it go out of Blakewood House. That is why Elizabeth and I thought it best for you to come here as we conclude Catherine's journal."

Seeing my anxiety, Henry was quick to soothe my concerns, "Yes, I understand."

He continued, "When Edward came into the office last, he seemed anxious. But it was clear he was pleased to have found his Catherine. It's odd that Catherine still suffers memory loss even though this ghastly ordeal is over."

Elizabeth volunteered, "I spoke with my doctor. He says it is probably due to the illness she had just before Edward arrived in Australia."

Henry remarked, "Edward said you were abused horribly. I can't imagine how you survived it. Edward said it was despicable. Is that true?"

Elizabeth answered his question. "Yes, Henry, it was. But we don't want to dwell on it too much tonight. Anyway, I told you Betsy is going to read the last few pages of Catherine's journal after our meal."

The table was set beautifully. I had been confident that Woods could be trusted when it came to fine dining. In a strange way, I felt like I was an intruder. Even though I was part of the story myself, I hadn't quite gotten used to the idea that I was home. I felt sure that Henry wished Edward and Catherine were there, but Elizabeth maintained a steady, comfortable conversation with both me and Henry, treating me like one of the family.

After drinks had been poured, Woods offered everyone little plates of delightful hors-d'oeuvres. He returned a little later and announced that dinner was served. I asked Henry to sit at the head of the table and Elizabeth across from me.

All through dinner I kept wondering at my change of fortune. This was another undeniable first in my experience, to be part of a gathering in a noble household and to be accepted in the conversation.

During a lull in the conversation, I volunteered, "I asked Mrs. Featherston to cook us a roast, but first we shall have vegetable soup."

Henry remarked, "That sounds good. I rarely get to have good, home-cooked food. My butler, Edwards, normally puts a few things together for me, but much of the time I eat out."

The soup was served in a tureen and Woods ladled some into our bowls. He also placed a basket of oven-fresh rolls and two little plates of butter curls on the table.

During the meal, Henry was jovial and quite the charmer. I understood more fully why he was considered a lady's man.

He asked. "What will you be doing now, Betsy? Elizabeth tells me you are no longer a servant and my brother is going to find a house nearby for you."

"Yes, that is his intention," I replied. "It's very kind, but I don't know that I'm deserving of it."

"If my brother says so, he has undoubtedly made the right decision," Henry replied cheerfully. "Edward is seldom wrong about such things and usually makes wise choices. He has worked with me from time to time and I have found him to be a reliable judge of character."

He frowned thoughtfully before continuing, "Nevertheless, it is troubling to me that he went away to India again, leaving you and Catherine to try an adventure which turned out so badly."

When Woods removed our soup dishes, I thanked him. He bought in dishes of roasted vegetables, green peas and gravy boats filled with delicious smelling gravy. He returned and bought in a sizeable roast of beef.

Turning to me he asked, "Would you like me to carve the meat Ma'am?"

"Yes, please do," I replied. "Thank you, Woods."

When each of us had settled into our meals, Elizabeth said, "My, Betsy what a delicious meal. I think your cook must be complemented yet again."

I was pleased. This was a dinner of my dreams. I said as much. "Yes, I agree with you. I will express my gratitude to her."

There was not a lot of time for talking. The meal was most enjoyable. Woods took our plates and removed the excess dishes from the table as we finished.

"I hope you have saved some room for apple pie," I said. "I asked Mrs. Featherstone to make it. She said she had little experience in preparing pastries. We will have to see."

Woods returned with the pie and three dessert plates.

"Would you like me to serve, Ma'am?"

"Yes, Woods. Thank you."

As Woods went to serve the pie, I said, "Not too much for me."

The pie was wonderful. I mentally contrasted it to the food on the convict ship. I did that almost every time I had a good meal. I hoped the need to compare everything to those days and those times would go away, that someday I would be able to just feel whatever feelings I had without that backward look.

After the meal, we returned to the drawing room where I had put Catherine's journal. Woods had a warm fire burning so the temperature of the room was comfortable.

As I walked over and gathered it up, I remarked to Mr. Banister, "These are just the final pages. Catherine has written a good deal more covering the entire period from the time we were imprisoned to her last days in Australia."

Henry said, "Yes, as I said, perhaps I could come by Blakewood House some time and read it fully?"

I could see no harm in that. "As you wish, Sir," I replied.

Henry caught the formality of my tone and smiled devilishly. "Oh, come now Betsy, don't Sir me. You are among friends here."

I flushed deeply, aware of the handsome man and his devilish smile in a way that made me feel …well I couldn't quite explain it. But looking around at both Henry and Elizabeth, and seeing their smiles and friendly faces, I realized that he was merely teasing.

Henry continued, "My brother, Edward, told me that you were no longer a servant and you were to be treated with respect. I will certainly do that. Anyway, let's hear what the final pages of Catherine's journal say."

I looked at Henry as I said, "When we were in Australia as convicts both Catherine and I were in service. I was a lady's maid, but poor Catherine was a kitchen hand. The woman who oversaw us had a high opinion of herself and treated Catherine poorly.

I began to read Catherine's journal.

"After endless days of following Miss Beatrice's orders, I half imagined that somewhere behind the harsh exterior she displayed there might be some understanding and tenderness. Eventually, these thoughts led me to confide in her about my identity.

You know, Miss Beatrice, I am not the person you think I am. It has all been a wicked mistake. Betsy and I were sentenced for a crime we didn't commit. I had my own household and my husband is Lord

Edward Bannister. He is the Lieutenant Governor over the North-Western Provinces of India."

"So then why didn't your husband speak up for you?" she asked skeptically.

"He was away at the time we were arrested and sentenced. The trial was a hasty affair based on trumped-up charges."

She replied, "That sounds a little trite. Where was he then?"

I replied. "In India, doing his duty for England."

She retorted, "Then you could have contacted him."

I said earnestly. "Believe me we tried! We tried to contact Edward's brother who practices law in London. My father is a baron.

Miss Beatrice seemed perplexed and asked, "What be your name then, before you married this so-called Lord?"

I quickly replied, "Kensington."

When I told her my family owned lands in Sheffield, she instantly took note of what I was saying. I even think I saw a tear in her eye when she told me, "I was born in Sheffield. That is where my parents were condemned to a life of poverty and shame. There was a Baron Kensington who caught them stealing food-stuffs from one of his properties. He immediately dismissed them and let it be known they were shameful, dishonorable people. They had worked in his employ for many years. They were only taking food to some of his tenants who were suffering because of the high taxes he had imposed on them. After being dismissed they could not find work in Sheffield so they moved to London. But work was scarce, so it was the workhouse for us. Both my mama and da died within a few months of each other. Perhaps that Kensington was a relation of yours?"

Her demeanor changed then. Her face hardened to an angry scowl. She became brusque and quickly dismissed me by saying, "You said you are not the person I think you are. You are wrong about that. I know exactly who you are. You are a dirty convict named Catherine Lancaster who cleans my kitchen and launders my clothes. I don't want to hear any more rubbish about how innocent you are. You must not continue with such ridiculous foolishness. It is complete and utter nonsense. Get to scrubbing the floor. Make sure you do a good job as I'll be inspecting."

I wanted to protest, but her scorn made me shiver with dread. That was a turning point. From that moment on her attitude toward me became decidedly worse. That night, I told Betsy what I had done, and how badly Miss Beatrice had spoken to me.

Betsy responded, "You know…you never seem to know when to hold your tongue. You have made things harder for yourself again. That Miss Beatrice, she thinks she is the Almighty's gift to us all."

By the time I finished scrubbing the floor my hands were bleeding. I washed them and then Miss Beatrice came in. She looked at the floor and noted there were a few drops of blood.

"What's this then?" She asked mockingly, "Pretending that you are bleeding too? I'll not be deceived by such stupidity."

Katty responded, "It's real. Look at her hands."

As Miss Beatrice looked at my hands, she responded, "Yes, Katty, don't you get in cahoots with her. She has taken some red dye from the pantry. What a fraud you are! Clean up those spots on the floor and then get on with your duties. Have you started the cheese today?"

Realizing that nothing good would come from any denial I might offer, I answered quietly, "Yes, Miss Beatrice, the milk is curdling."

I was grateful that Katty had explained what I was expected to do and how to do it.

I wasn't well, I decided. I felt faint and tired and a cough I had acquired on the ship before we reached this God forsaken land continued to plague me. While we had been on the ship it was a nuisance, but now the cough tore at my chest as I tried to do my work. As my body began to fail me, my failing mind fixed on one single idea, if only Edward would come.

Occasionally Betsy came down to the kitchen, braving the wrath of Miss Beatrice and coming to my defense. While being browbeaten by Miss Beatrice because I had been slow in doing the household's breakfast dishes, Betsy happened to come along.

Miss Beatrice remarked coldly. "Catherine Lancaster, you are slothful and lazy. You should have been done by now."

Though I knew it was hopeless, for the first time I defended myself, "I have been working hard. You can see my fingers are bleeding".

It was clear she wasn't having a bar of this. Miss Beatrice continued "There will be no dinner for you unless you put your mind to what you are doing."

What little food I had for a day was mainly eaten at dinner time. For breakfast, I was permitted to eat the scrapings from the pot which had been used to make porridge. For lunch, I was told I could take a slice of bread and cheese. And, if I was lucky, a cup of tea. For these meals, I was not permitted to eat my food with the other servants. I had to eat my food while I was working. When I was able to complete my work in good time, I was permitted to eat at the servant's table.

Betsy pleaded leniency for me, pointing out to Miss Beatrice that I was a real lady in every sense of the word. I can well remember her words.

"What is wrong, Miss Beatrice?" she said. "You know she does the best she can. You can't expect her to adapt to this sort of work so quickly. Whoever heard of a real lady scrubbing floors and doing servants work? Back in England, she could have had a thousand servants. Now she is treated as if she is the lowliest of them all. She never complains, never talks back to you. Haven't you noticed she always tries to be pleasant no matter how harshly she is spoken to?"

I looked at Betsy with admiration and thankfulness. Having stepped into the fire she added yet more fuel to it, "She is to be admired. She is a woman of great integrity and she is very dear to my heart."

Miss Beatrice replied scornfully, "She has talked you into making up this ridiculous tale. It is all a lot of nonsense. No magistrate would dare convict a lady! Some lady she is! Ha!"

She continued contemptuously, "What's made you two think up a story like that then? The way she talks? That is all a part of this stupid nonsense."

Betsy replied with such a look of earnestness, "Catherine's father is a Kensington. Haven't you heard of the House of Kensington?"

It is odd, that remark made Miss Beatrice flash those dark eyes of hers in sheer hatred. She could barely control herself as she continued, "For some reason, unbeknownst to me, she has you under her thumb.

Both of you are stupid and your beloved Lady will be dealt with accordingly."

I didn't know what prompted these remarks, though she clearly associated the Kensington name with something very evil. Surely, I thought, it must have stemmed from some past event in her life, though I was in no position to ask.

Poor Betsy became the subject of more ridicule from Miss Beatrice than she had possibly anticipated.

Miss Beatrice continued "You are to stop helping her. It is your responsibility to prepare the household's table, assisting Robert and helping the real lady of the house, not fussing over some 'would be lady' who is nothing more than a gutter tramp."

I confided in Betsy that night with tears in my eyes, "I just feel as if I can't go on. She treats me as if I were swine. Despite her ill-treatment of me, I have struggled to go on. I don't seem to be getting any better. My coughing and chest pain are unceasing."

Though Betsy listened sympathetically, she seemed pre-occupied. I wasn't sure why she seemed hesitant to talk to me. But, when she finally decided to share what was bothering her, what she said re-kindled a glimmer of hope within me.

"I overheard something tonight amongst the talk of the dinner guests. Can you imagine what it was? Evidently, there is news that a lady of nobility has been sent to Australia as a convict."

I quickly hastened to ask her if she had said anything, but I should have known better. She had learned early in life that servants remained silent during dinner. She had not responded to the news in any way.

Nevertheless, the next day, it was my dear Betsy who knocked on the master's study door to ask that he would listen to what she told him and to hear what I had to say.

CHAPTER

13

Recognition at last

I don't know what Betsy said to the master, but that very same day I was sent for by the master himself. As I walked behind Betsy towards the study door, my heart was beating so hard I almost couldn't breathe. As we knocked on the door, I asked myself if this was really happening. As we approached the door I was beset with a bout of coughing. Betsy left me with a smile and a hug as I heard a voice bid me come in.

The master and I greeted one another, though I could barely respond without falling into another bout of coughing.

"Betsy has told me you are the lady of nobility whom my guests and I were talking about last night during dinner. I suspect you both have conjured up a tale. If it be true, what is your real name?"

"I am Lady Catherine Bannister."

Although I could tell he suspected that I was lying, he continued questioning me.

"Are you married?

"Yes, sir," I replied.

He prompted, "Your husband must have a name?"

"My husband is Sir Edward Bannister, Lieutenant Governor over the North-Western Provinces of India."

His face darkened somewhat, as though weighing what questions he might ask that he knew the answers to. "Are your parents still alive?"

"Yes," I replied. "My dear mother and father sold Blakewood House and its properties to my beloved Edward and they have moved to their country estate as my mother's health is poorly."

He prodded, as though this was a question that might sift the wheat from the chaff. "And where in the country?"

His questions seemed endless. Finally, he asked, "How long have you been in service here?"

"I can't answer that truthfully as the days have seemed to run into each other. The work I have been required to do is monotonous and tiring."

He continued, "Do you remember a great event in England two years ago?

I kept going over it in my mind and then finally it came to me, "King William the 4th was coronated as King, As I remember it was during the month of September 1831."

He seemed frustrated for a moment. "That was a silly question, I suppose. All of England will know that."

After another moment, he continued, "There were celebrations amongst the nobles. What do you remember of them?"

Hope beamed even more brightly when I remembered, though I had difficulty speaking because of my coughing, "I remember now. Duke Marsden held a party that went until dawn. Everyone was there."

I think he was trying to trick me when he asked, "Was it a 'Lloyd Marsden?"

I knew perfectly well it was Henry, his older brother. I remembered that Lloyd had gained fame because of his political writings. He had a twin brother whom Edward and I had never met. We had heard that he came to help colonize this country. I told him so. "No, No! It was his brother, Henry."

He asked, "What about Henry? Was he married when he held this party?'

I told him what I thought. "I don't think Henry married until sometime later."

I thought to myself this master knew a lot about goings-on back in England. How is this possible?

I ventured to say, "I was there. I remember these things. How is it that you know so much about that party? I don't remember seeing you there."

The master spoke quietly, "It is true. I wasn't there. But I am in contact with my brothers often."

This remark made me wonder.

More questions followed. While I realized the reason for his questions, it was also very fulfilling to be able to talk about such wonderful old times, things I had no reason to discuss for many months.

After much talk, there was a profound stillness in the air apart from my coughing.

Then he stood and walked over to me and said, "Yes, I believe you."

I was overjoyed.

He asked, "Do you know my name?"

"No, I don't know your name, I only know you as the master."

When he told me who he was, I felt that somehow, in a way that I couldn't understand, fate had redeemed me!

"I am George Marsden, brother of Henry, and twin brother of Lloyd. I am known in Australia as George Mars. While there is much to be said for this country, I sometimes miss the lush countryside of

England. Anyway, I will send word to England immediately. They say your husband has been searching everywhere for you."

"You need to be somewhat healthier before we can send you back," he said. And then, with a growing awareness of my present state, he continued, "Or perhaps he would like to come to get you. I'll get a runner to take word to Sydney now, but it will be three months before your husband receives it. Ships leave Sydney regularly."

As my coughing continued, he became concerned. "You are shivering on such a warm day and your cough sounds dreadful. I'll fetch my wife. She will ensure that you are well looked after. As he went off, I felt delighted. Of course, it meant that Betsy and I would have to wait until Edward came for us. Thoughts of Miss Beatrice drifted in my mind. At least I knew I would no longer have to serve under her.

I had never seen Lady Mars. I had always imagined her as being a tall big-boned woman with an air of grace about her, so I was naturally surprised to see a rather stout little woman who looked more like a duck than a swan. Nonetheless, she proved to be a kindly soul and asked me how long I had been feeling so poorly. I could hardly answer for my coughing. Fortunately, Betsy joined Lady Mars and related many of the ordeals which we had been through. I must have looked ill because she ordered that one of the guest bedrooms be made ready for me and then ordered me to bed. Lady Mars told me she had sent for the doctor.

The next thing I remember, I was in a bed like the one I had back in England and the doctor was standing over me saying, "You have a fever and must stay in bed for as long as it takes to return to full health."

He hadn't told me anything I didn't know. Lady Mars had told me the same thing. The doctor gave Lady Mars a bottle of medicine and instructed her how often I was to take it. I was to be fed soup and, as

I could tolerate it, other wholesome foods. I had grown weary of the plain bland food Miss Beatrice had permitted me to eat. But now, as I was allowed a wider variety, and it was presented in a more appealing manner, I began to enjoy it more. I also rejoiced that Edward would soon be on his way to get me. I decided I would try to eat and get well for his sake.

It was at this point that I decided to write this narrative of my experiences over these past many months. I was determined to tell Edward all about our sad experiences. Betsy insisted that she would only help me find writing materials if I gave her my assurance that I would eat what she brought to me.

I began to improve a little. I decided that my improvement must have been because of the quality and quantity of the food that Betsy bought for me several times during the day. Most of all, I believe it was the knowledge that my dear Edward was coming for me.

As I was writing one morning, the master knocked on the door and came in and shared the good news that my dear Edward was bound for Australia. There was a good deal of cargo and human traffic arriving in Australia. The captain of the most recent ship, the HMS Portland notified the Governor and he notified me. Your husband will arrive on board the HMS Morton which is expected to dock within a month's time. This news cheered me as nothing else could. I was happy even despite the interminable coughing which seemed to be my constant companion.

The master came to my room one morning and asked, "What are you writing?"

"I am putting some of my experiences on paper, so I will remember to share them with Edward."

He looked a little concerned. Undoubtedly, given my circumstances for the past year, he was wondering if he was responsible for my condition. I could tell he was only half jesting when he said, "I hope you have good words to say about my wife and me."

I immediately tried to ease his concern. I knew he might not have been aware of me personally, even though I was a member of his household. "Indeed, I will speak highly of both you and your dear wife. You have been nothing but kind to me. However, in all honesty, there is one in this household who treated me harshly and with inhuman contempt."

He asked, "And who might that be?".

I debated whether to answer his question. I appreciated the hospitality he had shown Betsy and I since learning of our plight. Nevertheless, the hatred and abuse Miss Beatrice had heaped upon me left me little choice.

I spoke solemnly, "Miss Beatrice."

"I don't understand," he said. "She has run this house for the past five years. Nothing has ever gone amiss while she has been in charge. I will have to speak to her."

He continued, "She came out to the colony with the first fleet as a girl. Her parents were both dead. According to her, some baron treated them very badly. Oddly enough, his name was also Kensington. Evidently, her parents were caught stealing from his household and she was with them. They had to move to London to try to get work but, because of the stories that had been spread about them, they ended up in a poorhouse and subsequently died within two years. She blamed her parents' ruin on the baron, I suspect that is why she doesn't care much for the upper class. I have given her every respect and she has done well by me."

My illness had taken a turn for the worse. I realized I could not follow the conversation any longer. I begged his understanding, "I feel very tired now, Lord Mars, if you would excuse me, I feel I must sleep."

Betsy closed the journal and spoke to Elizabeth and Henry, "Unfortunately, Catherine never made another entry to her journal before Edward came to join us. But while we were on the ship coming home, I tried to complete Catherine's story."

Henry and Elizabeth listened attentively.

"As I read the final chapter," I said, "I shall try to hold back my tears. I don't know why it has that effect on me. Surely, we were saved, and our future looked reassuring. This is what I wrote."

Dear Catherine wrote no more. For the rest of that day she slept. In the days following, both Lady Mars and I tried to get her to eat, but it was with mixed success. The only food she was able to keep down was broth. She slept fitfully over the next two weeks, and sometimes when she spoke, her words were understandable, but at other times she was clearly delirious.

The master sent for the doctor again, but he could do little. We all thought she was close to death. I kept reminding her that Edward was on his way to take us back to England. Surprisingly, over time she began to keep more food down. I think that saved her. Gradually she strengthened. Both the master and his wife encouraged me to sit with her. They were worried and hoped that her health might not deteriorate.

With unmistakable emotion, Henry interrupted my narration. "Understandably so."

I continued, "I prayed to the good Lord, 'Please keep her alive so she can see her dear Edward.'

I sat by her bedside for several weeks. Indeed, the weeks turned into a month. As I talked, I reminded her that Edward was on his way to take us back. I reminded her of Blakewood House and the games we used to play when we were children. I reminded her of her mother and father and their home in the country. I just kept talking because I didn't know what else to do. I don't know if she heard anything I said, but I felt encouraged when she started to eat more. Soups, custard, and jellies. One or two slices of bread."

Elizabeth remarked, "Yes, it must have been encouraging to see her eat a bit more."

I continued reading.

"Often Catherine would eat but then return to her pillow and sleep. She was never awake for very long and, when she woke, each time there was a sense of alarm about her. She no longer seemed to recognize her surroundings, asking each time she woke, "Where are we? Is this where we live? I don't recognize this room. Tell Miss Beatrice I will scrub the floor as often as she wants, but I'll have to put bandages on my hands."

It pained me to see her worry. "Hush. Don't worry Catherine. It will be all right. Don't you remember? We live in England. There was a terrible mistake. Try to remember the ship journey and how we were half starved. Try to remember the journey from Botany Bay to here with Alf and little Toby in the carriage. Remember how hard you have worked."

Catherine looked at me blankly. "Betsy we will have to ask Miss Beatrice if we can have some blankets as it's getting cold at night now. I hope my dear muma and da will visit soon or maybe we should visit them. You arrange it, Betsy."

I panicked. What was happening? Was Catherine losing her mind?

Catherine made similar comments over several days. I told the master and his good wife of my fears. Each day they would go into her room and remind her of her identity and ask questions to try and recover her memory, but they tried in vain. Catherine's comments didn't make sense.

The doctor was called again. He sat at her bedside asking questions. "Do you remember your name?"

Her reply, "Betsy keeps telling me I'm called Catherine."

"Do you not remember coming to Australia on the ship?"

She was muddled, "No, not me. We came in a carriage. Can you make sure Toby is safe! Betsy, you are going to be his mother."

She rambled on, "Miss Beatrice will be wanting me to set the table. Would you tell her I'll do it tomorrow?"

Again, the doctor questioned her, "And what do you remember of Sydney town?"

"I remember the old ships and the cruel ropes."

The doctor asked, "Do you remember Edward, your husband?

At least I knew I had a place in her life when she said "Betsy keeps telling me I have a husband. Who is a husband?"

"He is the man you love, and he loves you. He will care for you and is on his way here now to take you back to England."

The doctor spoke to the master, his wife, and me in the hall.

"I think it's some form of shock. Just be caring of her. Keep reminding her of who she is. Talk about good times and good memories. I'll give you a tonic. It might help. When she sees the people she loves, she might pull out of it. You'll need to be patient with her. It might take some months. But she seems well enough now. I suggest you get her up for a few hours each day as she gets a bit stronger physically."

The master had already excused me from any household duties. My place was at Catherine's side for as long as she needed me. Occasionally her words made sense, but I felt sad and hoped she might be a little more recovered before Lord Edward arrived.

After breakfast the following day, I told Catherine, "The doctor suggests that you get up for a few hours each day."

Catherine asked, "You will help me, won't you?"

"Of course. You have no need to fear, Catherine."

She asked, "Can we go out in the yard together?".

My response was always the same, "Yes, but not for too long. You need to regain your energy."

As the weeks passed, Catherine continued to recover physically. She spent some of the days sitting with Lady Mars, but generally spent more time with me each day as we walked in the garden.

George Mars kept tabs on when the ships were due to arrive in Sydney and notified the governor that Lord Edward would be among the arrivals on the HMS Morten. When word came that the Morton had docked in Sydney, Edward was received formally by the governor and provided with accommodation while he was in Sydney. The master sent Alf and Toby to bring Lord Edward to the property.

I heard the master tell Alf to make sure he told Lord Edward Catherine had a memory problem, and the doctor believed it to be a type of delayed shock.

I asked Catherine often, "Do you remember your husband, Lord Edward?"

The oddity of her response brought sadness to my heart, "Do you know him too?"

"Catherine, do you remember the day you were married?" I asked.

She offered a hesitant response, "Not really."

Several weeks before Lord Edward's arrival, I felt the need to start preparing Catherine. I worried his arrival might cause her more trouble. "Lord Edward will be here soon, Catherine. He has come all the way from England to take us home."

Catherine frowned a little, not really grasping the situation. "But this is our home. What will Miss Beatrice say?"

I had a satisfying answer to that question. "We will never, ever, have to do what Miss Beatrice says again."

Over the following days, I continued to tell Catherine that Edward was coming. I asked her if she could remember what he looked like?

Of course, given her memory lapse, I felt certain it was a silly question. But Catherine's answer surprised me. She answered, "I only remember that he has blond hair."

I can't remember if that was something I had told her, but I hoped to myself that she was starting to remember.

Later in the day, I asked Catherine, "How do you know Lord Edward has blond hair?"

She replied, "I think I can remember Mother and Father. I was sitting eating food with them and a man was there with blonde hair. Maybe that is the Edward whom you say is my husband. I feel sure when I see Mother and Father I will know.

I asked, "So you remember your parents then?"

She answered, "Not really, but I do know they love me and you too Betsy."

As the time drew nearer for Lord Edward's arrival I continued to be worried for his sake. How I hoped Catherine would feel joy to see him.

As the days passed, I continued to encourage Catherine to remember. Still, I didn't want her to feel stressed. I think her only memory of Edward was the one she had described. She didn't seem to recollect anything else.

As the sun was going down, I looked out to the vast expanse of untamed land and felt melancholy. There would be joy in seeing Lord Edward again. But how would Catherine greet him?

The following morning, I told Catherine that Edward would be with us that night.

"I know he will be looking forward to seeing you," I declared.

Her innocent reply worried me, "And you too Betsy."

I repeated, "He is your dear husband, Catherine."

Her reply wasn't one I wanted to hear.

"Does that make a difference?"

Much later in the day, I exclaimed, "Catherine, come look out the window. There is a carriage coming toward the house!"

She looked but said impatiently, "Where? I can't see it."

I pointed to a mark on the horizon.

She said, "I am very curious. You say that he is my husband?"

I tried ever so much to get Catherine to remember, "Catherine, don't you remember how he loves you and you love him!"

Her response saddened me, "I love you, Betsy. You care for me."

"Edward cares for you too. He has come all the way from London to take us back with him."

As the carriage came nearer, we saw it pull up at the main entrance. Catherine's Edward got out and the carriage pulled away.

I think he must have shared words with the master, as he didn't come in to see Catherine straight away. But when he did, he walked up to Catherine and sat on the bed and circled her in his arms.

"Here's my dear and wonderful wife." He continued. "How I have searched for you! How I have missed you, my dear sweet Catherine."

I didn't think Catherine recognized him, but she too put her arms around him. I felt I should withdraw and allow them to be alone together.

"Catherine, I'm just going to the other room. If you need anything, just call. I am sure Lord Edward will help you also."

I stood up from my chair to go but then Edward turned to me and gave me a hug,

"Oh, Betsy I have also missed you. I've heard you have been at Catherine's side since this whole ghastly mess began."

"Yes, that is true, Lord Edward. We have been fortunate to stay together throughout all this time. We have had a difficult time but are so pleased to see you. How we appreciate you coming to take us home! I'd best be going now. I'll be in the next room if you should need me."

"Betsy you care for me. Why do you want to leave?" Catherine asked plaintively.

I think Edward realized why I felt I should go. He said, "I'm sure Betsy has much to do. Anyway, since I am here now, I can be with you all the time."

"But Betsy loves me." She replied sadly.

"That is true, but I love you ever so much also. Let me care for you, dear Catherine. Betsy can be here for you as often as you wish."

I retreated and know nothing of what Lord Edward said.

Perhaps he shared memories with her. I don't know, but Lord Edward asked me to stay with her for a few hours each day. I would take her lunch and just sit and talk. During such times Lord Edward would either read Catherine's journal or spend time with the master looking over the property. Lord Edward always shared breakfast and the evening meals with Catherine.

A few days later I was asked by the mistress to take Catherine's tonic to her. Lord Edward must have forgotten it when he took her breakfast.

At first, I listened at the door because I didn't want to intrude. I heard Edward say, "I have read your journal, Catherine."

"Yes, I have also," Catherine replied. "Betsy wanted me to. I don't remember it. It sounds like a nightmare. We are fortunate that we live here, and Betsy helps me."

"We live in England, dear one" Edward began. "After reading your journal I am really troubled. You were treated very badly. I would like to avenge you for all those who treated you so badly. I am truly sorry to think I left you to serve our country and by so doing allowed my fellow colleagues, if I can call them that, to turn your life into misery. I should have stayed with you. If I had stayed with you, none of this would ever have happened."

Sadly, Catherine's reply showed little understanding, "Well I don't know what you are talking about, Edward. That's all I know about it, and I have no idea what Miss Beatrice will say."

He reassured her, "Oh, Catherine, you shall never need to see that Beatrice woman again. Seeing that your health has improved, I will arrange for our return to England in a few weeks."

"Betsy, will she come? I can't leave without Betsy." Catherine declared.

"Of course," he replied. "Everything will be the same. I'll call for Betsy now. She will help you dress, and we shall have a look over this property again."

After a moment I knocked on the door and entered the room.

"We were just talking about you, Betsy," Edward said. "Would you help Catherine dress? We are going to look over the house and the buildings nearby. I am going to talk to George to organize our voyage back to England. I'll be back within the hour."

As Edward left the room, Catherine asked, "Will you be coming with me Betsy? Edward said you would."

"Of course," I replied. "All will be well. I am so pleased your Edward has found us and we three shall return to our beloved England."

"Is England so far away then? Even though you say I was born there, I can't remember."

I responded, "Yes, it is a long way, three or four months by ship, but the time will go quickly. You will share a nice cabin with Lord Edward. You need not fear. I will be in the next cabin and will see you often."

Catherine said thoughtfully, "I don't care much for the food they give you when you are at sea."

I noted that was another memory, but I didn't pursue it. I expect Catherine had tried to remember and I was hoping that she would when it was the right time.

In reference to the food, I responded, "You'll be pleasantly surprised. Things will be better than you can possibly imagine."

When Edward returned, he told us that Alf and Toby would be going to Sydney to arrange our voyage. "They are going to arrange a double cabin for you and me, Catherine, and an adjoining cabin for Betsy."

Catherine responded. "I really think we should ask Miss Beatrice. If not, I suspect she will make me scrub the floor twice".

I could sense Edward was feeling a little impatient, but he told Catherine quietly, "Forget Miss Beatrice. Forget all the bad things that have happened here, dear Catherine!"

"I shall try," she said timidly. "Will we be seeing Mother and Father soon?"

"If that is what you want, my love, yes indeed we will."

Lord Edward asked me, "Betsy, you can sew, can't you? The Mistress here says she has a few dresses that don't fit anymore. She said she would gladly give them to Catherine, but they would certainly need altering because Lady Mars is much heavier than Catherine. Could you see to them? We would surely appreciate it. I don't know if we will have time to purchase anything in Sydney."

"Of course," I replied. "I am not much of a seamstress, but almost anything would be an improvement over the rough clothing we've been required to wear. It is kind the mistress to offer clothing for Catherine. I'll see to them now and then join you at lunchtime, Catherine."

So that was the agenda for most of the remaining days in Australia. I worked to alter some of the mistress's dresses so that Catherine might have appropriate clothing, and Edward helped Catherine and encouraged her by his love and support to continue to improve.

When the time finally came for us to leave the property, I was sad to leave Toby. Of course, I believed it was for the best. He and Alf had grown very close.

Dear Katty, what a lifesaver she had been to Catherine! She came up to see Catherine before we left. That was a sad parting, but she had good news for us. She was allowed to leave the kitchen and take on my job as a lady's maid. Miss Beatrice had been sent back to the workhouse in Sydney and a new housekeeper had been found.

CHAPTER

14

Home

T he trip back to Sydney was as tedious as it had been the first time. It wasn't so much the heat on the return journey, but the flies were all over us, even in the carriage. Then too, it rained so hard that Alf stopped the carriage and told Toby to sit inside with us. I wasn't sorry. Spending a little time with him during our last few hours in Australia was a joy.

As he took the seat next to me, I sensed he felt some discomfort, so I told him, "I'll write to you and tell you how everything is going! You never know how the future will unfold. You might be a land owner one day."

Lord Edward added amiably, "You've surely got a good head on your shoulders for a young'un. Your master back at the property says he's going to get some schooling for you. If you can read and write you'll get on well lad, remember that!"

"Yes, sir. I'll do my best," Toby replied, acting older than his six years would suggest. One thing about little Toby, he was always polite and friendly.

As we came into Sydney, I said to Catherine, "The trip was long and difficult, but at least there is a bright light at the end of the tunnel. Sydney has grown since we were here before. Look, Catherine, there are a lot more houses."

Catherine frowned deeply. "I have never been here before. I don't know what you are talking about. When are we going home? You promised, Edward!"

Edward responded cheerfully. "Don't worry, my sweet. Our ship leaves in a few hours." His cheerful confidence turned Catherine's frown into a small smile.

When it came time to part with Alf and Toby, I was more emotional than I should have been. We all agreed that we would write to one another, but that didn't satisfy the hurt I felt. Catherine hugged Toby and told him she loved him. It was very like her I thought, but a little strange because of memory problems.

Lord Edward singled out Alf. "From all that I have read in Catherine's journal, you have been a great help to my wife and Betsy. I do thank you. You are a good man."

As he thanked Alf, Edward put a wad of money into his hand. "Keep up the good work with Toby. He needs you to set a good example."

Alf blushed. "Thank you, Sir. I've come to see Toby as one would a little brother or a best mate."

There was a big difference in age between them, but I could see Alf spoke from the heart.

Edward and Alf took our luggage down from the top of the carriage.

Catherine and I both hugged Toby. There was a tear in his eye, and, indeed, a tear in mine.

Alf looked a little upset when he said, "Toby and I had better be getting back. Take care, ladies. May you enjoy your trip."

As we walked onto the ship, I was grateful Lord Edward had his arm around Catherine. At first, she didn't want to board the ship, but with Edward's encouragement, she soon relented. A ship's officer greeted us and said he would accompany us to our cabins.

It was a far better-looking ship than we had come to this country in. Our cabins were delightful in comparison. Having a cabin for myself was remarkable. The only time I had ever had a room of my own was back at Blakewood House when my sister, Aggie, moved on to be with her husband. When last at Blakewood, I shared a room with Emmy, a parlor maid. I wondered if she would still be there when we returned.

I heard Edward say to the ship's officer, "They are staterooms I trust?"

The officer smiled. "Yes, of course, Lord Edward, they are the best cabins on board."

The officer escorted us downstairs to a corridor which had a series of doors. The first one he opened was for Lord Edward and Catherine, and the second door he opened was to be my home for the next three months.

To my surprise, staterooms, although tiny, came equipped with a mattress, linens, a washbasin, and some drawers. There was also a tiny mirror and a small desk. After I had unpacked my few belongings, I made my way to the top deck. There was a chill in the air, so I was grateful for my shawl.

As I walked about the deck, there was some resemblance to the HMS Barringer. There were three masts standing tall, and ropes of all sizes. Looking up at the forecastle, my thoughts immediately went back to that hard-hearted captain and that rogue Mr. Tottenham. They had made our existence like hell on earth. I walked from the stern to the bow. As I looked back at Sydney harbor, I remembered the heart-ache Catherine and I experienced. I recalled our fear of being separated. Now, on the verge of our departure, I felt that fortune had finally smiled on us.

After gazing a while at the harbor, I thought I should return to Lord Edwards and Catherine's cabin to see if they needed my help.

When I knocked on their cabin door, Edward quickly opened the door, greeting me cheerfully, "So pleased to see you, Betsy," he said. "Come in. Do you like your cabin?"

I smiled. "Yes, it is far better than I could have ever imagined."

Lord Edward responded agreeably, "Yes, Catherine and I are pleased as well. I have been trying to explain to Catherine. This voyage will be far different from her previous one."

Catherine remarked, "We don't have to sleep on a bench again."

I walked over to Catherine and put my arm around her. "We are no longer convicts or servants. We are traveling back to England where you will be treated like the lady that you are. That is why you have such a fine cabin."

Catherine looked pleased. "Thank you, Betsy. You have always told me the truth."

I thought perhaps Lord Edward might feel annoyed by Catherine's response. I immediately said, "Your dear husband, Edward, will always tell you the truth. He loves you so."

Catherine responded, "Yes, I know, but he didn't come with us on the other ship. So how can he know?"

"He has read your journal. He knows. He cares."

I thought to myself that Catherine must be starting to remember small snippets of the past. She remembered the convict ship. That was a start.

"We are invited to eat at the captain's table," Edward said. "But I would rather not. It could prove difficult for Catherine and I would rather not do that. Catherine and I will have our meals bought to us in our cabin. But you, Betsy, you may eat at the captain's table."

I felt alarmed, and I expect Lord Edward could tell from my expression that I feared the thought of sitting at the captain's table.

He said, "You may also have your meals bought to your cabin if you wish."

I replied quickly, "I am sure I would like my meals bought to me. I think I would feel uncomfortable sitting at the captain's table."

I would not have enjoyed the sort of questions I might be expected to answer at the captain's table. I could foresee too many ways for that to become awkward and uncomfortable for all concerned.

Edward put a hand on my shoulder gently and said, "Don't worry, Betsy. I will go up and notify the officer now. Could you stay with Catherine while I am gone?"

He really didn't have to ask as I still loved and enjoyed being with Catherine even though she had little memory of the times we both went through together.

After Lord Edward left, I put my arm around Catherine and said, "We are going home, Catherine. Isn't that what you have so dearly wanted?"

Her response was not very encouraging, "I don't know where my home is. Will Miss Beatrice be waiting for us? I long to see Mother and Father. Edward said we would see them."

I replied, "Yes, you surely will see your parents. You can forget Miss Beatrice. You will never see her again!"

Catherine's response, "That's what Edward keeps telling me. I will try and forget her. Now I am feeling tired. Would you mind if I slept for a while?"

I answered promptly. "Why would I mind? Can I help you take your dress off?"

Catherine murmured, "You have always cared for me. Thank you."

Lord Edward returned while Catherine was sleeping. As the cabin door opened, I put my finger to my lips to warn Edward not to speak too loudly as we shouldn't wake her. Lord Edward stepped closer and quietly whispered to me, "I have arranged for your meals to be sent to your cabin, but they will bring your evening meal here so we three can eat together."

I smiled and whispered back, "Thank you, Lord Edward, it's very kind of you."

One day stretched into another. I often went up on deck to feel the fresh air against my face. It felt good to be going home at last. I enjoyed looking at where the sea met the sky. It was a stark contrast to our journey to Australia.

Lord Edward came up to me asking, "What have you been thinking?"

I replied. "Oh, I have myriads of thoughts. They take me back to our past and forward to England. I keep thinking it's a miracle that you found us."

He responded, "Call it Providence, good luck, call it what you may. I can't imagine life without Catherine. I hope her memory will return soon, perhaps when she sees her parents."

Occasionally Lord Edward and Catherine walked together on the deck. Often Catherine was reluctant to do so because her memories of sea life were distorted. I hoped that was a good sign and that it meant her memory might be returning slowly.

One afternoon I came upon Lord Edward by himself looking out to sea. Without looking at me he said, "I have re-read Catherine's journal. I cannot understand how my own country-men could inflict such cruelty on their fellow men. I hope to cause havoc among them when we return, but I don't want it to reflect badly on Catherine. I wonder if there is any true justice to be had."

I replied cautiously, "People are the same the world over. You know that, Lord Edward. Many people are cruel and evil, yet others are quite the opposite. Even so, I can understand your feelings."

He suddenly pulled himself together as though it was inappropriate to be talking thus in front of me.

He said, "Yes, you are right of course. I sometimes let it get the better of me. I have been wanting to chat with you, Betsy."

He said, "When we return, you will no longer have need to be a servant again. I intend to provide a proper endowment for you that will allow you to live comfortably. You must stay at Blakewood House until I can find a small house for you."

I felt I was not deserving of such kindness and said, "Oh Lord Edward, it would not be appropriate for me. I have been a servant all my life. What will people think?"

He replied quickly, "I don't care what people think. Indeed, Betsy when it is appropriate, I will make it known that my wife wouldn't be alive if it weren't for you."

He continued, "You mustn't consider yourself unworthy. How many servants would defend someone in such circumstances? How many would stand up for those they served in such life-threatening circumstances? While I love my dear wife, it is you who have been the heroine. I forbid you to say anything else. Now I must go to dear Catherine. It has taken a little while for her to regain her trust in me. But I do believe she is starting to come around. I'll see you at dinner."

How pleased I was to enjoy my meals with Lord Edward and Catherine! For a while, Catherine didn't seem to want to join in any of our jokes. But, as time passed, Lord Edward and I could see that familiar gleam in her eyes when we were sharing some silly anecdote.

On our journey to Australia, I had no time or desire to enjoy the trip, but now everything was totally reversed. It was a pleasure to meet some of the other passengers and learn of their lives and joy as they returned to England. It was wonderful to know that I wasn't being watched by some trooper or that evil little man, trooper Tottenham.

I was chatting with a young trooper who was returning home when the seaman from up on the crow's nest called out, "land ahead," I ran to the starboard side to view our homeland. Both Lord Edward and Catherine weren't far behind me. Someone must have knocked on their cabin door to let them know. Catherine was so pleased. Yes, Lord Edward was correct. She looked more herself than she had in the past several months. This was indeed true as we docked.

There were crowds of people everywhere, but it was good to be on English soil again. Catherine seemed a little befuddled, but I saw Lord Edward put his arm around her and whisper some kindness to her.

One of the officers from the ship helped Lord Edward with our luggage. We had several cases. Lord Edward couldn't manage them all by himself. The officer flagged down a coach for us. They loaded our luggage and Lord Edward encouraged Catherine to step into the coach. She looked at Lord Edward and me, "You are both coming too or else I won't get in."

Lord Edward smiled as he stepped in front of Catherine, "Look, see? I shall go before you, and Betsy will come behind."

As the coach left the busy confines of the harbor front, the noise from the crowds diminished. The streets of London were busy as well, but the sounds seemed comfortable and welcoming. It felt good to see familiar buildings and to hear the horse's hooves on the cobblestone roads.

I think we were all excited when we finally reached Blakewood House. Catherine quickly alighted from the cab and ran up the steps and rang the bell. Lord Edward looked anxious and went quickly after her. But it was too late, Woods had opened the door. I heard him say, "Madam it is so wonderful to see you."

Catherine's quick reply must have been confusing to him. "While I don't know you, I wish you well. Where are Mother and Father?"

By that time Lord Edward had reached them. He nodded to Woods, who seemed totally mystified.

"Come, Woods, help me with the luggage."

I saw Lord Edward speak quietly to Woods. I imagine he told him of Catherine's condition.

I followed Catherine into the house. She had already looked into one or two rooms. She looked at me and said, "Edward has been telling me lies. Mother and Father aren't here."

I hastily reassured her. "No, No. You must have got the wrong impression. Your parents live near Sheffield. It's a good distance away from here. Don't you remember? This is our home, Blakewood House."

As Edward came into the foyer, Catherine cried impatiently, "You promised we would see Mother and Father. They are not here. You promised."

Lord Edward looked troubled, "No, my love, I would never lie to you. We will go to see them as soon as we possibly can."

He continued, "Let's go into the parlor, Woods told me there is a warm fire burning for us."

Catherine responded, "Betsy must come!'

Lord Edward looked at me for support, and I reassured Catherine again, "Of course I will come."

As we sat down, Lord Edward spoke patiently. "Yes, dear one, we will soon go to see your mother and father. Don't you remember? Blakewood House is our home. Your father sold it to us, and your parents have returned to their home in the country because your mother's health is failing."

Catherine replied in a matter of fact tone. "Well, that seems odd. I thought they would be here. Still, I am sure you must know. I hope mother's health has improved. You must take me to see them now."

Edward and I exchanged glances. I said to Catherine. "It is much too far to travel today after we have had such a long journey."

Lord Edward said, "Surely we should rest before we make the journey."

Catherine's asked, "Do we have to go on a ship?"

"Not at all," Edward replied. "We shall go by coach. But we will have to stay a night at an inn along the way. It is too long a journey to complete in one day. The horses and you and I will be tired."

"Very well," Catherine announced. "Then we shall leave tomorrow."

"As you wish, dear one." Edward replied wearily. "We will leave tomorrow."

"Will Betsy come?" Catherine asked.

"Betsy has things she needs to do in London." Edward said. "But you needn't worry. I will be with you and we will have a very fine trip."

I felt sorry for Lord Edward. He, like me, must have been tired of traveling. It's not an easy thing to deal with someone who has lost their memory.

Woods knocked on the door and came in. When Edward asked him what was needed, he asked, "Lord Edward, where would you like me to put the luggage?"

Edward replied, "Put Betsy's bag in the guest bedroom next to our room. Her case is the gray one. Put the others in Catherine's and my bedroom. I would appreciate it if you would unpack my bag. I shall unpack Catherine's a little later."

Woods bowed and said, "Very good, Sir."

When Woods left, Catherine asked, "Miss Beatrice won't be with Mother and Father will she?"

Lord Edward looked wearily at me as he reassured his wife, "Have you forgotten, dear Catherine? You can forget about Miss Beatrice forever. You will never have to speak to her again."

I excused myself, as I was feeling tired. I was pleased we had a few hours to rest before dinner but wondered why I was to sleep in the guest bedroom.

Woods knocked on my door and addressed me as 'Miss Betsy'. It felt strange to be addressed that way. He was senior staff and all the staff were required to obey him.

He told me, "Dinner is served. You are invited to eat with the master and mistress in the main dining room."

We three sat in the grand dining room for our dinner. Soup and bread, cottage pie and vegetables and a meringue pie for dessert if we wanted. Lord Edward and I declined dessert, but I was pleased to see Catherine enjoyed both the meal and her dessert. I was pleased, she needed to eat as much as she could. Her sickness and deprivation had taken their toll. It had been three months since we left Australia and she still seemed very thin.

I think Lord Edward must have told Woods to ensure that none of the servants bothered Catherine, for none could be seen apart from Woods himself. As we were drinking our tea, he told me, "While we are gone you are to act as mistress of the household. I have told Woods, and he will notify all the servants. When we return, we'll find a small home nearby for you."

Catherine looked puzzled and asked, "Isn't Betsy coming with us to see Mother and Father?"

Edward replied, "No, she has some things to do here in London."

I couldn't help saying, "Don't worry. I will be here when you return."

"Thank you, Betsy. I'm feeling rather tired. Could you help me get ready for bed?"

I presumed Lord Edward wanted to help his wife, as he had done so for the past few months. I didn't want to upset him. He had shown me a lot of kindness. I replied, "I am tired also. Perhaps Lord Edward could help you."

He hurriedly agreed. "Indeed, I would love to help you, Catherine."

He whispered to me, "Before you retire for the evening, meet me in the parlor."

I nodded my assent.

I wondered what he wanted to speak to me about. He had told me his expectations at dinner. I wondered if I had acted inappropriately. I certainly didn't want to offend Lord Edward. He had been very kind to me. I picked up a book while I waited. Although I thought I could read, the words seemed to run into each other, I was just too tired.

A half-hour later Lord Edward came into the room. He said, "I am pleased you waited, I know you must be tired. I wanted to ask you if you would help Catherine dress in the morning and see to it she eats a good breakfast. Woods will pack a bag for me. Could I prevail upon you to pack a bag for Catherine? I will leave early because I want to see my sister, Elizabeth, and then I need to stop and see Henry, my brother. But I will be back by ten. We will have to stay overnight at an inn on the way."

I instantly replied, "Of course, Lord Edward. I will be happy to help."

"I'll tell Catherine, so she won't worry. I know she loves to have your assistance, so I expect all will be well."

I woke early and felt greatly refreshed. Lying in the huge eiderdown bed in the guest room, I felt a comforting sense of peace, being in the land of my birth, and reveled in all the familiar sights and smells of Blakewood House. As I lay there, I heard Lord Edward make his way past my door and down the corridor. I dressed quickly and looked in on Catherine. She was fast asleep. I thought to wake her a little later and went down to the kitchen and met the new cook. Several of the servants were just finishing breakfast, and we were able to renew acquaintances. I rather enjoyed that. I told Mrs. Featherstone that Catherine and I would want porridge with honey, toast, and a pot of tea for breakfast. I also asked if she had any jam, as I knew Catherine had a liking for it on her toast.

An hour later I went into Catherine's room and opened the blinds. She lay in bed yawning and said, "Where are we?"

I answered her quite cheerfully, "We are home! Isn't it wonderful?"

Her reply was not reassuring, "I don't recognize anything. Please tell me where we are."

I responded, "We are at Blakewood House, in London. This is the home you grew up in and now share with your husband, Lord Edward."

She answered, "Oh yes! I remember Edward. He is very kind to me. Where is Edward? He generally wakes me for breakfast."

I answered, "He had a few errands to do and left early, but he will be home soon."

Catherine responded, "He promised we would see Mother and Father today."

I said, "Don't you remember? Lord Edward said you would start your journey today, but you would have to stop over somewhere on the way for the night. It's a long trip."

Catherine looked a little downcast and said, "Yes, I remember. It's a pity we need to travel so far."

I told Catherine, "I have put your clothes out for today. You will see them. They are laying on the chair. Lord Edward asked me to pack a bag for you. Woods has left a bag outside your door, so I will pack for you now, while you dress, and then we shall have breakfast together. I have asked for your favorite."

Catherine looked puzzled. "I can't remember my favorite," she said. "How do you know?"

I told her. "We have been best friends since we were young. There is very little I don't know about you."

After breakfast, we went into the parlor. Woods had a fire burning for us. It felt wonderful to be home.

A short time later I heard the front door open. Lord Edward's footsteps could be heard on the floor as he made his way to the parlor.

His smile beamed as he looked at Catherine. "Are you ready then, my love?"

Catherine was clearly pleased when she told him I had packed a bag for her.

Lord Edward told us, "I spoke to Todd and told him to have the coach ready to leave by ten-thirty. He will take us all the way to your parents place and will doubtless stay until we are ready to come home."

Then Lord Edward looked at me. "Betsy, if you should need to travel anywhere, there is another carriage and one of the stable hands can drive you."

Catherine was tearful when we said good-bye. She looked earnestly at me and said, "You will be here when we come back won't you, Betsy?"

I replied, "Yes, of course. I will look after your lovely home. I hope you have a happy time."

I stood watching as their coach drove away.

Betsy closed the journal and looked up at Henry and Elizabeth. "Either Catherine or I will complete the journal. I hope it will be Catherine."

Henry said, "Both of you have many years ahead of you. I feel there will be many more adventures ahead, but I am sure you would prefer them to be far less traumatic."

I chuckled a little and said, "I don't know how we did it, but thank goodness it is past and gone."

Elizabeth stood up, "It is way past my bedtime, my man is undoubtedly in your kitchen, Would you ask Woods to tell him we are ready to leave?

I rang the bell and Woods appeared soon after. He asked, "How may I be of service, Miss Betsy?"

I asked him to inform Miss Bannister's coachman she was ready to leave.

While we were waiting, Mr. Bannister said, "So I'm to call you 'Miss Betsy' from now on?"

I replied a tad shyly, "No. You must just call me Betsy, as always."

Mr. Bannister grinned and said, "I will on one condition. You must call me Henry!"

I think I blushed a little, but I agreed.

Elizabeth asked, "When might we see you at the Manor? You said you would read to me!"

I responded, "Perhaps Tuesday. Would that suit?"

Elizabeth smiled and said, "Yes, come by ten-thirty and then you could have lunch with me. It gets kind of lonely eating by oneself so often."

At that same moment, Woods called out, "Your coach is waiting."

I assured Elizabeth, "I'll be there."

As we were walking to the door, Henry said, "I'll make time to come to read Catherine's journal soon. I will be in touch."

Elizabeth hugged me and Henry thanked me. I smiled to myself as they were leaving, perhaps I had a new friend in Henry.

The time moved slowly with no one to talk to or to share time with. Thank goodness for the servants. I still felt like I was one of them. I often found myself in the kitchen either in the morning or late afternoon spending time chatting with Mrs. Featherstone as she and the pantry maid prepared our meals. When I saw the pantry maid at her work, I immediately thought of Catherine and what a trial it had been for her. Thank Goodness the pantry maid at Blakewood House would never be treated as badly as Catherine had been.

On Sunday I went to church with the servants. I doubt Lord Edward would have approved. I expect he would have wanted me to sit with those of the upper class. But I cannot be what I'm not.

It strikes me as rather odd. There are many people who seem to be one thing, perhaps a noble by birth, and, in reality, they are no better than the lowest of the low. I didn't want Lord Edward to feel that he was beholden to me for the care and love I had shown Catherine. I thank my dear parents, Baron Kensington and his dear wife, and those around me for being fine examples of showing love and care to all those who crossed their paths.

I looked forward to visiting with Elizabeth. I had one of the stable hands take me over in the extra coach. Fortunately, Elizabeth's home was just a short distance away, as I sensed the stable hand didn't have much experience driving a coach.

Elizabeth's home was somewhat smaller than Blakewood House. Nevertheless, it was quite stately.

After ringing the bell, I waited for a short time and was welcomed by a stout gentleman. I expect he was Elizabeth's butler.

He said, "You must be Miss Betsy. Miss Bannister said you would be here this morning."

I nodded in reply. "Yes."

I started to remove my cloak.

He was as well-mannered as Woods, immediately saying, "Please let me take your cloak, Miss Betsy."

As he hung it up, he said, "There's a fire in the library. Miss Bannister is waiting for you."

As we were walking, I caught glimpses of Elizabeth's house. It was very elegant and reflected her stylish sense of decor.

She welcomed me as I entered the library. "Dear Betsy, it is so nice to have you here."

"Indeed. It is a joy to be here." I replied.

With a glowing smile, Elizabeth asked, "I hope you are here to read to me?"

I replied, "That's what we had planned isn't it?"

"Yes, of course, Betsy, I was only trying to be humorous. I am afraid my humor is somewhat lacking these days. Don't grow old too quickly, Betsy. One needs to be brave in one's more mature years."

I said, "I've heard others who have spoken those very same words. But I don't think of you as old at all. They say you are only as old as you feel. You are very alert and caring towards those around you. Certainly, that is all we can ask for as the years roll on."

Elizabeth responded, "Yes, I suppose you're right." She looked away at a nearby desk. "I have chosen a book which you might read to me. That is if you haven't already read it? It was only published recently. 'Persuasion', written by Jane Austen. Have you read it?"

"What a coincidence!" I remarked. "I was going to read it just before Catherine and I started our ordeal. So, I'm pleased to be able to read it with you now."

Elizabeth beckoned to me, "Come, dear, sit down here by the fire."

"Thank you, I will," I replied. "What a cozy home you have."

Elizabeth replied, "Yes, it suits me. Not that I clean it myself, but I can't see the reason for a larger house for one person."

I walked over to the desk and picked up the book and smiled inwardly. In my wildest dreams, I could have never imagined that I would ever be reading to Miss Elizabeth Banister in her home.

Elizabeth asked, "Did you know that Persuasion is the last novel written by Jane Austen? It was published at the end of 1817, six months after her death."

I opened the book and suggested, "Perhaps we can read three or four chapters today?"

Elizabeth replied, "Yes, we will need to watch the time, as I have told Mrs. McDonald, we will want lunch at about twelve thirty."

As I read, I listened for the chime of the clock in Elizabeth's Hallway.

When it struck twelve, I thought we could finish the fourth chapter.

We shared a delicious lunch, little egg and bacon pies, some sweet cakes and a delicious cup of tea with sugar and milk.

As we concluded our lunch, Elizabeth asked, "Have you heard any word from Edward and Catherine?"

I responded, "No. Nothing. I keep wondering myself. I hope Catherine is enjoying herself."

Elizabeth replied, "I hope her memory returns."

I agreed, "Yes, most certainly, but what I really hope is that she will find peace in her soul again."

I stood to leave. "I'd best be off. My coach will be waiting,"

"Thank you, Betsy. I do appreciate you reading to me!"

I replied, "It is my joy to do so. Shall I come again on Friday?"

Elizabeth smiled, "That would be wonderful."

Apart from the time I spent reading to Elizabeth, the weeks went by slowly. After each visit, Elizabeth would ask, "Have you heard any word from Edward and Catherine?"

We were reading a third book by the time I received a note from Catherine. "All is well, Betsy. We shall be home in less than a week."

The following day, I took the note with me as the stable hand drove me to Elizabeth's house. As her butler escorted me to her library, I didn't wait for a proper greeting. I blurted out, "I have a note from Catherine. Let me read it to you."

As I did so, Elizabeth stood up and we hugged each other.

"What do you think of Catherine writing 'all is well'? Do you think her memory has returned?"

Elizabeth beamed as she said, "Yes, but don't put much faith in my words. Whatever the case, we will have them in our lives again."

9 798890 315656